CLUSTER DWARF

CLUSTER DWARF

DWARF BOUNTY HUNTER™ BOOK SEVEN

MARTHA CARR

MICHAEL ANDERLE

DISRUPTIVE IMAGINATION

LMBPN Publishing
PMB 196, 2540 South Maryland Pkwy
Las Vegas, NV 89109

First Version, April 2021
ebook ISBN: 978-1-64971-647-7
Paperback ISBN: 978-1-64971-648-4

THE CLUSTER DWARF TEAM

Thanks to our JIT Team:

Diane L. Smith
Dave Hicks
Jackey Hankard-Brodie
Kelly O'Donnell
Deb Mader
Peter Manis
Dorothy Lloyd

If We've missed anyone, please let us know!

Editor
SkyHunter Editing Team

CHAPTER ONE

"Which way did he go, boys?"

Johnny Walker crouched behind the low-hanging branches of a huge tree that had rooted itself at the edge of the island in the swamp. Beside him, Rex and Luther sniffed furiously in an attempt to find the trail they'd followed for the last hour.

"He's real close, Johnny."

"Yeah, could be right behind us."

"But he's not."

The dwarf tightened the grasp on his hunting rifle, a regular, human-made 7mm-08 Remington used to hunt large game. "Y'all find that trail. I ain't goin' back home without somethin' to show for it."

"Yeah, yeah. We're on it, Johnny."

"Don't know how we lost the trail in the first place. Deer don't...disappear. Right?"

"Keep lookin'." He peered through the thick underbrush, alert for the telltale rustle of any creature moving through the Everglades. If there were any others out there in their hiding place, the hounds would pick up the scent.

More importantly, he was merely glad to be out of the house

and off his property. It was good to be on the hunt and alone with his hounds again instead of surrounded by way too many magicals who all wanted something from him.

Hunting provided a small relief and maybe the only one he'd had since he'd returned from the last major case that had taken him and Lisa up north. Tracking and apprehending an ex-CIA scientist gone rogue was one thing. Bringing four brain-addled magical cyborgs to the Everglades with him was something else entirely.

I think I'll probably grow old and die before I get my privacy back.

Luther whipped his head up, stiffened, and uttered a low chuff, his tail stiff and raised vertically. "Got it!"

"You sure it's the buck, bro?" Rex sniffed around his brother. "You don't exactly have the best track record with—hey! He got it, Johnny. We got it!"

"Then get along, boys." Johnny stood from his crouch as both hounds uttered bloodcurdling bays and barreled through the underbrush.

When he brought that two-hundred-pound buck back to his cabin, trussed up on the airboat and ready to be used for meat and a helluva mounted trophy, he'd find a little more peace.

They raced through the swamp, splashed across waterlogged berms, and sloshed through tributaries as the hounds followed the trail. He lifted his rifle when he saw a flash of tan hide through the trees at the top of a slightly elevated mound twenty yards ahead.

"We'll get him, Johnny."

"Yeah, yeah. You hang back and shoot. We'll bring him right to ya!"

The hounds separated and raced wide to each side of their target as the dwarf steadied the rifle butt against his shoulder. Screw using a sight or a scope. The bounty hunter rarely missed without them anyway, especially at this distance.

Still downwind of the buck, Rex and Luther closed in on their quarry and he waited for it to move. Only another half-inch to the left would give him a clear shot.

The animal raised its head abruptly. It had caught the sound of the hunt but still seemed unsure where it came from or whether the danger was headed toward it.

Johnny's finger tightened on the trigger, almost ready to squeeze and put a round into its hide.

A crackling buzz filled the swamp a split second before a crackling blue light illuminated the small island. A moment later, a massive explosion wracked the vegetation and a burst of soggy earth, mud, swamp water, and decimated tree branches scattered in its wake.

With a shout of surprise, Johnny ducked a thick tree limb that hurtled toward him. "What the fuck?"

"Johnny!" Rex barked wildly. "Johnny, it's getting away!"

"Hey, I thought you had regular bullets in that," Luther added and his wild baying ended any hope of silence.

"To me, boys!" The dwarf raced toward the explosion site and caught a fleeting glimpse of the buck as it darted away through the underbrush again. "Stay on him!"

A roar of engines broke through the noise from the hounds and June landed in front of Johnny with a crash. The sputter of her jetpack cyborg boots winked out against the mud.

He staggered to a halt and scowled at her. "What the hell are you doin' here?"

The augmented Crystal woman sneered at him and gestured toward the escaping buck.

Leroy and the twins Brandon and Clint darted out of the next thick stand of trees. Their feet trampled reeds and ferns and launched huge sprays of swamp water. The shifter cyborg raised his fully mechanical arm and the click and whirr of all the segmented parts made a massive racket as he transformed what had looked like a robotic hand into the barrel of a huge hand cannon.

"Got it." Leroy aimed into the swamp as his weapon powered up.

"No, no. Wait a goddamn—"

Johnny lunged at the shifter borg, but Leroy fired before he made it halfway to him.

A churning bolt of crackling magic propelled by technological force blasted after the buck that raced through the swamp. The charge struck the base of a mangrove stand, which erupted in splintered fragments and smoking leaves.

The hounds bayed in the distance. "What the hell, Johnny?"

"Yeah, you said this was hunting. Not target practice with new bombs!"

"The buck's getting away, Johnny!"

The dwarf swung his rifle into the air and fired. "Y'all need to cut it out!"

Brandon and Clint fired their magical blasts into the trees and thick underbrush, heedless of the fact that no one had any idea where the buck was. All Johnny knew was that it wasn't where he had intended to shoot it and bring it home.

"This ain't war, numbnuts. It's a goddamn hunt!" He strode toward the cyborg twins, skidded to a stop in front of them, and raised his rifle. They stared at him in silence and without emotion, and he uttered a piercing whistle. "Rex! Luther!"

The hounds splashed through the water toward their master, covered in mud and shredded foliage, and panted heavily. "What gives, Johnny?"

"We were this close."

"And then you go and blow up the whole—oh. Hey. Where did they come from?"

Johnny glared at the four cyborgs who'd crashed his hunting party. "Y'all cost me a monster of a four-point buck. There'd better be a damn good reason for it."

The twins shrugged.

Leroy and June shared an emotionless glance, and the shifter gestured toward Johnny. "You forgot to invite us so we decided we'd come help anyway."

"Forgot?" He growled in annoyance. "I didn't tell you on purpose."

Luther trotted to his master's side and gazed at the cyborgs who stood in the swamp. Their metal gears clicked and whirred and the internal mechanisms of their augmented limbs lit up with a silver glow. "Johnny, I don't think they know how to hunt."

No shit.

Leroy shrugged as his hand cannon morphed into something resembling fingers. "Better luck next time, right?"

"No. This ain't about luck and there ain't a next time." The dwarf glanced over his shoulder at the destroyed mangroves and the giant crater June had blasted into the berm. "Shit. All right, boys, we're callin' it off. Let's go."

"But Johnny, the buck—"

He snapped his fingers and swung the rifle to rest it against his shoulder as he brushed past the cyborgs. "Now."

"Aw, man…" Rex sniffed the ground as he shuffled after his master. "We were this close."

"Yeah, I wanted a buck neck between my teeth."

And I wanted the thing gutted and quartered with a trophy on my wall and meat sent out for processin'. These damn borgs can't leave well enough alone.

Another massive explosion detonated behind him and he whirled to scowl at the small mushroom cloud and the spray of swamp water before June's jetpack boots kicked off and she launched herself skyward. The twins stared at Johnny. Leroy's gaze followed June's flight before she disappeared above the thick trees and a smirk played on his lips.

"What the hell are y'all still doin' here? Let's go." The dwarf strode through the mud and backtracked to where he'd left his flat-bottom airboat tied off on the riverbank.

I ain't gonna last much longer than this with four cyborgs buttin' in where they ain't needed. Or wanted.

The hounds trotted beside him. "We gonna try again, Johnny?"

"Yeah. We'll get it next time. You watch."

"Not today, boys." He gritted his teeth and tried to ignore the crashes and splashes of Leroy and the twins behind him. It was impossible.

Do the right thing, she said. It'll be good for you. Help the damn borgs discover what they are. Give 'em a purpose. The next hair-brained idea Lisa throws my way, I ain't listenin'.

When he reached the riverbank and the airboat that was still tied to a thinner tree trunk, Johnny undid the rope and hopped aboard after the hounds. He took his place at the stern beside the throttle control stick, ready to rev the giant fan to get the hell out of there. Despite his inclination to ignore them, he paused when he noticed Leroy and the twins standing at the edge of the bank. All three simply stared at him.

The dwarf's upper lip curled into a sneer beneath his wiry red mustache. His eyes watered with the itch under his nose he refused to scratch. "Aw, hell. Get on, huh?"

The borgs stepped none too lightly onto the airboat and made it rock dangerously beneath their unnaturally heavy weight. Johnny grunted and used the throttle to get the airboat away from the bank so he could turn downriver toward his property.

Brandon—and he only knew it was Brandon because Clint hardly ever said a word—turned toward him and nodded at the rifle in the dwarf's hand. "Want someone to hold that for—"

"No." He stared straight ahead and maneuvered them in a wide U-turn on the water. The hounds had all but forgotten the disappointment of an interrupted hunt as they sat at the bow, their ears flapping in the wind and their noses pointed down-river. The airboat's bow was slightly elevated with all the weight distributed toward the stern. "Y'all need to spread the hell out. If you sink my boat, I'll have Lisa fry your gears."

Leroy snorted but stayed where he was as the twins took two steps forward. The airboat settled again into as close to level as they were likely to get.

Two months of this and I've regretted it the whole time. Amanda was rough too, but at least she tried to talk her way out of a mistake. These bozos don't even give a shit.

His irritation faded as they skimmed across the water to his swamp-front property. Adopting a group of cyborgs who couldn't remember who they'd been before all the illegal experimentation wasn't one of his more carefully considered plans, mainly because it had been Lisa's. Where else were the clueless and ridiculously powerful magicals supposed to go? Admittedly, they were somewhat trained, at least when it came to using their biotech enhancements. But they were more unpredictable and harder to wrangle under control than a pack of wild boars.

Harder than havin' a baby shifter around the place over the summer, and I'll be damned if I ain't missin' that kid somethin' fierce right about now.

Johnny pulled back on the throttle when the monstrosity that was his pipedream houseboat made reality—as payment from the FBI—came into view. The vessel rose at least six feet above the tops of the trees surrounding his property and two months before, the sight of it had made him smile.

Now, it was fully overrun by the borgs. Where the hell else was he supposed to keep them?

Sunlight glinted off the head of June's shoulder cannon as she stood on the craft's second-story balcony.

Watchin' us roll on in like she owns the goddamn swamp. It ain't hers. It's mine.

The airboat knocked against the dock despite all his efforts to bring them in gently. The hounds leapt off first and raced toward the back yard, barking and jumping around each other.

"All right, now." The bounty hunter grasped the docking rope and pointed at Leroy and the twins. "Y'all step lightly. This thing ain't—hey!"

All three borgs stepped onto the dock at once and the airboat bobbed frantically on the water after the sudden release of so much weight. He staggered across the deck and stamped on the butt of his rifle as it skittered away to stop it from toppling over the side and into the water.

"Y'all need to pull that stuffin' out your ears!"

The borgs ignored him and headed across the yard to where Lisa Breyer sat at a large table Johnny had cobbled together. They'd argued a little over whether it was even worth it to put anything else in the dwarf's back yard.

"We can't leave them on the houseboat," she had told him.

"Why the hell not? I already gave it up for 'em to use."

"They're not tenants, Johnny. You're training them. And you don't even have a dining table inside the house."

No way in hell would Johnny Walker host fun family dinners inside his cabin, so he'd relented and built the massive table in the center of the yard.

Out of everything I've had back here, that damn thing's the biggest eyesore yet.

"Clint's hungry," Brandon muttered as he approached Lisa seated at the table.

Johnny finished tying the airboat off and rolled his eyes.

"Only Clint, huh?" The agent set down the eighteenth-century rifle from Johnny's collection she'd finished cleaning and reassembling. She raised an eyebrow at the twins and smirked.

"No." Brandon slumped in one of the chairs Johnny had to reinforce with a steel plate beneath the seat after the first two had broken beneath the cyborgs' weight. "Me too."

"I could eat," Leroy added, although he chose to stand beside the table with his arms behind his back, his organic hand clasped around the wrist of his robotic appendage.

Lisa stood when she saw Johnny march down the dock and across the back yard toward them. "How many jars do we have left?"

"A fair amount." *And it still ain't enough.*

"I'll come help you." She pointed at the dwarf's rifle collection spread out at the head of the table. "These are off-limits."

"Yeah, we know." Brandon nodded as Clint slumped into the chair beside him with a metallic clang.

The half-Light Elf studied the shifter borg who still stood at attention beside the table. "Okay, at ease, Leroy. You can sit without a command."

His mechanical eye whirred and spun as he studied her before he lowered himself slowly into one of the chairs.

With a chuckle, she turned and headed after Johnny. "We'll be right back."

CHAPTER TWO

The bounty hunter threw open the door to his storage shed which was hidden by Margo's massive steel frame. The satellite intelligence hub took up the far side of his back yard and separated the shed from the hulking wooden table. If not for that, he would probably have shouted at the borgs to quit staring at his back and let him walk around his property in peace. With the shed out of the borgs' view, though, he finally had a moment to himself.

"How did it go?" Lisa asked as she appeared around the side of Margo and joined him.

"It didn't." He grunted and stepped inside the shed.

"What?"

He retrieved two jumbo-sized jars of pickles and nestled one under each arm as she entered. "The damn borgs ruined my hunt."

She stepped aside to let him exit the shed again, and the two pickle jars clanged into the wheelbarrow parked beside the structure. "Oh."

"Yeah, that's one way to put it."

Lisa took two more pickle jars down from the shelves, which

they'd had to rearrange quickly when the borgs first arrived. Now, the back two-thirds of the shed held nothing but giant glass jars of pickles she'd ordered wholesale for their unlikely guests. "I thought you told them not to come with you."

"I didn't tell 'em nothin'." Johnny sniffed and stepped inside again to collect two more jars. "And those…dingdongs decided I forgot to invite 'em along."

With a short laugh, she placed her jars in the wheelbarrow and frowned playfully at the open door to the shed. "Dingdongs?"

"Well, what the hell else am I supposed to call 'em?" he snapped from inside. "They ain't listenin' to a word I say and blow the swamp up at all damn hours of the day and night. I ain't runnin' a damn frat house for college kids, darlin'. And I can't get one damn hunt on my own with the hounds without those…cyborgs gettin' in the way."

"You merely have to be firm with the rules."

"I am firm!" The dwarf appeared in the doorway with a scowl and she took the jars from under his arms with a patient smile. "A fella should be able to go out and mind his own business without havin' to shout to all of creation that he needs a little time and space to his own damn self."

"They're still learning things, Johnny."

"They're grown-ass adults."

After she packed the next armload of pickles into the wheelbarrow, she stopped in front of the door again, folded her arms, and waited.

When Johnny reappeared with another armload, he stopped, frowned at her, and grimaced. "All right. That look means you have somethin' to say, so what is it?"

"You're right. They're adults." Lisa shrugged. "But they've been through hell. And the only exposure they've had to life as what they are now was being locked in that lab for who knows how long and experimented on by a psycho scientist who cared more about results than the living, breathing magicals who gave her those results. They're missing whole pieces of their memories, Johnny."

"Do you think I don't know that?" He handed her the jars and disappeared into the shed for two more.

"I know you know it. I'm only here to remind you."

When he stepped out with the last of their load, she tilted her head, stood her ground, and blocked him from the wheelbarrow. Johnny scowled at her. "I don't get it."

"What?"

"How you got all this damn patience."

Lisa stepped toward him until they stood only inches apart and cupped his red-bearded cheek. "I've had considerable practice over the last eight months."

He snorted. "You're talkin' about me, ain'tcha?"

"Yes, Johnny. And no, I'm not saying you're worse than four cyborgs still trying to discover who they are now that they're... different. But if anyone can help them get a handle on themselves and find a purpose after being nothing but a seriously messed-up science experiment, it's you." She took the giant pickle jars from him and smirked as she turned toward the wheelbarrow. "Honestly, you're doing better than I expected."

"Oh, yeah? How did you think I'd take it?"

"I thought you would have tried to kick them off the property by now. Two months in, and you've only threatened their lives half a dozen times." The jars clinked into the wheelbarrow with the others and she turned to face him with a coy smile. "I'd call that progress."

With a grunt, he closed the shed's door with a bang and strode toward the wheelbarrow to grasp the handles. "Well, I'm callin' it an early grave. Mine."

She forced back a laugh as the dwarf pushed the load around Margo's glinting, curved metal hull and toward the three borgs seated at the giant table in the center of his yard.

They all watched him intently until he lowered the wheelbarrow and tossed a flippant hand toward its contents. "Lunch."

"Awesome." Brandon stood first to unload and set two huge pickle jars in front of four chairs. Clint snatched the closest one and flicked the sealed lid off with the tip of his finger. It clattered across the table, wobbled for a few seconds, and finally settled. By the time it stopped, he had already taken a bite of the huge pickle clenched in his hand. More jar lids popped off and were tossed aside, and Leroy and Brandon dug into their meals as well.

Johnny watched it all with a grimace of disbelief. "Y'all sure you ain't ready for somethin' else? It's been two months and you've had nothin' but those giant-ass pickles."

Leroy swallowed thickly and washed his mouthful down with a swig of pickle juice. "I wouldn't mind a different flavor every once in a while, but these are all right."

"Do you think they come in spicy?" Brandon pointed at the shifter borg with his half-eaten pickle. "I like spicy."

"Or maybe garlic?"

The dwarf shook his head. "I meant other than pickles."

"No can do, boss." Leroy speared another out of the jar with his shifting robotic limb and took a huge bite. "Salt and water's the trick. Electrical conductor and all that, right? And I don't feel like drinking seawater."

"Potatoes have ions. Have you ever tried that?"

"Uh-uh." Brandon drank from his jar next. "Nothing else works, Johnny. Potatoes simply clog the gears up. Know what I'm saying?"

"I ate a sandwich once."

Everyone looked at Clint in surprise. The borg stared at his pickle, shrugged, then popped the rest of it in his mouth.

The guy won't say jack else but a sandwich has meanin'. Christ, what the hell did I get myself into?

The crackle and roar of June's jetpack feet grew louder before the Crystal borg pounded onto the grass beside the table. She jerked her chin at Leroy, tossed her ice-flecked bangs out of her eyes, and popped open the lid of her jar before she slumped into a chair. "This blows."

"Hey, it ain't my fault. Blame the psycho who set you up with a new diet for the rest of your lives." *I guess that'll be much longer than before they were half-machine.*

She looked sharply at the dwarf. "You got us cooped up here in a stupid boat with nothing to do. I want action."

He pointed at her. "It ain't simply a boat."

"Yeah, when's the next big job?" Leroy asked around a mouthful.

Brandon nodded. "We're ready."

Johnny scowled at them. "No, you ain't."

Lisa nudged him gently with her elbow.

"Aw, hell." With a sigh, he ran a hand through his auburn hair. "There ain't no big job, all right? Nothin's come through, so y'all gotta deal and keep it together until somethin' comes up."

"Well, when it does, don't forget to tell us again."

The bounty hunter clenched his jaw and glared at Leroy, but the shifter borg was too focused on fishing out and devouring pickles to notice. Instead, Johnny turned his attention to his collection of old and rarely used rifles spread out at the other end of the long table. "Darlin', what are these doin' out here?"

"Oh, right. I'm almost finished." Lisa grinned. "You know, I wanted to start with the musket but I thought I could get the others done faster. Maybe I'm saving the best for last."

"For what?"

She gestured toward the cleaning box that lay open beside the guns. "Cleaning them."

"They don't need cleanin'."

"That Sharpshooter begs to differ. It was almost rusted shut."

He gave her a sidelong glance. "Gettin' real cozy with my things, huh?"

Lisa fought back a smile and caught his hand. "Well, when you tell me to make myself at home, I'll hold you to it."

"That don't include grabbin' my collection and doin' who knows what with 'em."

"Johnny, I know how to clean a few old rifles. I'm very sure I made that clear the day we met."

"Uh-huh. Sure." He rubbed his mouth and wiry red beard and watched the hounds as they trotted toward the table, drawn by the smell of over half a dozen open pickle jars.

"Hey, guy." Luther sniffed around Leroy's boots in the grass. "Don't worry about dropping an extra pickle. I can help with the cleanup."

"Do you guys have anything else?" Rex wormed his way under the table and inspected the dirt for scraps. "Hey, Johnny. Is this what two-legs mean when they talk about pickling their brains?"

"No, that's their liver, bro."

Johnny ignored them and turned toward Lisa. "I know you're only tryin' to help—"

She laughed. "No, I'm making myself at home."

"That ain't—" He grunted and scowled at his collection spread across the table.

"Okay, fine." She turned toward him and took his other hand before she planted a quick kiss on his lips. "So what's your definition?"

He frowned at her and shrugged. "Hell, I gotta spell it out?"

"Well, there does seem to be an unusually high amount of miscommunication lately." She cast the feasting borgs a sidelong glance and tried not to laugh.

"Aw, come on. Make yourself at home means take a shower whenever you want. Help yourself to the fridge. Don't bother knockin' on the front door 'cause it ain't only mine anymore."

"Yeah, neither is the bed," Brandon muttered. The other borgs sniggered.

"And he already mentioned the shower," Leroy added.

June slurped more pickle juice. "I'd say get a room but you already covered that."

"Goddammit." Johnny turned away from Lisa and pointed at the borgs. "Y'all need to mind your own business."

Brandon pointed at him in response. "Or you need to grow a sense of humor."

"I swear, y'all are worse than the damn hounds."

Luther darted around the table toward a nonexistent pickle, still looking for scraps. "Aw, thanks, Johnny."

Rex emerged from under the table. "Yeah, you mean it? We're flattered."

"That's it." Johnny marched toward the table and stacked the old rifle collection in his arms. He slammed the cleaning box shut and snatched it from the table, then shook it at the borgs. "When y'all finish your gourmet meal, come let me know. We have work to do."

Without even a glance at any of them, he stormed toward the stairs onto the back porch and struggled to balance everything in his arms so he could open the door. It creaked and slapped shut behind him.

The borgs continued to eat without a care in the world.

Lisa scrunched her nose as she considered the back door. Finally, she leaned toward June's freshly opened second pickle jar. "Do you mind if I..."

The Crystal borg slid the jar toward the edge of the table and she selected one. "Thanks." She took a large bite and headed to the back door. "Give him half an hour, guys. He'll get over it."

"Or not," Clint muttered before he drained the rest of his pickle juice.

Leroy sniffed the air. "Why does it still smell like chickens out here? And where the hell are they?"

"Yeah, that's only the shit." Luther sat at the shifter borg's feet and stared at him as his tail swished across the grass.

"Chicken shit," Rex clarified. "They all packed and went home."

Leroy leaned sideways in his chair to focus on the large coonhound and muttered, "Tell me that's a euphemism for you ate them."

Luther uttered a high-pitched whine. "No. Major buzzkill, you know? Hey, how about those pickles, though?"

Inside the cabin, Johnny laid his antique rifle collection out on his worktable and checked the bolts and chambers of each. No, Lisa hadn't told him she'd go through his things and work on his weapons. But when he saw how well-oiled the parts were and how cleanly the old pieces slid together and clicked into place, he couldn't help a tiny smile.

Shit. I can't be mad about this and couldn't pay anyone to do a better job. And I ain't got the time to do it all myself without gettin' interrupted by—

"Johnny?" The back door opened and shut again, and her footsteps drew closer from across the kitchen.

He stared at the far wall of his workshop and sighed. *Everyone. Interrupted by everyone.*

Lisa stopped in the doorway between the kitchen and his workshop and wiped pickle juice off her hand with a paper towel. "They look much better now than they did an hour ago."

"'Course they do. Most times folks are touchin' my things, it all goes to hell."

She approached him and rested a hand on his shoulder. "I'm not trying to get in your way."

"Yeah, I know that too." He set the firearm he held down and turned to face her. Only when he met her gaze did his scowl finally disappear. "And you ain't. But I got four borgs livin' on my property and drivin' me up the wall 'cause I didn't sign up for babysittin'."

"Nope. You signed up for doing the right thing."

"Uh-huh. It feels more like someone signed up for me and forged my signature."

Lisa chuckled. "You can complain about it until the cows come home, Johnny, but if deep down you didn't want to do this, you wouldn't have. You would have let the CIA or the Bureau deal with them instead. But you know this is the right thing to do. For all of you."

He grunted. "You gonna keep lecturin' me on how I'm growin' a heart?"

"Nope." She gave his shoulder a reassuring squeeze. "You already know that part too."

"You sound way too damn sure of it."

"Because I am. And I know I'm right."

"Yeah, we'll see." He shoved the cleaning box onto the shelf, snorted, and cast her a sidelong glance. "There's one thing I wanna know, though."

"And what's that?"

"Since when did you start sayin' 'until the cows come home?'"

Lisa laughed. "I've lived down here since we brought Amanda back. It was bound to happen sooner or later."

"Well, we oughtta find you a better sayin'."

CHAPTER THREE

When Johnny and Lisa stepped outside again, the borgs had finished eating. The empty pickle jars now rested in the wheelbarrow, all the lids accounted for and screwed on tightly.

June still sat at the huge wooden table, her legs kicked out in front of her and her arms folded. Leroy stood in the center of the yard and stared at the swamp and the massive houseboat rising above the treetops. The twins stood at the base of the back porch's stairs and inspected each other's metal plates embedded on the sides of their necks like they were interacting with a mirror that responded.

Johnny strode down the stairs and pointed at them. "Did y'all get those up and runnin' again?"

"I think so," Brandon muttered and looked questioningly at his brother. Clint shrugged. "It's worth a shot if you wanna try it."

"Yep. Y'all need somethin' to do besides sittin' around here with your thumbs up your asses and gettin' in the middle of my business."

"I thought you wanted us in your business."

"The workin' kind, sure. Not the personal kind." Johnny headed across the yard toward Margo and ignored the scathing glance from June. It appeared to be her go-to no matter what kind of mood she was in. From what he could see, the Crystal borg only had one mood—pissed off. "Where did the hounds get off to?"

A sharp bark rose from the swamp, followed by splashes and the scurry of paws.

"Hey, no fair!" Luther shouted. "You cheated."

"Being faster than you isn't cheating, bro." Rex darted through the reeds at the edge of the yard and raced across the grass toward Leroy.

"But you've gotten it every single time!"

"Again, because I'm faster." Rex trotted to a stop in front of the shifter borg and dropped the huge stick at his feet. "You can throw it as far as you want, guy. I'll get it."

"Come on!" Luther yipped and jumped around at the edge of the swamp. "Throw it! I'm gonna win. You watch."

The dwarf studied the shifter for a long moment. "You playin' fetch with my hounds?"

"Yep." Leroy bent to grab the stick and shoved it into the narrow barrel of his mechanical hand, which he had turned into a stick launcher.

"Leroy, they're huntin' hounds. The only thing they fetch is the game I shoot. And the occasional asshole who rubs me the wrong way and had a beatin' comin' anyhow."

Without a word, the shifter borg aimed far above the treetops and fired. His arm thumped with a hydraulic hiss and the stick arced over the treetops before it vanished into the swamp. The hounds howled and chased after it.

"I got it, I got it, I got it!" Luther shouted.

"Bro, you don't even know where it landed."

"Yeah, but I'll—" The smaller hound stumbled over his feet as he launched himself into the swamp and landed face-first with a gurgling yelp. He thrashed, leapt to his feet, and raced after his brother. "Rex, wait up!"

"It's fetch! Keep up or lose the stick!"

Leroy turned toward Johnny and gestured at the rustling underbrush and the quickly fading sounds of stick-maddened coonhounds. "It sure looks like they're fetching hounds."

"And your arm sounds like a damn potato gun."

The shifter smirked. "It's better than any gun you could make."

The dwarf opened his mouth for a biting retort but shut it again and clenched his jaw.

It ain't worth the headache. It's not like any of them are gonna listen to a word I say anyhow.

"Wonder twins! Get over here!"

Brandon frowned at him. "Who?"

"Do y'all see any other twins on my property?" Johnny waved them closer and headed toward Margo. "We have work to do. And none of that moseyin' over either. Get a move on."

The twins shrugged at each other, crossed the yard, and followed him around the curve of Margo's metal hull before the dwarf stopped them outside the dark entrance.

"I'll grab the hookups. Y'all stay put, ya hear?"

"Why can't you hook us up inside?" Brandon asked.

"And risk y'all blowin' up one of the best damn intelligence units on this planet? No. Stay."

Clint stared blankly at him. The segmented metal rod melded to the flesh of his arm from his shoulder to the tip of his middle finger flashed with silver light and threw off a few sparks.

"See? Don't get cute." Johnny pointed at him. "I assume that's you tryin' to make a point, but I ain't fixin' to test it. No sparks on the job unless I say so."

He turned, walked into Margo's dark interior, and completely missed the smirk the twins shared at his expense.

The bounty hunter flung the panel of Margo's power breaker open and turned her on. The overhead lights flickered and the buttons and dials on the control panels lining the slightly curved walls blinked to life. The monitors mounted on the far wall flashed before they turned on with a light-blue glow.

"Hello, Johnny."

The tinny female voice designed to sound like Mila Kunis as much as was technologically possible echoed around him. Despite his irritation, the dwarf smiled. "Yeah, hey, darlin'."

He went directly to the cabinet he'd built beneath one of the control panels and opened it to rummage around for the gear he wanted.

At least I have someone who listens to what I need and doesn't do a damn thing else. And it's a beautiful hunk of metal. It's the best idea I've had all month to make her talk like that.

When he found the connection cables and the stabilization patches, he stood, closed the cabinet, and gave the control panel a loving pat. "I guess you could use a project too, huh?"

"All systems operational and awaiting instruction."

"Yeah, that's what I thought." With a smile, he plugged the business end of the cables into the panel and strode across the metal floor.

The twins sniggered at him when he stepped onto the grass. "Does Lisa know about your little crush on Margo?"

He stopped and gave them both a blank stare. "Yep. And the one on Sheila, the airboat, all my guns, my privacy, my property, and damn near everythin' else. Quit bein' smart and open up."

Still sniggering, the twins stepped toward him to give the connection cables enough slack. Moving as if they were two different bodies with the same mind, both borgs tapped the metal panels embedded in their necks and their fingers moved in a complicated pattern Johnny didn't pretend to recognize. The panels swung open to reveal thinner cables inside.

They had to bend over for him to attach the stabilization patches over the technology implanted in living, breathing magicals where flesh and muscle and a surprisingly large number of veins and arteries should've been. He set the first into the hole in

Clint's neck and wrinkled his nose when he felt a hint of the guy's pulse flare beneath his fingers in the cables themselves. Ignoring it, he hooked up the much narrower end of one cable and gestured for Brandon to step closer.

This time, his curiosity got the better of him and he took a moment to study the augmented technology in the guy's open neck. "So those little bastards go all the way into your brain, huh?"

"Probably." Brandon seemed to be fighting a smirk. "I haven't exactly tried to pull them all out to make sure."

Johnny snorted. "Good thinkin'."

He attached the stabilization patch and the cable and clapped both of the twins on the shoulder. "Y'all are lookin' for anythin' that—"

"Mentions genocide, explosions, spies, large-scale illegal activity, you, or Amanda." Brandon scratched his neck below the cable that dangled from it. "I'm fairly sure we know the drill by now."

The dwarf cleared his throat. "Yeah. That."

"Who's Amanda?" Clint asked dully and his eyes widened as Margo's information connected with his head—however the crazy-ass scientist Dr. Monroe had set that up to work.

"A name y'all are screenin' for and that's it. Let me know if you find anythin'."

"You should make these cables longer." Brandon tested the length of his cable that stretched through Margo's open doorway. "It's weird back here. We're stuck between the shed and a giant talking Airstream on wheels."

"Airstream." Johnny clicked his tongue. "Lemme tell you somethin'. The goddamn FBI built me a—"

"Satellite intelligence unit copied from theirs and probably a leftover from the CIA," Brandon droned and stared blankly at Margo's outer wall. "But you rigged the whole thing to be bigger, better, faster, stronger, sexier, and less of a pain in your ass because you're smarter than every fed out there and now you have your own super-computer. Did I miss anything?"

"Yeah, smartass. She ain't merely a computer." Before he said or did anything he'd probably regret—or that Lisa would remind him he should regret—the bounty hunter hurried around Margo's rounded corner, shaking his head.

I can't get nothin' outta my mouth without someone openin' theirs for somethin' smart. This is why I don't take trainees in. Or strays.

Leroy blasted the giant stick into the air again as Johnny headed across the yard. The hounds splashed after it while they barked and bickered with each other. Lisa now sat at the table across from June, who hadn't moved an inch.

"So what now?" his partner asked and turned to him with an eager smile.

"Now we wait. I have the twins hooked up and they're scannin' the channels as we speak. I think that was what the psycho doc had planned all along." Johnny tugged his thick beard. "Those two are wired and primed for this. I couldn't do it much better myself."

"That's it?" June lowered her head and stared at him. "We simply wait until something comes up?"

"Yep. Y'all wanted a big job, right?"

"You can't wait for cases. You'll drive your business into the ground. Go bankrupt. You have to bring money in. Have you ever heard of it?"

Johnny tilted his head. "Well, it's a good thing I ain't in this business for the money. And I ain't fixin' to go all out on a local case to chase a cat out of a tree or help find the grocer's missin' truck of apples. That's a lawsuit waitin' to happen."

Lisa snorted and immediately wiped the smile from her face when June glanced scathingly at her.

"This place blows." The Crystal borg stood abruptly and her chair, despite its heavy metal plate, catapulted behind her across the yard and toppled end over end until one of the thick legs finally snapped.

"You ain't hardly given it a—"

Her feet lit up with propulsive fuel and the noise drowned out the bounty hunter's words before she elevated sharply and sailed overhead toward the second-story deck of the houseboat. Her feet landed with a metallic clank and she stormed inside. The sound of buckling metal echoed toward the yard across the swamp and Johnny grimaced.

"I swear if she breaks anythin' in that boat—"

"I don't think they've had enough time to discover how strong they are," Lisa said. She tried to keep her voice low as Leroy stood close by in the yard and continued to fire sticks across the swamp for the hounds.

"Great. I might as well have a group of moody teenagers squattin' all over my property. Only these have magic and more firepower than I can fit onto Sheila."

"It's a good thing the actual teenager you have coming back isn't all that moody. As far as teenagers go."

"Yeah, but she has her own baby-shifter firepower—wait." Johnny looked pointedly at her and frowned. "Comin' back? She's at the boot camp."

"The Academy? Yep. And she's coming home at the end of the week."

"Huh? Why the hell would she do that?"

She studied him with a confused smile until she realized he was serious. "Because it's winter break, Johnny. She said she wanted to come home over break and you said it was a good idea."

"Aw, shit." He rubbed the back of his neck and growled in irritation. "You mean I gotta deal with all five of 'em here at the same time?"

"Unless you want to explain to Amanda why you're revoking your invitation for her to come home whenever she wants to."

"Now don't go sayin' it like that. I ain't gonna keep her away. It's her home as much as it is mine." With a sidelong glance at Lisa, he cleared his throat. "Ours."

"She knows that. It'll be fine."

"No, it'll be a goddamn mess. How the hell am I supposed to keep track of everyone around here when no one listens to a thing I say?"

She leaned back in the chair and chuckled when the hounds burst out of the swamp again for another round of fetch.

Luther jumped around his brother and yipped as he tried to snatch the stick away. "Come on, Rex. Lemme have it. Only for a second."

"No." Rex panted happily toward Leroy and his wagging tail flung water in all directions.

"Just to drop it at his feet, huh? A little—"

His brother snarled at him and chased him off before he deposited the stick at the borg's feet.

"It looks like they're having a good time," Lisa said.

"Sure. Such a good time that at the end of all this, I'll have lazy-ass pets who roll over and play fetch instead of the hounds I raised."

"Everything will be fine, Johnny. You're overthinking it."

"I can't overthink a single thing with all this damn noise. Add Amanda to this crazy mess out here, and we'll be trampled by all the neighbors comin' to ask about explosions and noise at all hours and why there's an unholy number of craters in the Everglades."

She chuckled. "If they haven't already, I don't think Amanda coming home will change that. The neighbors love her."

Leroy fired the stick cannon again and chuckled when the hounds got into a snarling scuffle over who leapt into the swamp first.

Lisa looked at Johnny. "Do you know what I think?"

"I'd say I wish I could, darlin', but I already know everythin' the boys think. I don't think I have enough patience for anyone else's constant talk in my head."

She smacked his arm with the back of her hand. "I think she's gonna love the borgs."

"Oh, sure. 'Cause there's so much to love, ain't there?"

"I mean it. They have so much in common."

"Like drivin' me into a homicidal rage."

The woman stood and gave his shoulder a sympathetic pat. "Like having nowhere else to go, no one else to turn to, and you right there beside them the whole way."

He grunted and folded his arms. "It doesn't mean I gotta like it."

"No. But we both know you don't hate every minute of it, either. So while Brandon and Clint are sweeping space for intel on this big job of yours, I'll go inside to make lunch. When you stop being pissed off about how much you can't control other magicals, feel free to join me."

The bounty hunter stood in silence for another minute as she headed up the stairs of the back porch and disappeared inside the cabin.

"It ain't about control," he muttered.

But she was right and as he'd come to learn, Lisa Breyer most often was—and he knew it.

I'm supposed to be the only one who breaks the damn rules. And now, everyone else is makin' it their life's mission to keep breakin' mine.

CHAPTER FOUR

That night, the borgs settled in their prospective suites inside the boathouse and there was still no word from the twins about anything big enough over the airwaves to warrant the intervention of Johnny Walker Investigations. But the bounty hunter didn't care one way or the other if they found anything to get them off his property. Not tonight.

Finally. Peace and quiet. And I aim to drown everythin' else out as well.

He finished pouring himself a glass of Johnny Walker Black Label and studied the amber liquid under the kitchen light. With a decisive nod, he retrieved the bottle, looked at it, and doubled his usual four-finger pour. With another nod, this time of satisfaction, he snatched the rocks glass up and headed into his workshop.

A glance at his worktable made him pause before he reached the hall. The small black box that rested on the corner of the table made him wrinkle his nose as he sipped his whiskey.

Aw, hell. I might as well get it over with now while I can still think straight.

He picked the little box up and jammed it into the pocket of his black Levis before he strode into the hallway.

Lisa sat cross-legged on the living room couch, sipping a glass of iced tea and reading another book on her tablet.

"You know, I remember a time when books came in paper." He sat beside her on the couch and took another sip. "Pages you get to turn with your own hand. A nice cover you can hold, and you ain't gotta worry about the damn thing's battery dyin' on ya."

She pursed her lips and closed out of her book before she put it aside on the table. "You aren't the only one who was born in the twentieth century." She regarded him with a slightly mocking glance that contained enough teasing to be appealing.

"If you hadn't told me about your kid, darlin', I'd tell you that was a flat-out lie."

"I still won't tell you how old I am."

The dwarf chuckled and took another sip of whiskey. "Why don't I ever see you readin' a regular book the way they were meant to be read?"

Lisa placed her cup of tea on the coffee table and tried not to laugh at his genuine curiosity. "I haven't had a chance to empty my apartment in Washington, but I emptied the hotel room the Bureau put me up in down here."

"Uh-huh..." He frowned. "What's your point?"

"You've done everything but outright ask me to move in with you."

"Well, shit, darlin'. It seems to me you already did." When she laughed, the overwhelming need to backpedal made him add hurriedly, "I ain't sayin' you crossed a line. I like you here. It's as simple as that and I ain't fixin' to complicate it. But I don't see what that has to do with books."

"If I bought a paperback of every book I read on a weekly basis, Johnny, there would be more books in this house than guns."

He stared at her, ran his tongue along the inside of his cheek, and immediately lifted his glass to his lips and muttered, "Point taken."

"And judging by that look, I should start looking for storage units."

The bounty hunter choked, swallowed his drink, and pounded his chest with a fist. "Say what, now?"

"Unless you don't truly want me to move in with you."

"All right, now wait a minute." He leaned away from her to study her warily. "I came in here talkin' about books, and you're spittin' out all kindsa somethin' I got no idea what to call."

"Well, I have another month left on my lease." Lisa shrugged. "So..."

"So what?"

"You won't say it, will you?"

"Darlin', the list of things I give a damn about is short. Yeah, you're on it, but riddles ain't. So say what you're tryin' to say."

"I'm saying I want you to tell me." She tilted her head and leaned back against the corner of the armrest when his only reply was to frown at her and drink more whiskey. "And don't ask me what it is. We've been talking about it."

Dammit. I ain't fixin' to go round and round on this ride all night. I thought I was done with headaches.

"All right." He nodded. "I guess I oughtta ask if it's what you want first."

A small smile twitched on her lips. "I'm here, aren't I?"

"Yeah, darlin'. I ain't forgettin' that anytime soon."

"Good. So..."

The bounty hunter shifted on the couch to place his whiskey on the coffee table. Something jabbed painfully into his thigh and he leaned back again to reach into his pocket with a frown.

"Are you okay?"

"Yeah, I only..." He pulled the black box out and stared at it. *Damn. I picked a hell of a time to bring this up. She's talkin' about*

33

livin' together and all I have is inside this dumb box. "All right. You want me to say it, darlin'? Fine. Lisa, I—"

"Whoa, whoa. Wait a minute." Her eyes widened as she stared at the box in his hand. A nervous chuckle escaped her. "Johnny, I was talking about me living here with you. That's it."

"Well, I know that."

"Okay, but now you're—"

"Jesus, you were grillin' me about sayin' it out loud and makin' it official. Now you look like someone's holdin' a gun to your head."

Lisa snorted. "Well, some people might view it that way."

"What the hell are you goin' on about?"

"I only…I'm not sure that's the best thing for either of us."

Johnny growled and dropped the box in his lap. "Make your mind up!"

"I didn't think you were going to propose to me!" The second she voiced the protest, she looked like she wanted to suck it all in again like it never happened. He frowned at her, and she lifted her gaze slowly to meet his. Her blush extended from the tips of her Light Elf ears and down to her neck until it disappeared under the neckline of her t-shirt. "I'm sorry, okay? You…I wasn't…"

"Hold up. You—" He looked at his lap and the black box there. Once he'd snatched it up again, he shook it and the contents rattled around inside.

"Oh, don't—"

"Is this what has you all flustered?"

She wrinkled her nose in confusion. "Isn't that the point? Maybe?"

The dwarf threw his head back and roared with laughter. It was so loud and sudden that she jumped and pressed herself against the couch cushions. "You thought… Aw, hell, darlin'. You—"

He burst out laughing again and grabbed his whiskey. The

laughter only stopped so he wouldn't spill his drink as he knocked back half of it in one swallow.

"I don't think it's that funny."

"That's 'cause you don't know what it is." He chuckled and shook his head. "Okay, I ain't sayin' it's completely off the table but come on. You're givin' me way more credit than any of this deserves. Trust me."

Lisa licked her lips and glanced from his crooked smile to the black box in his hand. "I'm so confused right now."

"Here." He tossed the box at her and she caught it with a startled yelp. "Open it and I'll explain."

She bit her bottom lip as she started to open the box, then snapped it shut again. "Johnny…"

"Go on. It ain't gonna bitecha." Another sip of whiskey cut him off in mid-chuckle.

Lisa opened the box and lowered it slowly into her lap. "Oh."

"Yeah. Oh."

"You're giving me a…bullet. In a jewelry box."

"Naw, I'm givin' you the same special dose of alchemy and tech I gave myself."

"What?"

He gestured toward the box with his rocks glass. "You and me, we've been through some shit together, darlin', and you stuck around through all of it. I reckon it's a good time to cut out the last thing we ain't sharin' at this point. Except for my toothbrush."

"Ew. Who shares toothbrushes?"

"Exactly."

She drew a deep breath and stared at the silver cylinder in the box. "Johnny, why am I looking at an alchemy bullet?"

"No, it ain't—" With a sigh, the dwarf ran a hand through his hair and nodded at the box. "It don't matter how much either of us do—or don't—wish we could read each other's minds. As far as I know, that ain't possible yet. But I reckon I'm done bein' the only one hearin' the extra voices in my head. I thought you might wanna…join in."

"What voices?"

He growled in exasperation. "We done passed the point of you thinkin' I lost my mind, Lisa. At least, I thought we were."

"Oh, the hounds." Her eyes widened in realization and a moment later, she burst out laughing.

Johnny scowled at her as she seemed to lose control entirely on his couch, and every time she settled, she glanced at the black box and lost it all over again.

"Well, shit. If I knew you'd laugh in my face about it, I wouldn't have offered. Hand it over."

"No, wait. You—ha!"

"Lisa. Give me the damn box." He lunged for it but she snapped it shut and whisked it away from his hand. "Don't make me wrestle you for it."

"Yeah, you'd like that, wouldn't you?" She grinned at him and held the box playfully out of his reach—unless, of course, he chose to wrestle her for it. "Okay, fine. What is this?"

He glowered at her, downed the rest of his drink, and thunked the glass on the coffee table. "I told you."

"You…wait. Truly?" Her smile faded when she opened the box again for another look. "You're serious?"

"Well, I thought I was, but it seems it's nothing more than one big joke."

"No, no. Hold on. I'm sorry." Lisa swiped her dark hair away from her face and laughed a little more circumspectly. "I thought you were kidding."

"Uh-huh."

"This is… Okay, did you have to shoot yourself with this to be able to hear Rex and Luther, or—"

"Stop." Johnny snatched the box out of her hand and picked up the small application canister that did, in fact, look like a bullet. "Put this in a gun, and yeah. You'll blow yourself up no matter where you're aimin'. It ain't a bullet. This right here? It's a one-time injection. I had Wallace whip me up the right kinda magical sauce to put in this and it only took us half a dozen attempts before we got it right. It works with—"

"The collars. Right. It's not a bullet."

"Nope." He wiggled the canister at her between his fingers and snorted. "And it sure as shit ain't a ring either."

Half-laughing, half-groaning, she buried her face in her hands. "I can't believe I went there."

"That makes two of us, darlin'."

"But you do see what pulling a box like that out of your pocket makes most people think of, right? It's not like I simply pulled it out of nowhere. We were talking about me living here with you. About us."

"Honestly?" He scratched his head and replaced the canister in the box. "It didn't even cross my mind."

"Oh, okay. Of course not." When the lid snapped shut again in his hand, they both laughed. "Wow."

"I ain't fixin' to push anythin' you don't want on you, Lisa. It was only a thought I had and I decided I'd let you decide."

"Well, that's a relief." She smoothed her hair away from her face and shook her head. "I need a drink."

"I'm right there with ya. Here." He handed her the box and she leaned slightly away.

"I don't know, Johnny…"

"Sure you do. Take the damn box. Keep it on ya. If you decide you wanna take the jump and enter my special world of crazy, all you gotta do is hold it against your neck and press the button to —what? Why are you lookin' at me like that?"

Lisa smiled as she studied his face. "I'm already in Johnny Walker's special world of crazy."

"You know what I mean."

"I do." She took the box from him and froze. "Okay, that was purely meant as me agreeing with you that I know what you mean. Not...you know."

He cleared his throat, stood abruptly, and snatched his rocks glass off the coffee table. "I'll get the drinks."

Her soft chuckle followed him as he hurried down the hallway and into the kitchen.

Jesus Christ, I thought both our heads were gonna explode. Mine ain't even in the right place. It was a stupid idea to put it in a box like that, Johnny. What the hell?

He took another glass from the cupboard and grimaced as he poured a healthy amount for each of them.

I blame the borgs. It's takin' up too much of my damn energy tryin' to keep 'em from killin' everyone in a hundred-mile radius.

The sight of Lisa standing in the doorway when he turned almost made him spill both drinks. "Shit, darlin'. You can't sneak up on a guy like that."

"I'm not sneaking." She grinned and entered the kitchen. "You're merely distracted."

"Damn right I am." When he handed her drink to her, the expectant look she gave him didn't exactly sit right with any part of their current conversation—two giant misunderstandings included. "What is it?"

"You still haven't said it."

"Aw, come on."

"I'm serious."

"You're killin' me, darlin'. You ain't said if you're gonna use that damn canister either. So we can call it even."

"Uh-uh." Lisa pushed his wrist down gently when he tried to drown the topic in more booze. He scowled at her. "We need to finish one conversation at a time and I'd rather do that now instead of having another talk like this that could go south in any number of ways."

The dwarf stared at his drink, then raised it toward her in a toast. "Drink with me first."

"And then you'll say it?"

"This whole thing is like pullin' teeth for you, ain't it?"

She clinked her glass against his and knocked back the whole double shot in one swallow.

With a chuckle, the dwarf nodded and followed suit. Unable to look at her, he turned to the bottle of Johnny Walker Black. "Yeah, darlin'. I want you here with me. Don't bother renewin' that lease in D.C. If it ain't gonna send you runnin' for the hills, pack the whole thing up and move in. I have more than enough room."

The pop of the stopper coming out of the whiskey bottle was the only sound in the kitchen as he refilled his glass.

There. I said it. It's time to move the hell on.

"Okay."

He slid the bottle across the counter and sighed. "Okay?"

"But I'm still getting a storage unit for my books. We'll leave all the extra room for your guns." Her glass clinked onto the counter.

Johnny turned toward her with a chuckle. "Well, ain't that a relief. Do you want another drink?"

"Nope."

"All right." His gaze flicked around the kitchen as he took a long sip, only because she still had a weirdly expectant look on her face. Finally, he shrugged. "So I said mine. It's your turn."

"You mean will I use what's in this box to hear your dogs in my head like you do?"

"Sure." He cleared his throat. "If that's somethin' you want. Or you can hand it back right now and I'll—hey."

Lisa had snatched the rocks glass from his hand and turned away from him with a coy smile. "I'll have to think about it."

He watched her sip his drink and shook his head. "What are you up to?"

"Well, I'm certainly not trying to get us both awkwardly confused again." She backed out of the kitchen and held his whiskey glass out to the side like a carrot on a stick. "So let's stop talking."

"Uh-huh." He followed her across the hall until she stopped in front of the bedroom door. "It's a fine idea, darlin'."

"I know."

The dog door clacked open and shut and both hounds raced into the house. "Johnny! Hey, Johnny!"

"You won't believe what Leroy just told us. Remember that —Johnny?"

Rex and Luther skidded to a stop when they saw their master and his woman tangled together in the bedroom doorway.

"Oh…" Luther sniggered. "Get it, Johnny."

As he ducked his head between his rear legs to lick himself, Rex chuckled. "You'd think after all this time, they'd learn how to close the door."

"Yeah, you both have opposable thumbs, right?"

"Shut it," Johnny muttered.

Lisa pulled away from him with a playful frown. "I didn't say anything."

"I'm talkin' to the hounds, darlin'." He wound his arms tighter around her waist and led her into the bedroom.

"Huh. It doesn't make a very good case for your little-black-box offer."

"It don't matter to me what you decide. For now, stop talkin'." Lisa burst out laughing before he swung the bedroom door shut with a bang.

"Wait, what?" Luther cocked his head. "What does any of that have to do with us?"

"It doesn't, bro." Rex finally stood and sniffed the bottom of the door before one of Johnny's boots thumped against it.

"Git!"

"Yeah, you too, Johnny!"

Laughing, the hounds scrambled to turn on the wooden floor

and darted outside. "Bet I can beat you to the empty pickle jars, Rex!"

"You couldn't beat me to the stick. What the hell are you gonna do with empty jars?"

"No clue. Let's sniff 'em and find out."

CHAPTER FIVE

Mornings had become Johnny's favorite part of the day over the last two months, and that was because the borgs tended to stay up late and sleep in late. Even when he woke at a little after 8:00 am the next morning, the promise of at least two blissful hours without being harassed by bored, grumpy, disrespectful, brain-scrambled cyborgs put some extra pep in the bounty hunter's step.

He stood in the kitchen and drummed his fingers on the countertop as he waited for the coffeemaker to finish brewing enough for his first cup of the day. A billow of steam emerged from the bathroom when Lisa stepped out, fully clothed but still towel-drying her hair. She grinned when he darted her a sidelong glance. "It looks like someone's enjoying the coffeemaker."

"You caught me, darlin'." He took two mugs out but hovered over the pot. "Do these always take so damn long?"

"Seriously? You've gone this long without making your own coffee at home and you're suddenly this impatient?"

"Naw, it ain't sudden." He leaned toward her when she stopped to kiss his cheek before she moved to the fridge. "It's two months of havin' the patience sucked outta me by my house bein' turned into a damn magical zoo."

The fridge opened and Lisa cast him a disbelieving glance over her shoulder. "Your house?"

"Fine. Whole damn property." The coffeemaker hissed and burbled even louder when he yanked the pot out to pour himself a cup. He returned it and let it finish the rest of its cycle.

"Let's call it the back yard, huh?" Lisa went to the stove with the carton of eggs and a huge packet of sliced ham from the deli.

"I ain't talkin' about you and me, darlin'. Maybe I could, after last night."

"In which case, I'd have to ask why you're pissed at the speed of the coffeemaker instead of enjoying the morning." She didn't turn away from the stove when she said it but instead, set to work making breakfast.

The dwarf snorted. "Well then, I ain't gonna say it. What are you doin' with that ham?"

"Frying it. With eggs. Why?"

"You have no idea how much I like hearin' you say that." He leaned against the counter and sipped the piping-hot coffee. "Shit. This is one fine cuppa joe."

"You know you've said the same thing about every cup since I got the coffeemaker, right?"

"'Cause it's true. Do you want any help with that?"

"Nope." The first egg cracked on the edge of the skillet with a sizzle and she tossed the shell in the trash.

"All right. Then I'm gonna—"

A loud, urgent knock came at the back door, followed by a swift bark from each of the hounds. "What're you doin', two-legs?"

"Yeah, get outta the way. That's our door."

The dog door clacked open and shut, and Rex and Luther skittered into the kitchen.

"Ooh. Hey, lady. Whatcha cookin'?"

"Luther. Is that ham?"

"Oh, yeah! Hey! Drop it right here. No, no, don't—aw, man. It's already cooked!"

Johnny sipped his coffee and tried to drown out the hounds' voices to listen to the sizzle of frying ham and eggs. *I ain't gonna let a little noise ruin my mornin'. No, sir.*

The knock came again.

Lisa turned from the stove and pointed at the back door with the tongs. "Are you going to get that?"

"Nope."

Whoever it was pounded on the door this time, followed by a gruff, "Johnny? Open up. It's Brandon."

"What the hell is he doin' up this early?"

"What?" She laughed. "It's after eight-thirty."

"Dammit." He stalked across the kitchen and ignored the hounds that scrambled out of his way before they converged at Lisa's feet again and stared at the sizzling stove. The dwarf twisted the lock—which he hadn't used once until bringing the borgs home two months before—harder than necessary and jerked the door open. "What?"

"Hey. G'morning."

"It sure was."

Brandon tapped the side of his neck, where the metal panel was now closed to hide his inner cyborg wiring. "You're gonna want to see this."

"I already know what your neck wires look like. Get off the—"

"No, I mean we found something. Or rather, Clint found it. I thought you wouldn't want us to keep you waiting on it."

"You thought wrong, pal. I ain't fixin' to start the day like this, so the quicker you git on, the sooner I can get back to enjoyin' my mornin'." Without giving the borg a chance to reply, Johnny slammed the door in his face and turned toward the kitchen. He took a long slurp of black coffee and closed his eyes.

"Even if we heard your name specifically?" Brandon called from the porch.

Lisa met Johnny's gaze and raised her eyebrows before she flipped the ham.

"Dammit." The back door opened again enough for him to scrutinize the cyborg with one eye. "What exactly did you hear?"

"Uh…Johnny Walker."

"Gimme five minutes." The dwarf shut the door again and locked it before he stormed across the kitchen toward the coffeemaker, which now sputtered at the end of its brew cycle. He added a little to his, poured a cup for Lisa, and filled the rest of his with whiskey. "I swear, they're turnin' me into a mornin' lush."

She snorted. "Since when did you start blaming that on anyone?"

"Since I had four assholes on my property to blame it on. Do you want some?"

"No, but I'll take the coffee." When he brought it to her, she reached out to take the handle without removing her attention from the stove. "Thank you. Do you have any idea why your name's on private airwaves or encrypted radio or…whatever?"

"I assume I'm about to find out. After the robot twins tell me what the hell they're doin' hookin' themselves up to Margo first thing in the goddamn mornin'."

"I'll keep your plate warm."

"I appreciate it." Johnny cursed when he jerked on the doorknob and it wouldn't budge. "Stupid locks in this—hell." He shoved the lock aside and tried again, this time successfully, before he strode down the steps and off the porch.

Once the door shut behind him, Lisa took another slice of ham from the deli package, ripped it in half, and dropped the two pieces on the floor one after the other.

"Oh, man…oh, man…oh, man. You're the best, lady!"

Rex snarled at his brother when Luther tried to gobble the

one half that didn't belong to him. "What's your problem? You got yours!"

"I love ham—"

"Hey." Lisa snapped her fingers. "Cut it out. If you guys start fighting over food you're not supposed to have, we'll all be in trouble."

Luther sniggered as he licked the linoleum floor in a wide circle where ham had most certainly not fallen. "Listen to her, bro. Talking like she can understand us."

"But she has a point."

Outside, Johnny sipped his coffee and wished he'd filled the mug with neat whiskey instead. *It's still too damn hot to chug and I ain't been awake long enough to handle this like someone tryin' not to be an asshole.*

"What the hell are y'all two knuckleheads doin' out here right now?"

Brandon poked his head around the side of Margo and frowned. "I told you—"

"I told y'all she's off-limits. And here you are with the cables out bright 'n early like I ain't laid down the rules."

"No, we didn't. The cables were out all night and we were up early to get back to work."

The dwarf stopped two feet from the metal hull and clenched his jaw. "Y'all didn't clean up after yourselves last night?"

"Not when you told us the Airstream's off-limits."

"She's ain't a—" With a growl, Johnny stalked around the other side of Margo. "Fine. Whatcha got?"

Clint sat on the grass in front of Margo's doorway, the cable connected to the open panel in the side of his neck. He glanced at Johnny, then at his brother, and spread his arms.

"Oh, yeah. Can you rig this for audio playback?"

"You mean Mr. Silence here can't open some other metal part and blast it out for everyone to hear?"

Brandon wrinkled his nose. "No. That's impossible."

"Huh. It worked on an armored worm."

The borg glanced at the bounty hunter's mug. "Are you drinking already?"

"It's coffee. Stay there." With another loud slurp of the spiked coffee, Johnny stepped into Margo and fiddled with the control panel until he found what he needed. He typed the command and stabbed the execute key.

"Audio replay initiated, Johnny. How else may I help you?"

The bounty hunter clicked his tongue in the side of his mouth and gave the control panel a little pat. "That's fine, darlin'. Just fine. All right. Y'all better have somethin' worth draggin' me outta my kitchen durin' the only hours of quiet I ever get around here anymore."

The second his boots touched the grass again, the squeal of feedback screeched through Margo's speakers. He ducked at the earsplitting sound and shouted, "Too damn loud, Margo."

"Would you like me to turn the volume down, Johnny?"

"That's what I said, ain't it?"

Static crackled through the speakers and reverberated around Margo's hollow interior.

"I'm sorry. I didn't understand that. Please repeat. Would you like me to—"

"Yes, dammit! Turn the volume down!"

The feedback and static disappeared and he gulped the rest of the coffee despite it being too hot to do so comfortably. "Clint. You had somethin' to share?"

Brandon nodded at his brother. "Go ahead."

The other borg's eyelids fluttered rapidly and his head jerked toward his shoulder. The cable connected to his neck panel wobbled with the movement and a moment later, Margo's Mila Kunis voice spoke again.

"Audio sync complete. Initiating playback."

After another quick burst of static, Margo filled with different voices.

"...so we need someone on the inside."

"We can't use any of ours, sir. It's too risky."

"You think I don't know that? Shit. Read me the list."

"Abernathy Incorporated."

"Not even close."

"Girard Holt. He has connections."

"With pencil-pushers and investment firms. He'd shit himself if he got caught up in an illegal arms deal. He wouldn't even know how to buy himself out. Who else?"

"Thomison & Hardy."

"Fuck me sideways. Those bastards tried—and I mean tried. I don't trust them to hold my pen without breaking it. Who made this list?"

"Private Ensen, sir."

"The research guy?"

"I think so, yeah."

"Is that it?"

"There's only one more. Johnny Walker Investigations."

"Never heard of—wait. Like the drink?"

"Like the bounty hunter, sir."

"Shit. The one who had that show?"

"I think he spent more time working for the FBI."

"Dammit. I'm not trying to screw around with all that. How did he make it onto the list, huh? I thought the guy up and disappeared decades ago."

"It seems he's back, sir. Unaffiliated."

"No feds?"

"It doesn't look like it. This is his firm."

"Ha. A dwarf bounty hunter with a firm. That's rich. Does he have a profile?"

"Private Ensen can't find it."

"Nah. Get Lance Corporal Hendricks to investigate him. If the whiskey dwarf pans out, we'll set a meeting up. No contact for now, Harper. Only a glance through the window. Got it?"

"Sir."

"All right. Get off the line, Sergeant Major. I gotta make some calls."

After a click and another burst of static, Margo announced, *"Audio playback has ended. Would you like me to repeat the recording, Johnny?"*

Johnny tugged his beard and scowled at Clint. "Whiskey dwarf? Asshole."

"Please confirm your request to search for whiskey dwarf asshole—"

"What? No. No search, Margo. Stand down."

Brandon sniggered and immediately lowered his head to hide his smile when the bounty hunter glared at him.

Clint's eyes snapped open when he sucked in a sharp breath. He looked at his brother with a questioning glance.

The other borg nodded before he turned to Johnny. "So? You wanted us to tell you about anything with your name on it, right?"

"Uh-huh. This has my name and a few other things." He pointed at Margo's open door. "You heard 'illegal arms deal' in there too, right?"

"Yep."

"Huh. It sounds like some military douche got his panties in a bunch." Johnny smirked. "And he's lookin' for a dwarf to unbunch 'em, ain't he?"

The twins exchanged a confused glance.

"We're still talking about a job, right?" Brandon wrinkled his nose. "Not panties?"

The dwarf grunted and didn't bother to answer. "Did y'all pick this up on a private phone line?"

Clint nodded.

"On a base in South Carolina," Brandon said. "I'm not sure which one but we can find it."

He folded his arms and couldn't wipe the smile off his face. "You know, the more I think about it, the better it feels."

"We have all the right guys for it too."

"If we were dealing with a nutjob CIA scientist, maybe. But this is the US Military. My guess is Marines or Navy SEALs."

Brandon shrugged. "I can ask Leroy."

"Why the hell would he know jack?" He pointed at him and squinted. "Did you play this for him first?"

"No." The borg frowned and gestured toward the monolith of the houseboat visible even behind Margo. "But he used to be military. If anyone knows how to—"

"Leroy was what?"

"Military. I already said that, right?"

Johnny flung his hands in the air and turned away from the twins. "You gotta be shittin' me."

"You didn't know?"

He stalked around Margo's metal hull. "Do I look like the kinda guy who'd act surprised if I already knew a thing like that?"

"Well, it's a hard thing to tell simply by looking at—"

"That was rhetorical!"

Brandon and Clint exchanged another wide-eyed glance before Brandon darted around Margo after the dwarf. "Hey, what do you want us to do with all the gear?"

"Unplug your silent half and leave everythin' where it is. I have some brainstormin' to do."

"Do you want me to get Leroy?"

"If I wanted that, I woulda said it. Jesus, does anyone know how to pay attention anymore?" Johnny marched up the stairs of the back porch and entered the house. The door slapped shut behind him.

Brandon returned to his brother and knelt at Clint's side to help disconnect Margo's cable and the stabilization patch. He grinned. "I think we found a big one. Are you ready to go in for this one?"

His twin clicked the metal panel in his neck shut and stretched his head from side to side. He smirked and made a childish explosion sound, miming the action with a raised fist exploding into an open hand.

"Yeah." His brother sniggered. "Me too."

CHAPTER SIX

"That was fast." Lisa lifted a forkful of eggs to her mouth as she leaned against the kitchen counter with her plate in her hand. "Did they find anything good?"

"Maybe." Johnny ran a hand through his hair and thumped the coffee mug on the counter before he filled it halfway with whiskey. He added a splash of coffee for good measure. "Some military hotshot basically put out a private APB on yours truly."

She choked on her mouthful, forced it down, and put her plate on the counter. "What?"

"They're lookin' for private contractors, darlin'. And somehow, my name came up."

"Well, you're not exactly low profile."

"And they mentioned the business too."

"Hey, that's good, right?" She paused to wash her food down with coffee, then cleared her throat. "I haven't checked in a while, but I bet the website's finally getting enough traffic to make a splash. Certainly enough to catch the military's attention. What's the job?"

"Dunno. Somethin' with illegal arms dealin' and that's as much as the twins had."

"Wait. Was this a direct message?"

"Not to me." He took another sip of his coffee-flavored whiskey and sighed. "But it has my name on it, darlin'. Literally."

"Well, if it's time-sensitive, I can't imagine they'd take very long. Okay. We'll wait for them to reach out and ask if you want the job—"

"Naw, I ain't waitin'."

Lisa folded her arms and raised an eyebrow. "Oh, so you'll go with your usual MO, huh? Storm onto a military base and say you'll take the case no one asked you to take?"

"I thought about it." He turned and glanced at her half-empty plate on the counter. She gestured toward the oven and he brought his mug with him before he pulled out the still-warm plate covered in tinfoil. "The asshole called me the whiskey dwarf."

She snorted and opened the silverware drawer to hand him a fork. "I assume that's because these people had no idea two cyborgs in Johnny Walker's back yard were listening to their conversation."

"What a guy does when he thinks no one's watchin' or listenin' shows everythin' you need to know about him." He crumpled the tinfoil in his hand and tossed it into the trash. "But I ain't headin' out to a base until those bastards realize they ain't got a choice."

With a resigned sigh, Lisa picked her plate up again and began to finish her breakfast. "I assume you already have a plan for how to corner them into hiring you."

"You're damn right I do. If Margo swings both ways, I reckon the twins do too."

"Wait, what?"

"Communicatin'. Receivin' and sendin'. What'd you think I meant?"

"Nothing." She forced a laugh back with another forkful of eggs as Johnny dug into his breakfast.

Chewing slowly, he stared at the plate of scrambled eggs and fried ham. "Lisa."

"What?"

He shook his head slowly and tapped his fork against the plate. "This is the best damn breakfast cooked in this house. I think you oughtta know."

"Thanks. Don't expect it to be a regular thing."

"Why not?"

"Johnny, I'm not—"

His sharp laugh cut her off. "Yeah, I know. You ain't a secretary or a cook or a maid. It's a good thing I ain't lookin' for any of 'em."

With a smirk, she returned her attention to the last piece of ham on her plate. "That's what I thought."

They ate in silence and ignored the hounds' wild baying outside as they raced after something in the swamp. And the loud crash and angry shouts to announce that June had woken for the day and was ready to destroy everything around her.

"Every damn mornin'." He shook his head, rinsed his plate in the sink, and traded plates with Lisa so he could rinse hers while she loaded the dishwasher. "You'd think after two months, she'd finally realize where the hell she is when she opens her eyes."

"We don't know how long they were down there with Dr. Monroe, but I'm willing to bet it was longer than two months." She closed the dishwasher and fixed him a knowing glance. "It'll take time, especially for June. She doesn't remember anything about her life before being half-machine."

"That ain't an excuse to tear my houseboat up."

"You know, not everyone is as adaptable as you want them to be."

The dwarf wiped his hands on a paper towel before he threw it in the trash. "I'm adaptable."

"I wasn't talking about you. But no, Johnny. You're truly not." She snorted. "Unless you're working a case and making everything up as you go. That's the only time I've seen you go with the flow."

"The flow." He nodded toward the back door. "I aim to go with the flow and stick it to whoever thinks he's so clever with that whiskey-dwarf bullshit. And you know what else?"

Lisa smiled as he held open the door for her. "What else, Johnny?"

"Accordin' to the twins, Leroy used to be military."

"Oh…" She looked directly ahead and hurried down the stairs.

"You don't sound too surprised."

"Should I be?"

"Aw, hell." Johnny stopped halfway down. "How'd you find that out before I did?"

"He told me."

"And you didn't think it was somethin' I oughtta know?"

She turned quickly to watch him stride down the steps and shrugged. "Johnny, if I'd told you when I found out, you wouldn't have brought them here."

"You knew before we left that damn base?"

"Yep. And I told the borgs not to tell you. You know, because of your…whatever against the military." Her eyes widened when he stormed closer to her. "Which, by the way, you haven't explained to me in any real detail."

"There ain't nothin' to explain, darlin'. I have a thing. That's all anyone needs to know. Brandon!"

"Yeah?" Both twins looked up from the huge table in the center of the yard.

"Where's everyone else?"

"On the boat."

"And they ain't comin' out here for this job or what?"

The twins shrugged.

The bounty hunter headed across the lawn again toward Margo, stepped into her dark interior, and swiped a hand across the control panel.

56

"Hello, Johnny."

"Yeah, hey. Call the borgs."

My scan shows two cyborg magicals seated in the yard and two in the houseboat. Would you like me to split and redirect two different—"

"The houseboat! That's it." He scratched the side of his face and stared at one of the overhead monitors as it lit up with a view of the swamp behind his house and the giant houseboat anchored in the river. *Why the hell would I need an alarm for the damn borgs seated twenty feet in front of me? I guess I still have a few bugs to fix here.*

A countdown from five illuminated in the center of the monitor and he sniffed.

The high-pitched whine he barely heard wasn't meant for him or Lisa or even the hounds. The frequency had been designed specifically for the borgs and it was about the only thing he'd come up with that made them listen to a single thing he said.

The bounty hunter heard June's angry shout and the slam of one of the houseboat doors before her figure appeared on the monitor. Her crystal body flashed with blue-white light and yellow sparks and propulsion fuel burst from the soles of her built-in cyborg shoes before she launched off the deck toward the yard.

Leroy opened the door on the lower deck and stood motionless at the railing.

Johnny swiped at the control panel for a quick command, and the monitor's view zoomed in on the shifter borg standing perfectly still. Leroy glared directly at the camera and his mechanical eye spun, widened, and narrowed again. His right cyborg hand was already raised in front of his chest, shaped as a hand this time with the segmented middle finger extended.

With a smirk, the bounty hunter turned the monitor off. "All right, Margo. That's enough. Kill the alarm."

"Alarm sequence deactivated, Johnny. Is there anything else I can—"

"If I need somethin', I'll tell you."

And I don't remember addin' a 'can I annoy you to death by tryin' to be helpful' line to that voice code. I seriously gotta fix that.

By the time he walked around Margo's hull and headed toward the table, Lisa, June, and the twins had already taken their seats. A heavy thump came from the dock, and Leroy stepped onto the grass at the end of the wooden walkway and flung water off himself with strobed bursts of some kind of energy shield.

"Huh. I guess that's about as close as a shifter's gonna get to actual magic."

Lisa frowned at him. "What?"

"It don't matter. Hurry up, Leroy."

The shifter borg didn't alter his pace as he approached the table and slumped into the last empty reinforced chair. Johnny studied the guy—the ex-military guy—and scowled.

It ain't like I have access to a better team at this point. I might as well see if they sink or swim with this one.

"Brandon."

"Yeah."

Johnny nodded at the twins. "Tell 'em what y'all heard."

Brandon shifted in his chair, shared a glance with his brother, and shrugged. "A private phone call from MCAS in Beaufort, South Carolina. Some top guy's looking for a contractor to help with an illegal arms deal—or stopping it, probably. Johnny's name came up. They're vetting him now, and…well, I guess that's it."

"Military." The dwarf pointed at Leroy. "Like you used to be. Ain't that right?"

The shifter borg's eyes widened and he squirmed in his seat. He darted a glance at Lisa and cleared his throat. "Yep. A long time ago."

"Uh-huh. Do you wanna enlighten us about how you went from military shifter to half-machine shifter who wasn't important enough to go chasin' after when you went missin'?"

"Not really."

"Did you get kicked out? Dishonorable discharge and time served? Or do I have a shifter soldier gone AWOL and hidin' out on my property?"

"Johnny…" Lisa gave him a warning look and shook her head slightly.

Leroy's mechanical eye whirred and clicked. "I don't know."

"I ain't buyin' it. Before I go playin' Hire the Dwarf with these guys talkin' about me out in Beaufort, I gotta know if it's gonna come back to bite me in the ass more than usual."

"He said he doesn't know," June snapped.

"Why the hell not?"

"I don't remember!" Leroy pounded his metal fist on the table, caused a flurry of thin splinters, and left an impressive dent in the thick wood. "None of us remembers everything we want to so leave it alone."

With his arms folded, Johnny studied the borgs and Lisa, who all glared at him. *If he ain't still loyal to chain of command, I can work with it.*

"Good." He stepped toward the head of the table and rapped his knuckles on the edge. "Y'all can retrace that little snippet of a phone call, yeah?"

The twins looked at each other and reached an answer without words before both nodded at him simultaneously.

"And send a message back?"

Brandon scratched his head. "Not through the phone, probably."

"But y'all can tap into somethin' that bigwig ain't gonna miss hearin' when it gets there, right?"

"Sure."

The dwarf regarded each of them calmly. "All right. Does anyone have a problem with taking a big job for the US military?" No one else around the table said anything, which was probably as good as he would get. "Clint, do you have recordin'…gear?"

The silent twin thumped his right elbow on the table and

raised his hand. The metal bar that stretched down his arm to the tip of his middle finger flashed with silver light. With another whirr and click of gears, a hatch at the edge of his metallic middle finger popped open.

Johnny stared at the display. "Is that a yes?"

"He's ready when you are," Brandon said.

"Uh-huh. Here's the message, then." He cleared his throat and couldn't quite hide the crooked smile that threatened to break through. "Johnny Walker, here. I heard y'all been lookin' for someone to help with your little arms problem. It might be that I can fit y'all into my schedule if you're interested."

The open hatch at the tip of Clint's finger blinked with a green light and continued to click intermittently. All the borgs stared at him.

"Is that it?" Leroy asked with a grimace.

"Yep."

"Do you…wanna leave a phone number or something?" Brandon asked.

"Naw. When y'all send this, go ahead and leave an openin' for them to get back to my secretary."

Lisa scowled and leaned forward across the table. "And who's that, exactly?"

"Margo." He gestured toward the curved metal hull behind him. "Who else would it be? Now go on. Send it. I bet we ain't got long to wait until they come snoopin' around wantin' to bite on my offer."

No one moved from the table.

The bounty hunter spread his arms in an impatient gesture. "I meant right now. Get it done."

The twins stood abruptly and headed toward Margo to hook up again and send his recorded message to…well, some asshole who would be very surprised.

Hell, I don't even know who's gonna see this. He smirked. *It makes it that much sweeter.*

"Why are we here?" June gestured toward herself and Leroy.

"I thought I'd let y'all in on the plan and give y'all a chance to say no thanks, you're out. But you're in, so we're good."

"Great." The Crystal borg rolled her eyes and stood. "Maybe call next time."

"On what? We ain't got phones hooked up in the—"

The ignition of her jetpack feet cut him off two seconds before she launched into a high arc toward the houseboat. A moment later, her metal boots thunked onto the deck and the sound echoed across the swamp.

Johnny sighed in exasperation and settled his gaze on Leroy. "What branch?"

The shifter borg regarded him warily. "Marines."

"'Course you were."

"Johnny." Lisa glanced at her wristwatch. "You have some-where else to be in half an hour."

"And where's that?"

She widened her eyes at him and finally gave in. "The Academy."

"Aw, shit. Is it time for that already?"

"Sure is."

"All right, fine." He pointed at Leroy. "Y'all stay here. If the twins can't get that message through—"

"It's already sent, Johnny," Brandon shouted and raised his hand as he stepped out from behind Margo. "We finished a second ago."

"Damn. Then…I don't know. Stay outta trouble while I'm gone." He headed to the side yard and Lisa stood to follow him.

"Do you want me to come with you?"

"To pick the kid up? Naw." He ran a hand through his auburn hair. "We'll be in and outta there faster than you can say, 'Pick the kid up.'"

With a smirk, she lowered her head. "Okay, sure. I guess it's probably good for you two to have some one-on-one time, right? I get it."

"What? That ain't it." Johnny snorted. "I can't leave these metal-brains here without someone keepin' an eye on 'em."

"Right."

She has me worked out like a damn kiddie puzzle. Shit. So what if I want a little time to prep the kid for all this mess?

"I won't be long." Johnny turned in a tight circle and scanned his back yard. "Where are those damn hounds? Rex! Luther!"

A quick series of thumps and the crash of shattered glass came from the other side of Margo, followed by two quick yelps.

"Shit," Luther whispered.

"Don't say anything, bro. Act natural."

"You think he noticed?"

"What the hell are y'all up to?" Johnny spun when another thump came from the shed's open door. "To me, boys!"

"Yeah, yeah. Coming, Johnny!" More glass shattered before Rex barreled around the side of Margo toward his master, panting and waving his tail. "What's up? Where we going?"

"Luther!"

The smaller hound yelped and trotted out after his brother. He looked repeatedly over his shoulder with wide eyes. "On it, Johnny. You say when, and I'll do it."

"It's time to pick the kid up from school." With a glance at Lisa, he turned and strode toward the side yard.

"We're getting the pup? Awesome!"

"I thought she lived there, Johnny. What happened?" Rex paused to sit and scratch vigorously behind his ear.

"Ooh, did she get kicked out? You know what? I bet she brought someone a dead rabbit or something." Luther snorted. "Two-legs. So ungrateful."

"She ain't kicked out, boys. She's on leave."

"What did she leave?" Rex caught up with them at a trot and his ears flopped against his head.

"Yeah, and where?"

"Break." The bounty hunter shook his head and headed to Sheila parked in the front dirt lot. "I meant break."

"I thought shifters could heal themselves."

"Dammit. No. School's closed for two weeks and we're goin' to bring her home. Before we take her back." He jerked the red Jeep's back door open and nodded for the hounds to hop inside. *Jesus. Why do I even bother tryin' to explain to a couple of coonhounds?*

"Oh…" Luther leapt into the back of the Jeep and his claws scrabbled across the bare plastic floor. "Is it a surprise?"

"No." After Rex bounded up, Johnny started to shut Sheila's back gate but paused to sniff the air. "Why am I smellin' pickles?"

"What? Where?" Luther whipped his head from side to side. "I don't smell anything."

The dwarf leaned toward the back of the Jeep, took another sniff, and scowled. "It's y'all."

"I'm not a pickle, Johnny. Be nice."

All their master had to do was fold his arms and the hounds caved.

"Come on, Johnny. It's not that bad."

Luther lowered his head. "And how come the metal two-legs get all of them?"

"'Cause it's all they can eat." He stepped back and pointed at the ground. "Get out."

"What?"

"But we wanna see the pup."

"There's a reason the air-freshener folks ain't made a pickled-coonhound scent. Git."

"Aw, man." Both hounds jumped from the back and Luther began to lick his brother's briny, dill-flavored back. "It's so good…"

"Get off me."

"Y'all stay here. I won't be long."

"Make sure she doesn't forget about us, Johnny."

"Yeah, and we won't forget about the pickles!"

He stopped at the driver's door. "Don't you—"

The hounds had already sprinted toward the back of the house again and howled fiercely as they raced each other.

The bounty hunter rolled his eyes, stepped into Sheila, and started the engine.

It ain't my house anymore. It's a damn madhouse.

CHAPTER SEVEN

"Boy, am I glad the semester's over." Amanda sat in Sheila's passenger seat, grinned at the road around them, at Johnny, and beyond them at the swamp. "Yeah, it was kinda crazy. You wouldn't think that, right? 'Cause I was already there for six weeks before school started but classes are so different."

He slid her a sidelong glance. "Are they hard?"

"My classes?" The girl leaned back in her seat and looked directly ahead and her smile faded a little. "Not really."

That's a sure sign she ain't fixin' to talk about it.

As Sheila bowled down the dirt road from the Academy of Necessary Magic in the swamp to his property, the dwarf slung his arm out his window and drew a slow breath.

It's been over five months without her and it feels like we're back at square one.

"Are the trainers treatin' you all right?"

Amanda looked at him in amusement. "You mean the teachers?"

"Sure."

"Yeah, they're fine. Petrov yells constantly but he's bald."

He snorted. "Are you makin' friends? Stayin' outta trouble?"

The girl shrugged slowly and turned to stare out her window with wide eyes. "Yeah. Yeah, it's all good."

"Good. You'll do fine at that school, kid. There ain't no doubt in my mind."

"Thanks." She drummed her fingers on the armrest, took a sharp breath, and turned toward him. "Hey, did you know there's a kemana in the Everglades? Like, right out in the middle of the swamp?"

"Yep."

"Have you ever been there?"

"I have everythin' I need at home, kid. I ain't had the need."

"But there's…well…way more out there than I thought, you know?"

"Do y'all take field trips at that school?"

"I can't go there this year. Freshmen aren't allowed." She darted him another sideways glance and cleared her throat. "Hey, how much do you know about the campus?"

"The one I built?"

Amanda laughed. "You didn't build it."

"My property. My wallet. Same difference. I know enough. Why?"

"No reason." She shrugged again but couldn't keep her excitement down. "So you knew about the kemana then. That's cool. We should go sometime."

"I'll…think about it."

"Hey, do you know anything about all the crazy-weird ancient stuff buried under the swamp?"

"The what now?" He finally looked away from the road and pulled his black sunglasses down slightly to look at her.

"The…never mind." She folded her arms and sighed. "I was curious, is all."

"Uh-huh. I'd say somethin's wrong if you weren't."

"You might be the only one," Amanda muttered.

"Say what?"

"Nothing." The wind gusted through Sheila's pane-less windows and whipped her hair over her face and across her neck. She brushed it aside and let herself enjoy riding in an actual vehicle again. "So what did you get up to while I was at school?"

"Me?" Johnny did a double-take. "Nothin' much."

"Lisa's still there, right?"

"What? Yeah. I reckon Lisa ain't goin' anywhere any time soon."

"Well, that's good."

"Ya think?"

The girl chuckled. "Duh. I like her. You like her. I guess it must have been boring without me, huh? Only you, Lisa, and the hounds."

Johnny cleared his throat. "It sounds like you're fishin' for somethin', kid."

"Me? No way." She couldn't hold a straight face, though, and they both laughed.

"Hell, I can't rightly say it's been borin' around here. But I tell you what. We sure as hell missed you."

"Really?" She gave him one of her winning shifter-girl grins and he forced out a cough to keep from choking up.

She's been gone that long and I'm still wrapped around her damn finger.

"Sure. But you oughtta be in school. It's good for ya. For now, you're right where you belong."

She wrinkled her nose. "I guess."

They rounded the bend in the road a mile away from his property and she looked out his window with an expectant smile. It faded as quickly as it had appeared and she pointed across the front of the Jeep. "Holy crap. What is that?"

"What?"

"That huge thing sticking up behind the trees."

"Huh."

The girl continued to stare at it and her eyes widened when

they finally reached the long dirt road that took them onto the property. Johnny took a sharp turn and Sheila's tires spat sprays of gravel and dirt as they fishtailed slightly.

"Um...Johnny?"

He tightened his hold on the steering wheel and sniffed. "Amanda."

"Why is there a giant building behind your house?"

"Oh, that. Well, that's been there for a few months."

"What is it?"

"Houseboat."

She laughed a little uncertainly. "You already have a house?"

"Yep." He scowled as they reached the end of the road and his property came into full view when they crested the shallow rise. *And here comes the shitshow.*

Sheila's tires roared again on the dirt drive when he braked sharply. He hopped out without giving her time to ask any more questions and muttered, "I'll get your bag."

"Okay..." Amanda stepped slowly out of the Jeep and shut the door behind her out of habit rather than conscious thought, her gaze fixed on the top of the houseboat. "It looks like a hotel."

He grunted and strode to the front porch with her duffel bag in one hand. "It's a houseboat."

"Hey, hey, hey! The pup!" Rex howled and darted down the side yard with Luther close on his heels.

"You're back! Holy shit, pup. You don't look any older than when you left fifty years ago!"

"Even shifters grow slower than hounds, bro. Everyone knows that. They live forever."

"You're here!" Luther leapt at the girl's chest and while he weighed at least half as much as she did, Amanda caught him around the middle and burst out laughing.

"Hey, buddy!" He licked her face until she lowered him to the ground and knelt. "Man, I've missed you guys."

"You don't even know, pup." Rex shouldered his brother out

of the way and stuck a paw on her thigh to get a better angle so he could lick her face too. "Wait until you see what—"

"Hey, look who's back." The screen door of the front porch clacked shut behind Lisa as she hurried down the stairs. "How was school?"

The young shifter pushed to her feet and threw herself at her.

"Whoa." The half-Light Elf laughed and hugged her in return. "That rough, huh?"

"No. School's great." The girl leaned away and grinned. "I missed you guys, is all."

"We missed you too. The next two weeks will be fun." She wrinkled her nose. "And a little different."

"Yeah, Johnny said you guys didn't do much while I was gone, but then there's that…" Amanda gestured toward the top half of the houseboat visible above the trees behind the house. "What's that for?"

"It's only something he's always wanted, I guess. Are you hungry?"

"Hey—hey, pup!" Luther darted around the girl in a frantic circle. "Wanna run?"

"Wanna hunt?"

"We can go right now!"

"Yeah, we found a rabbit burrow yesterday."

Rex sat on his haunches and yipped. "We'll show you. You've been gone forever. I bet you don't even remember what's back here."

The girl snorted and looked at Lisa. "I'm not hungry right now, thanks."

"Okay, sure. Do you wanna come inside?"

"No!" Luther howled.

"Come on, pup!"

Both hounds bounded away toward the side yard, paused to wait for her, and barked in encouragement.

"Yeah, I…" Amanda smiled sheepishly and moved slowly toward the hounds. "I'm gonna go—"

"Rex! The rabbit! Get it!" Both hounds darted into the ferns off the side yard and Amanda didn't finish her sentence.

She shifted and left her clothes in a pile on the ground as she darted after the hounds with a bloodcurdling howl of her own.

Before the small gray wolf darted into the swamp with Rex and Luther, Johnny marched down the stairs of the front porch and stuck two fingers in his mouth for a shrill whistle. "Y'all be back by suppertime, ya hear?"

"Got it, Johnny!" Rex barked back.

"Yeah, if we're even still hungry by then— Hey, wait up!"

"Damn, pup, you got fast."

As the hounds raced beyond the limits of their translation collars, their voices faded from the dwarf's mind. With a sigh, he ran a hand through his hair.

"Well, at least she's happy to be back."

Lisa finished picking up the girl's pile of clothes and joined him with a laugh. "Why wouldn't she be?"

"Hell, I don't know. It might be she decided bein' at that school with other kids is better than bein' stuck with a washed-up dwarf and his hounds."

"I'm here too, you know."

"Yeah, darlin'. But you're good with kids."

"Okay, give yourself a little more credit." She nudged him with her elbow and winked. "She's here because of you."

"Uh-huh. And I'm—"

A massive explosion wracked the air from the swamp behind the house, followed by a blazing mushroom cloud of crackling blue-and-silver light and thick white smoke.

"There ain't a goddamn minute of peace around here." Johnny trudged down the side yard as the hounds howled and bayed in the distance. Amanda's howl and snarl joined the din before another handful of smaller explosions lit up like fireworks behind the houseboat.

Lisa raced after him. "Did you tell her about them?"

"I was workin' up to it."

"Did you tell them about her?"

"What?" He spun to frown at her. "She's none of their goddamn business—"

"And they probably think a wolf is attacking your property and your dogs!"

"Shit." The second he rounded the back corner of the house, June landed in the center of the yard beside the huge table and lifted her sparking, glowing hand.

"Watch out, pup!" Rex shouted. "She's got lasers. I think."

"Yeah, but if you find her battery, rip it out!" Luther added and darted in a frenzy behind the gray wolf.

Amanda crouched at the end of the dock, dripping with swamp water, and snarled ferociously at the Crystal cyborg woman who aimed a weapon at her.

"Stand the fuck down!" Johnny shouted.

June fired a burst of crackling silver light at Amanda, who dodged it easily enough. The grass and earth where she had stood erupted and showered clods of dirt over the hounds.

Leroy's shifting mechanical arm clicked noisily as it shifted into a narrow-barreled gun. He aimed at the young gray wolf too and fired electric-blue pellets of energy as she darted across the yard.

"Get him, pup!"

"Holy crap! We haven't seen a fight like this in forever!"

The shifter ducked beneath June's next blast and vaulted onto the giant table. Her claws dug into the wood and threw shavings and chips up before she redirected her momentum and launched herself at her large adversary's head.

The Crystal borg couldn't react fast enough and staggered

back across the lawn, caught off-balance by a face-full of baby shifter.

Johnny growled at them. "Goddammit, that ain't—"

"I got it." Leroy snarled and aimed his gun-hand again as Amanda darted away from June and howled. "Someone has to learn to not trespass."

"Y'all need to cut this shit out!" Johnny roared and leaned toward the back of the house to snatch up the high-voltage blaster he'd made two months earlier for this very reason.

"Johnny, she's fine," Rex shouted and added a howl.

"Yeah, the pup can handle it."

"I ain't worried about her." Johnny swung the weapon toward Leroy first and fired a crackling blast of high-powered energy coupled with an alchemized ensnaring spell.

The yellow-white light grew as it raced toward the shifter borg and separated into lines of netting. When it struck its target, Leroy grew rigid in a second and his arms were clamped at his sides by the magical net that wound around him and pulsed with electrical shocks only strong enough to disable him, not injure him.

June ignored her fellow borg's incapacitation and aimed at Amanda again.

The bounty hunter slammed a hand against the side of the specialized blaster with a loud crack. "The settin's much higher for you, June. Don't even think about it."

June thought about it anyway, then she did it.

Amanda dodged the Crystal borg's next blast as the dwarf launched a much stronger charge. June had already activated her propulsion boots by the time the magical net twisted around her body, but the units snuffed out instantly and she dropped all of six inches to the earth. She fell forward onto her knees with a grunt beside Leroy, who'd already fallen prone and was now recovering from the limited effects of the electrified net.

When the magical entrapment gave out around June, she sat back on her heels and glared at him.

He swung the weapon from her to Leroy. "Don't make me do it again. You know I will."

"Well, what did you expect us to do?" June hissed and jerked her head toward the gray wolf who crouched and snarled twenty feet away.

"I expect y'all to not kill my fuckin' kid. How about that?"

Leroy propped himself on his elbows and stared at him. "Your what?"

"My ward." The dwarf cleared his throat. "It's the same damn thing."

Amanda shifted and stood there buck-naked, breathing heavily. "Who the hell are they?"

"Aw, hell, kid." Johnny looked away quickly although Lisa hurried toward the girl to hand her clothes to her. He rubbed the back of his neck and set the blaster down against the side of the house. "These are the borgs."

"The what?" The girl finished dressing but left her shoes in the grass and brushed her hair out of her face.

"Cyborgs," Lisa muttered and placed a reassuring hand on her shoulder.

"That's a real thing?"

"Do we look real enough to you?" June snarled.

"Yeah, real screwed!" Amanda shouted. "You tried to shoot me!"

Behind her, the hounds sniggered.

Johnny snorted but a warning glance from Lisa yanked him into peacekeeper mode. "All right, y'all settle down."

"Why are two cyborgs trying to shoot me?"

"Um…there are four of us." The twins emerged from behind Margo and walked slowly across the yard. Brandon raised a hand sheepishly. "Yeah, hey. Hi."

The girl stared at them. "Why are four cyborgs hanging out in your back yard?" She turned toward Johnny and did a double-take at Margo's glinting metal hull on the other side of the table. "And what is that?"

"Yeah…" The bounty hunter scratched the back of his head. "I guess we should start with the introductions, huh?"

"Good idea, Johnny," Lisa interjected and fought back a laugh now that the immediate danger to all of them was over.

Leroy stood quickly and offered June a hand up. She ignored it completely and jumped to her feet.

"All right, hell. Kid, these are the borgs. June, Leroy, and the mirror—uh, Brandon and Clint."

Amanda shifted her weight onto one hip and raised a hesitant hand. "Hey."

"And y'all better get it in your heads right now. The kid's with me and she was here way before y'all. This property's as much hers as it is mine, understand?"

June picked a clump of dirt off her hip and shook her head. "Whatever."

Her propulsion shoes activated again with a roar and she streaked across the swamp and the river to disappear somewhere behind the houseboat.

The girl watched the Crystal borg's trajectory and grinned. "That is too cool."

"We don't have anything fancy like that," Brandon said as he stepped toward the shifter girl. "But we can do tech stuff."

She studied the metal patch on the side of his neck and took his extended hand without hesitation to give it a firm shake. "Yeah, that's cool too."

"Hey, thanks." He gestured behind him at his brother. "That's Clint. I'm Brandon."

"Amanda."

"Nice to meet you—"

"You're a shifter." Leroy glared at the girl.

"Yeah." She shrugged. "Exactly like you."

"Not exactly." He turned his frown onto Johnny. "I didn't come here to be around other shifters."

"Oh, it's okay. I don't have, like, a pack or anything. It's only me out here in the swamp." She wrinkled her nose. "Unless you count the local pack, but they mostly stick to themselves."

"So do I." With his lips pressed together, Leroy stalked past everyone and headed to the dock. The blue energy shield flared to life around his entire half-mechanical body again, and he disappeared into the swamp with a splash.

"Wait, did I say something?" Amanda turned from the twins to Lisa and finally to Johnny. "I didn't mean to—"

"Naw, kid. Don't you worry yourself about any of that. The borgs have their own bugs to work out."

A tiny smile tweaked the corner of her lips. "Funny."

"How's that—oh."

"'Cause we're half-machine," Brandon clarified with a chuckle. "Yeah. Clint and I probably have more of those kinda bugs than anyone else."

The shifter girl pointed at the top edge of his metal chest panel and smirked. "I hope there aren't any real ones crawling around in there."

Clint burst out laughing and startled his brother before he joined in.

With a grimace, Johnny wiggled a finger around in his ear. *Oh, sure. We only need to add the sound of donkeys to all the other noise around here.*

"You're okay, kid," Brandon told her.

"That's what people tell me. Sometimes."

"And now I'm tellin' you to come on inside," Johnny interjected. "We'll get you settled in and somethin' to eat. You can tell Lisa what you told me on the drive back."

"There's not much to talk about—"

"The twins have incoming messages to monitor." The dwarf nodded toward Margo. "Let me know if we get any hits."

"Yeah. Sure, Johnny." Brandon smiled at Amanda. "See ya."

Clint shot her the guns with both hands, clicked his tongue, and winked.

She laughed and followed Johnny and Lisa up the back porch steps into the house.

"Hey, wait for us," Luther called as he darted after them.

"Yeah, we're hungry too."

"Glass and pickle juice can only go so far."

Johnny stopped at the open back door and scowled at the hounds. "Tell me that ain't what y'all ate today."

"Um…it's not?"

"Only a joke, Johnny." Rex chuckled nervously. "Yeah. A joke."

"It ain't funny." Their master headed into the house and the hounds crept up the back stairs.

Amanda turned to look at them both and whispered, "But if you start having eaten-glass problems, you should…you know. Tell someone."

"Hey, don't worry about us, pup."

"Yeah, we're invincible." They trotted through the door behind her and everyone moved to the living room. "This one time, Luther ate a pound of oyster shells. Only the shells."

"I did not." The smaller hound snorted and waited until he was halfway down the hall before he shook the last of the swamp water off. "It was almost two pounds."

The girl shook her head and laughed as she stepped into her bedroom beside Johnny's and looked around. "Yeah. It's good to be home. Hey, Johnny?"

"Yeah."

She poked her head out of the room as he and Lisa sat on the couch. "You should probably start with telling me how the cyborgs and the giant boat and that weird spaceship got here. You know, so you don't have to keep ignoring the weird explanation all the way through break."

Lisa burst out laughing and leaned against the armrest of the couch.

Rubbing his mouth and beard, Johnny scowled at the boar's head mounted above the empty fireplace. "How about you get yourself settled in and then I'll tell you what you wanna know."

"Okay, that sounds good."

He pointed at her and raised his voice slightly. "And it ain't a weird explanation. Not if you know the whole story."

"Yeah, okay."

The agent crossed one leg over the other and nudged his calf with her shoe. "It's good to have her back, right?"

"'Course it is," he grumbled. "But I think I'm the only one feelin' like I'm raisin' a kid in a zoo."

"I don't know, Johnny. I don't think it matters how many kids there are." She scrunched her face up and tried to fight back a laugh as she added, "Or...cyborgs."

"Aw, Jesus." The bounty hunter rolled his eyes but couldn't hold back a crooked smirk.

CHAPTER EIGHT

They still hadn't received a reply from the Beaufort base about Johnny's offer to help, but the next morning, the young shifter revealed that she had plans for how she wanted to spend her winter break away from the Academy.

She practically skipped into the kitchen as Johnny flopped another two pancakes onto the stack beside the stove and Lisa poured herself a cup of coffee. "Morning. Ooh, hey. That smells good."

"Good morning." Lisa watched the girl with a curious smile as Amanda found a mug and sloshed hot coffee into it. "They don't serve you guys coffee at that school, right?"

"No way. Are you kidding?" She sniffed the contents of her mug and sighed. "That's why this is so good right now."

"Since when did you start drinkin' it?" Johnny asked and ladled more pancake mix onto the skillet.

"Um…since you gave it to me and said it would wake me up."

Lisa tried to hide her smile in her mug.

"And you ain't had coffee since you started there?"

"What? No. I…well…I have."

"You said—"

79

"Lisa asked if they serve us coffee. They don't." Amanda took a loud slurp and sighed again. "But that doesn't mean I don't ever have any."

"And where the hell are you gettin' coffee on a base—I mean a damn school?"

She shrugged and stared at him like he'd grown two extra heads. "From the kitchen pixies. It's no big deal."

"Oh, sure." He turned to the stove and tried to focus on the pancakes. "It's always the damn pixies, ain't it?"

Lisa and Amanda exchanged a glance behind his back and both smirked into their cups. "So here's a question," the half-Light Elf said.

"Okay." The girl leaned back against the counter.

"Johnny and I wondered what you'd like to do for your birthday."

"We did?" The spatula dropped out of his hand and clattered on the floor. He grunted and stooped to retrieve it before he gave it a quick rinse in the sink. "I mean...'course we did. Thirteen's a hell of an age, kid."

His ward watched him with a playful frown. "I guess."

Lisa ignored the dwarf's agitation and didn't look away from her. "Do you have anything in mind?"

"Yeah, I do. I'm glad you asked." Amanda set her coffee down and took a folded piece of paper out of her back pocket. She opened it quickly, tried to smooth the wrinkles out, and handed it to Lisa. "I wanna build this."

"Now there's a birthday present I can get behind." Johnny clinked the spatula on the counter.

The agent inclined her head and squinted at the paper. "What is it?"

"Okay, so at school, there's—"

"Lemme take a look at that, darlin'." With a grin, Johnny headed across the kitchen, wiped his batter-covered fingers on a rag, and tossed it onto the counter. "Whatever she wants to put together, I got everythin' we need right here." Lisa handed him the paper and he simply stared at it for a moment before he frowned. He turned it sideways, then cleared his throat. "What is it?"

Amanda looked at him in amazement and sipped her coffee. "It's a copy."

"Of...a swing set?"

"No. That's the obstacle course Mr. Petrov has us run every single morning for his class."

"Who's Mr. Petrov?" Lisa asked.

Johnny tugged his beard. "The one who yells all the time. And he's bald."

"The Combat Training teacher," Amanda added.

"What? Are you tellin' me you're playin' on a jungle gym and they're callin' it combat trainin'?"

"Oh, my God. No. Johnny, please..." Amanda rolled her eyes, stepped beside him, and pointed at the drawing. "This is the obstacle course. We only pass his class if we can run it."

"Uh-huh. I assume you've passed his class...what? Two dozen times already?"

"I wish." The girl shook her head. "No one's been able to finish this. I've only gotten to maybe three-quarters of the way to the end, and I'm the one who's gone the farthest."

"Well, at least you're winnin'." He pointed at the areas along the drawing highlighted with bright-orange arrows. "What are all these here?"

"Oh, yeah. The guns."

Lisa choked on her coffee and snatched the rag up to press it over her mouth.

The dwarf stepped away from Amanda with a raised eyebrow. "The kind y'all shoot or the kind shot atcha?"

"The second one."

"What school in their right mind would shoot at children?" the woman shouted.

"No, they're not real guns. They...uh, have no bullets or anything. Only magical darts that knock you off the course or freeze you so you can't get out of the way of a different one that shoots you off the course."

The half-Light Elf shook her head slowly. "How is that better?"

"It's fine. It doesn't even hurt. Mostly."

"Good kid." Johnny chuckled when Lisa threw the rag at his chest. "It's bounty-hunter school, darlin'. Those kids have been through way worse. They can handle it."

"It sounds like torture."

Amanda laughed. "Yeah, sometimes. But how else are you gonna learn, right?"

He stuck his thumb out toward the kid and looked pointedly at Lisa. "See?"

She shook her head and hid an exasperated smile behind the rim of her mug.

"So." Johnny flicked the sheet of paper. "You wanna build the same thing here because..."

The girl's eyes lit up. "Because I wanna practice. I drew this up as close as I could get to the real thing. And if we build it here, I can get a head start on it before next semester and finally finish the stupid thing."

He chuckled and handed her the sketch. "I like the way you think, kid."

"Yeah, me too."

Lisa slid the last of the fresh pancakes onto the plate. "I thought we were talking about what she wants for her birthday."

"That is what I want." Amanda sipped her coffee and slapped the obstacle course plans on the counter. "I don't need a big party or anything. Or presents. This can be my present."

"Amanda—"

"You heard her, darlin'. The kid wants to build an obstacle course herself so she can kick ass at school. It's fine by me."

"Awesome. Do we need to go get anything or—"

"Naw. Like I said, we already got everythin' we need right here." Johnny joined Lisa in front of the stove, where they had a clear view of the entire back yard and all the eyesores in it. "And I think I know exactly where to start, too."

After breakfast, it took them an hour to disassemble the massive wooden table that had all but filled the entire back lawn. All the borgs were banned from helping with the destruction part —although only Brandon and Clint wanted to help—and Johnny finally had to remove the sledgehammer when Amanda went completely nuts on the chairs.

"Whoa, whoa. Hey." He caught the handle before she could swing it again and tugged it away. "I said break it down. You're breakin' it."

"But it's fun."

"Uh-huh. I get that, kid. I do. But we're usin' the pieces, understand?"

"Oh…"

Handing her the power tools to start sawing and drilling and nailing might not have been any safer but at least she was productive with it. The hardest part was keeping the hounds out of their work area and reminding her that the hounds did not, in fact, understand power tools and couldn't hand her what she wanted.

After months of putting up with the borgs' explosions, shouting, banging, and general destructive noisiness, Johnny had absolutely no qualms about driving Sheila to the back yard and blasting Pantera through the speakers while he and Amanda worked. Leroy and June would have stayed well enough away without the heavy metal drowning out almost every other sound, but at least it kept them away entirely. The twins spent most of their time huddled behind Margo while they scanned for incoming messages or any other trouble on the airwaves that possibly needed the assistance of Johnny Walker Investigations.

When Lisa left at midday, she returned with lunch for all the non-cyborgs—who still had a good supply of pickles—and heavy-duty noise-reduction earmuffs. Even with those on, she spent the rest of the afternoon inside the house.

By dinnertime, Johnny and Amanda had half the obstacle course built. Once they'd finished attaching the last row of monkey bars, he stepped back and folded his arms to study their work. The shifter girl mimicked his posture unconsciously and tilted her head. "Does it look a little crooked to you?"

"What? 'Course not. That there's as level as it gets."

"But we didn't use the level."

"Kid, are you tryin' to tell me I can't create a straight line all on my own?"

She smirked at him. "Honestly? I don't know. We didn't use the level."

"And we ain't gonna." He clicked his tongue, wiped the thin layer of sweat from his forehead, and turned toward the back of the house. "I think we'll have this up and runnin' for you by tomorrow. It's time for a drink."

"Wait, for both of us?"

"Yeah. You can have a pop." Before the dwarf reached the back stairs, both hounds barreled out of the swamp, raced down the side yard, and howled at the top of their lungs.

"Someone's here, Johnny!"

"Coming up the drive!"

"Sounds like a real idiot!"

Johnny and the kid exchanged a confused glance. "Can you hear the sound of an idiot?"

Amanda shrugged. "Only if one opens their mouth."

"Yeah. It takes one to know one for them hounds. Come on."

They walked around the side of the house together and emerged in the front yard as a beat-up station wagon pulled to a stop at the end of the dirt drive. The hounds barked and ran around the vehicle.

"Who's the idiot, Johnny?" Luther shouted.

"Yeah, he's got no idea who he's messing with!"

"It's Arthur, boys. Leave him be." Johnny folded his arms and watched the local old-timer unfold himself from the station wagon.

Arthur's long white handlebar mustache twitched as he stared at the houseboat behemoth visible over the trees behind the house. "Well, I'll be..."

"Arthur. What are you doin' here?"

"I thought I'd—" The man shut the driver's door absently and couldn't pull his gaze away from the houseboat. "I'd...uh, come see how things are movin' along for ya out here."

"Things are fine. I appreciate you stoppin' by."

"Uh-huh." After a low whistle, Arthur finally looked down. "You know, me and a couple of the fellas been hearin' some—oh." The man's face lit up with a rare grin when he saw the shifter girl standing beside her guardian. "Hey, Amanda."

"Hi."

"How's school?"

"It's good." She looked from Johnny to his old friend. "It's nice to be on break now. I'm home for two weeks."

"That's good to hear, girl. Good to hear." Arthur cleared his throat. "Johnny, do you mind...steppin' aside with me for a spell?"

"All right." He nodded at Amanda. "Go ahead and grab that pop if you want it. And stay outta my whiskey."

The shifter scoffed as she headed toward the front porch. "Why would I wanna drink your whiskey?"

She didn't wait for an actual reply before the screen door clacked shut behind her and she disappeared inside.

Arthur chuckled. "You keepin' pop around the house now?"

"The hell I am. Lisa brought it back with lunch. So what's on your mind?"

The man rubbed his finger over his mustache and nodded toward the houseboat. "That beast, for one. I heard a few things about you gettin' somethin' on your land that could take up its own spot on a map. That might have been an understatement."

"It's only a pipedream, Arthur. And a houseboat."

"Uh-huh." The man scratched his head. "See, here's the thing, Johnny. We know you have all your gear and fancy gadgets here. There's Sheila and the airboat, and it's all good. But there's been an awful lotta noise kickin' up across the swamp lately. You know, more than usual."

"Well, sure. Things get noisy."

At that exact moment, Leroy barreled through the wall of ferns at the side of the house and his weaponized arm spun maniacally as he raised it at Arthur's chest.

"Holy catfish on a cracker." The man stepped slowly away from the borg and raised both hands in surrender. "Johnny?"

"Hell, Leroy. Put that shit away, will ya?"

"He's trespassing—"

"No, he ain't! Arthur's a friend, and if any of y'all stopped to think about what you were doin' before you damn well did, we wouldn't be gettin' noise complaints from all the neighbors." Johnny shooed the borg toward the back yard. "Go on."

Leroy shrugged. "How are we supposed to know the difference, huh?"

"As long as you quit tryin' to shoot first." The bounty hunter sighed, hooked his thumbs through his belt loops, and shrugged. "What can ya do, right?"

"I got no damn clue." Arthur scratched his head. "What did I see?"

"A cyborg."

"A what?"

"Listen, Arthur. Everythin's under control out here, all right? Amanda's home for winter break, we have some…construction projects out in the back yard—"

"And a giant man with a machinegun for a hand." The old-timer frowned. "It seems a little reckless, Johnny. Even for you."

"Naw, it's all part of the business. You know, interns." The dwarf slapped his friend's arm and nodded before he turned toward the front porch. "We'll keep the noise down. Tell anyone who complains that I said so."

Arthur moved slowly to his station wagon. "Interns, huh?"

"Yeah, and real cheap too. I pay 'em in pickles." He raised a hand in farewell as the local slipped behind the wheel and turned in the lot. As soon as the station wagon disappeared behind a cloud of dust, he lowered his hand with a grunt and stormed into the house.

Those damn borgs are more likely to get me killed by an angry mob than kill anyone themselves.

CHAPTER NINE

The obstacle course was finished two days later, complete with replicated gadgets from the weapons at her school that Amanda described.

"And what's at the end of it?" Johnny asked and gestured toward the blank wooden platform with no booby traps or magic traps or anything remotely worth the time and effort of practicing.

"I don't know," the girl muttered. "No one's ever got that far."

"Huh. Do you think we should leave it as it is?"

"Yeah. I don't wanna learn the end of it wrong, you know?"

"Good thinkin'." He clapped a hand on her shoulder and gave her a little shake. "Well go on, then. Give it a run."

"Cool."

"Hey, Johnny?" Brandon headed across the yard and craned his neck to study the underside of the obstacle course. "Nice playground."

The shifter rolled her eyes. "Seriously. Have you ever seen a playground rigged with automatic weapons?"

He smirked. "Have you ever seen a wizard cyborg hack

through military security by sticking a cord in his neck and fluttering his eyelids?"

A bark of a laugh escaped her. "No. I haven't. It sounds awesome."

"You can come check it out if you want." Brandon nodded at Johnny. "We got a response."

"Well, let's go hear it."

"Do you want us to hook up to one of Margo's monitors or something?"

"For what?"

They headed across the yard toward the silver hull and where Clint was seated on the ground on the other side. "It's a video message. Kind of."

"Great. Everyone and their mama have to see who they're talkin' to these days. What happened to a regular phone call? Hell, mail a letter."

"Ha. Right." Amanda's smile faded when the dwarf scowled at her. "Oh, you meant... Yeah, okay."

"Ain't no one steppin' inside Margo. I tell you what, though. I think we got the next best thing right here." Johnny stuck two fingers in his mouth for another loud whistle. "Leroy!"

"Yeah, boss." The shifter borg leaned against Margo's hull next to Clint and looked up as Brandon, Johnny, and Amanda rounded the corner.

"Have you been here the whole time?"

"Maybe an hour."

"All right. What's the message?"

Clint's eyelids fluttered and a moment later, he nodded. The cable that connected him to Margo's power and her sound system enabled the audio to come through loud and clear.

"Johnny Walker, this is Colonel Bartlett at MCAS Beaufort. I don't know how you found out that we're looking into you or why, but I don't like it. Which makes me think you're the perfect guy for the job. So let's cut out the endless messages and arrange a visual conference call, huh? I sent you the link to join me. It's the twenty-fourth today, and I'd like to get this over with before I have to handle my personal obligations. Fifteen hundred hours. I'll wait to see you there and we can discuss the next steps."

The audio recording ended with a click and the bounty hunter raised his eyebrows. "Someone's gettin' a little bossy, ain't he? Huh. Did y'all get that link?"

Clint nodded and glanced at his twin.

"Yeah, we're ready to go when you are," Brandon said.

The dwarf glanced at his wristwatch and sighed. "All right. We have an hour."

"You're gonna need something to see the guy with, boss," Leroy added. "And you don't even have a computer. Or a camera."

Johnny pointed at the shifter borg. "Does that eye work both ways?"

Leroy's mechanical eye clicked and spun until the lens was a tiny dot in the center. "I dunno. I never tried it."

"It's a good thing we have an hour, then."

Amanda laughed.

Johnny turned toward her and frowned. "You don't think we can get it all rigged up in an hour? Lemme tell ya something, kid. There ain't nothin—"

"It's the twenty-fourth." The girl met his gaze slowly and her face colored as she fought back another laugh by holding her breath.

"Uh-huh. All the dates got numbers. What's your point?"

"The twenty-fourth of December."

"Well, hell." With a grin, he nudged her shoulder with the back of a hand and snorted. "Merry Christmas to me."

It only took forty minutes to learn how to hook both Leroy and Clint up to Margo's power source and servers to get the job done. The tricky part had been to find out how to get the shifter borg up and running for the use of his mechanical eye when he didn't have the same hookup hardware as the twins.

Johnny found it particularly hilarious when they discovered that all four borgs could be linked together by extra pairing nodes embedded in their fingers like the recording device in Clint's. "Y'all gotta hold hands and sing 'Kumbaya' to get up to full team power. That doc was batshit crazy but parts of this are pure genius."

Brandon's uncharacteristic frown brought the dwarf's laughter to a halt. "Genius and ruining someone's lives aren't exactly the same thing."

"Oh, sure." He cleared his throat and slapped the connection panel on the other side of Margo's outer hull shut. "Was that insensitive?"

The twins exchanged a glance. "Was that a rhetorical question?"

"I dunno."

As Johnny double-checked the settings on Leroy, Clint, and Margo, they decided that they needed more space and had to set up their live virtual meeting on the side of the metal intelligence hub that faced the rest of the back yard. "Typical. I can't get privacy any other damn day. Why would I get it in a little sit-down with a war dog?"

But privacy wasn't much of an issue. Lisa was inside, June was sulking in the houseboat—as usual—and Amanda raced through the swamp as a wolf with the hounds.

At 3:02 pm, Johnny planted his feet squarely in the grass and folded his arms. "All right. Open the damn meetin'."

Clint's eyelids fluttered. Leroy's mechanical eye spun madly for two seconds before the shutter opened wide to its fullest extent and glowed blue. A cone of light burst from the lens and in the next moment, Johnny stared at a projected image of a middle-aged man seated behind a desk, who scowled at him.

"You're late."

The dwarf glanced at his watch. "Two minutes. You're all right. Colonel Bartlett, I assume."

The man's mouth twitched. "If I were anyone else, Mr. Walker, I'd be screwed."

"Yeah, it's only Johnny."

"Great. Let's get down to it, then. If your schedule allows."

The dwarf smirked. *We're gettin' off to a perfect start.*

"I have a few minutes. I heard you have a little problem."

"So I've gathered. Here's what you need to know." The colonel shuffled through a few papers on his desk and opened his mouth to speak.

The hounds chose that moment to race into the yard from the swamp. They bayed noisily as they jumped around and shook themselves with matching sprays of water. The gray wolf bounded out of the water after them. Amanda shifted in mid-stride and laughed as she walked quickly to the narrow wooden stand with a shower curtain she'd built herself for when she shifted and had to dress in the middle of the yard.

The colonel saw all of this behind Johnny and tilted his head. "Is that a teenage shifter on your property?"

The bounty hunter scoffed. "If you wanna have a meetin' on teenage shifters, we'll have to schedule another call. Get talkin'."

Bartlett shook his head slowly and drew a deep breath. "We have an arms problem."

"Uh-huh. I picked up on that."

"Our people are in the middle of preparing for the wrong kind of weapons being smuggled into this country. As far as we can tell, they are still offshore but not for much longer."

"I ain't hoppin' across a pond to snag these for you if that's what you're tryin' to say."

"No. You absolutely would not be my first choice for that."

Johnny responded with a crooked smile. "So what the hell do you need me for?"

"The weapons and the organization trying to sell them on US

soil are magical-related. Admittedly, we don't enlist many magicals in any branch of the military, but those we do have aren't enough to handle this issue. We know when it's time to step aside and contract outside help."

Leroy cleared his throat and remained perfectly still as his mechanical eye projected the live image. "Ask him how many he has on this already. Magicals on the inside."

Bartlett scowled and leaned to the side to try to see behind and around the dwarf who filled his computer screen. "Who's that talking?"

"No one." Johnny pointed at his face. "Stay focused."

The colonel looked like he was about to throw everything off his desk, end the meeting, and start over again with someone else. "None of our people with an ounce of knowledge about how to handle this are available or expendable."

"If you're tryin' to tell me I am expendable, Colonel, this little talk ain't goin' nowhere."

"It has nothing to do with you. We merely can't have this traced back to us before the weapons are secured and we're in the clear. And we need you to come in with an outside perspective."

"Uh-huh."

Bartlett stared blankly at him and his lips pressed tighter together with every second. "There's a deal going down at a weapons convention in Philadelphia. The most detail we've managed to confirm is that these scumbags are meeting with a high-level buyer. The arms most likely won't be there, but we need someone to go in and find out where they are and exactly when they'll be brought Stateside. If you feel like you can apprehend a few assholes without blowing your cover or the entire operation, go for it. Otherwise, we need you to infiltrate theirs so we can nip this in the ass before it gets any closer to home."

Johnny nodded slowly while he considered the implications. "What kinda weapons?"

"Of mass destruction, Mr. Walker. Is there any other kind?"

"You're the goddamn US Military. You tell me."

The colonel sighed heavily and pinched the bridge of his nose. "We went through several possible independent contractors to approach for this work and seriously considered all of them. Then your name appeared on that list."

"It tends to do that, Colonel."

"You spent most of your time working for the feds, didn't you?" The man paused and took a breath. "And now you have your own business."

"And?"

"And there's much more at the bottom of that rabbit hole, Mr. Walker. What we found solidified our decision to bring you in on this. It looks like your brief career as a Marine is coming around full circle, doesn't it?"

The bounty hunter hissed a breath and scowled. *I thought that shit was buried.* "I have no clue what anythin' looks like to you."

"Well, because you couldn't make it as a Marine doesn't mean we don't have use for you. If you think you can handle this job without the same body count."

"The difference between me and that little cult y'all are runnin' is that I have become smarter over the last fifty years. I can't say the same for y'all 'cause now you're here beggin' me to come save your asses. Colonel."

Bartlett chuckled. "We'll send a team to your location for a briefing—"

"Nope. I have my own team."

"Oh, really? What branch?"

The dwarf jerked his head up at the projection. "Mine. I ain't goin' in with your people and I ain't goin' in without mine. It's a package deal."

"Fine. It's your head if this goes south."

"It won't."

"I'll send the details of the conference on this same...private chat line or whatever the hell we set this up on." Bartlett rifled through the papers on his desk again. "One more thing. We heard you have your dogs with you all the time and even take them on your cases with you, is that right?"

Johnny grunted. "My hounds, my business."

"Sure. But that won't fly at the convention. You won't get a foot through the door with your pets. Ditch 'em before you go in—"

"Hey, no one tells me what to do with my hounds. They're better than any team you could send of yours anyhow."

"They're dumb animals who don't have a place in a high-stakes operation like this one and you know it."

"Fuck you."

Colonel Bartlett raised an eyebrow and a tiny smile bloomed across his lips as he spread his arms mockingly. "No hounds or no deal."

The asshole's squeezin' me for everythin' he has. And if he's callin' me for this op, there ain't no one else who's gonna keep those weapons outta the wrong hands.

He scowled as he tried to find a loophole but came up empty. "Fine. I'll get your weapons—"

"They aren't ours."

"—and I'll leave the hounds. But my fee tripled."

The colonel didn't bat an eyelid. "Done. However the hell you managed it, don't tap into my private line again."

The man leaned forward to switch his computer off and the projection flickered and sputtered out before Leroy's mechanical eye went dark.

"Goddamn Marine." The bounty hunter dragged a hand through his hair in frustration and looked at Leroy and the twins and their expectant faces. "Well, shit. Are you fellas up for a party?"

The shifter snorted.

Brandon shrugged and glanced at the massive houseboat that marred the view of the swamp. "Are you gonna tell June?"

"I won't have a home to come back to if I don't." Johnny pointed at the borgs and turned toward the house. "This is what bein' invited looks like."

CHAPTER TEN

As it turned out, the weapons convention in Philadelphia was a week-long event. Johnny only had a week to brief the borgs—or prepare them as much as possible with what little intel Colonel Bartlett had given him—before they had to ship out and get this done.

Which meant the two weeks he had to spend with Amanda before she returned to the Academy had almost been cut in half.

"At least we still have Christmas," she told him that night over hamburgers for dinner in the living room. Grease and melted cheese dripped from her hands and onto the plate.

"And I ain't even fixed up anythin' for that either." The dwarf scanned his neat, clean cabin completely devoid of any holiday cheer—exactly the way he liked it.

The girl snorted and set her burger down as she chewed. "You don't even celebrate Christmas, do you?"

His eyes widened as he raised his whiskey glass slowly to his lips. "Do you?"

"Well..." Seated on the floor on the other side of the coffee table, Amanda shared a knowing glance with Lisa, who sat beside him on the couch. "I used to."

"Uh-huh. And here I am stealin' the magic outta your upbringing."

The half-Light Elf leaned away to fix him with a firm look. "You're coming down a little hard on yourself."

"Well, you know what, darlin'? No one said a goddamn thing about Christmas comin' up and I damn near missed the kid's birthday. That ain't the right way."

"Johnny, it's okay." Amanda drank the rest of her water and wiped her mouth with the back of a hand. "Seriously. Christmas is weird, anyway. And it's not like I believe in Santa or anything. We never did, to be honest."

"We can still do something." Johnny placed his drink on the coffee table and slapped his thighs. "I ain't bringin' a tree inside. That's temptin' fate and two coonhounds. But we'll getcha some of that glittery stuff."

The girl laughed. "You mean tinsel?"

"Sure. Stick it in your room, though, 'cause I ain't fixin' to pull that shit outta every rack of this place for the next twelve months." He scratched the back of his head and frowned at Lisa. "What else goes into this?"

She pursed her lips and tried not to laugh. "Presents, for one."

"No, we already built that obstacle course. I don't need anything else."

"That was for your birthday, kid."

"Yeah, when your birthday's five days after Christmas, they tend to get lumped together anyway. It's fine."

Lisa took another bite of her burger. "And music."

"Hell no. I ain't playin' that jingle bullshit in my house. No way." Johnny snatched his drink up again and looked sheepishly at his ward. "Don't repeat that."

"I never even heard it." The girl clapped her hands over her ears and grinned. "Seriously, though, I'm tired of Christmas stuff anyway. It was always fancy parties and wearing itchy dresses and trying to smile when all my parents' friends wanted to talk about was the stock market and where I'd go to college. And they all smelled like sweaty feet. Honestly, this is way better."

Johnny snapped his fingers and pointed at her. "Eggnog."

"What?"

"That's a Christmas thing, right?"

Amanda smirked. "Yeah, that usually comes with rum in it."

"Kid, you're killin' me. No way in hell am I puttin' rum in your drink." The dwarf lifted his glass under the low overhead light and shrugged. "I guess whiskey will do the job."

"Johnny." Lisa shook her head.

"What? She's on break."

"She's twelve."

"Thirteen." Amanda took another huge bite of her dinner and added around a mouthful. "Almost."

"Right. A teenager already." Johnny swallowed thickly. *She's almost older than Dawn was. There oughta be some kinda irony in that.* "Yeah, we'll do the eggnog."

"Without whiskey," Lisa added.

"Yeah, okay."

Lisa gave each of them a small gift for Christmas the next day simply because she could. Amanda had no idea what the black skort was until the half-Light Elf explained its usefulness. Johnny received a three-inch-long metal rod the width of a pen with a ring attached to one end and a hole on the other.

"It's a fine penlight, darlin'."

"No, Johnny, it's not a—" Lisa sighed and mimed bringing the silver rod to her lips. "You blow on it."

"Oh, yeah? Like a dog whistle? I already made one of those and it had a trigger. I like somethin' more when it looks like a gun."

She rolled her eyes and couldn't look at Amanda for fear she and the girl wouldn't be able to restrain their laughter. "It's one of those frequency whistles. You blow on a different one and the different frequency and vibration are supposed to make you feel different things."

"Yeah." He looked from his partner—business and personal now—to his teenage ward. "Like the kind I already made."

"It's for you, okay? No explosions and no death and destruction for shifters or hounds."

Amanda dropped the skort into the box on her lap. "Wait, what?"

The hounds were stretched nearby and chewed on two massive rawhide bones the size of their front legs. "Hound-whistle gun," Luther muttered.

"Scrambles our brains. And shifter brains too."

"He put it away, pup. Don't worry."

Johnny stared at the alleged whistle in his hand. "So what's it for?"

"That one's supposed to promote peace and calm." Lisa nodded encouragingly. "Go ahead and try it."

With a snort, the dwarf raised it to his lips and blew. The hounds laughed.

"Wow, Johnny. She has no clue."

"Yeah, I don't know about you—" Luther burst into high-pitched giggles. "Oh, man, that tickles!"

"Well...thanks, darlin'." Johnny deposited the whistle into the front breast pocket of his button-down shirt and nodded. "I appreciate it."

"Uh-huh." She raised an eyebrow and didn't look like she believed him even slightly. "Merry Christmas."

"Where's Lisa's present?" Amanda asked and settled the lid of the box onto her gift.

The dwarf smirked. "She already has it."

Lisa smiled coyly at him. "Oh, so we're calling that my Christmas present now too?"

The shifter girl grimaced. "Ugh. Forget I asked."

"You get your head outta the gutter, kid." He pointed at her.

"We're talkin' about a real present with a little black box and everythin'."

"Wait—like the kind with a ring in it?"

"No!" Johnny and Lisa shouted it at the same time, and Amanda fell back against the armchair beside the hearth in a fit of laughter.

"Okay, okay. I get it. You—" She shrieked another laugh and pointed at them. "You should see both your faces right now!"

The bounty hunter couldn't keep a straight face when he darted Lisa a sidelong glance. "Yeah. Merry Christmas."

Four days later, Johnny had the borgs ready to head out for their "big job" in Philadelphia. He was the only one with any luggage to take with them, which Clint held on his lap as he was forced to sit in the back of the Jeep where the hounds usually rode.

Johnny said his goodbyes to Amanda first, shuffled his feet, and looked everywhere but at her face. "If it weren't for this job, kid, you know I'd stick around until you had to get back to school."

"Yeah, I know."

"And for your birthday."

"Yep."

"And—"

"Don't try to pretend you're not excited about it." The girl folded her arms and glanced at all four borgs who waited in the Jeep. Their combined weight forced Sheila's undercarriage a full six inches lower than usual. "And honestly, it'll be much quieter around here for a few days. Only me, Lisa, and the hounds, so that'll be nice."

"Uh-huh." *It should have been me sayin' that.* "Well, you be good, understand?"

"Yeah. Easy." She threw herself at him for a huge hug. "Have fun with all the weapons."

The bounty hunter snorted and hugged her briefly in return before she pulled away and grinned at the hounds.

"Do you guys wanna run?"

"We thought you'd never ask, pup." Luther panted in excitement.

"What? She asks all the time." Rex scratched his ear with a hind paw. "So do we."

"See ya, Johnny." The girl raced across the yard toward the swamp and the hounds darted after her with sharp barks.

"Hey, no fair! You didn't give us a head start."

"Yeah, it's not like you need it when you can go all wolfy and —yep. There she goes. Hey, wait up!"

Lisa laughed and stepped toward Johnny and they watched the hounds and the small gray wolf race through the reeds. "We'll be fine."

"I know. And listen, once you get her to the Academy, I'll have Felix come pick y'all up. You and the hounds." He reached for her waist and pulled her toward him. "Then it's back to the whole team on the job, yeah?"

"No problem. And be careful." She kissed him with a little more intensity than he would've liked with a whole Jeep full of cyborgs waiting for them, but he wasn't about to complain. She pulled away and shrugged. "You know. Careful for you."

"What's that supposed to mean?"

"You know exactly what it means." She winked, stepped back, and raised a hand in farewell to the borgs. "Try to keep this guy out of trouble, okay?"

In the back seat, June rolled her eyes and stared ahead. The twins nodded wordlessly but shared matching goofy grins as they stared at the couple in the front yard.

Leroy sniggered. "I'm very sure he's in more trouble if he stays. Let's get a move on, boss."

"All right, you listen here." Johnny pointed at him. "I'm the one who calls the shots. It ain't like we're gonna miss the flight when I own the damn plane."

The shifter borg raised both hands in surrender and buckled his seatbelt in the front passenger seat.

"Go crash an illegal arms deal." Lisa gave the dwarf's hand a little squeeze and turned toward the front porch. "I guess this means you have to break your own rules, right?"

"Huh?"

She chuckled and spread her arms in an offhand way. "Well, someone has to feed the hounds."

"That ain't—" The dwarf gritted his teeth, sighed heavily, and moved to Sheila's driver's door. "There's only one exception to that, darlin'."

"Yep. And it's me." She watched them from the front porch and laughed as Johnny accelerated down the dirt drive and the borgs clamped their hands around any part of the steel frame they could reach.

Felix wasn't especially thrilled to hear he had to fly Johnny across the country with all four cyborg magicals again. But the bounty hunter had paid him three times his usual retainer two days before and the captain of the private jet couldn't exactly turn it down.

Once the borgs had filed onto the jet—which shuddered a little under their heavy footsteps until they'd all settled in their seats—the captain stopped Johnny outside the cockpit and folded his arms. "We'll have to stop halfway to refuel, exactly like last time."

"That's fine, Felix. As long as we touch down in Philadelphia by the end of the day, you do what you gotta do."

"All right." The man rubbed the back of his neck. "You realize you overpaid me for this flight, right?"

"Naw. That's only for the first half." He clapped a hand on the captain's shoulder. "Let's get outta here."

Felix cleared his throat as the dwarf headed down the cabin, took the intercom from the wall, and spoke directly into it over the roar of the jet's engines. "We'll be in the air shortly. A reminder, please, that any...heavy movement in the cabin will affect our altitude, so please refrain from getting up and moving around unless absolutely necessary." He hung the intercom speaker on its receiver and turned toward the cockpit with a sigh. "This guy needs a bigger jet."

CHAPTER ELEVEN

Their rental in Philly was ready and waiting for them when they landed, although the driver from the rental company who had been paid to bring the car to the private runway didn't look especially pleased to see the dwarf and four weirdly outfitted magicals heading toward the Humvee.

He couldn't stop staring at Leroy's swiveling mechanical eye as he handed Johnny the keys. "So what...brings you Philadelphia?"

The bounty hunter snatched the keys from him and studied him carelessly. "Do you ask everyone this?"

"I'm...uh, being friendly."

"Good for you."

The Humvee rocked violently when Leroy climbed into the front passenger seat and the other borgs followed. The man's eyes widened and he opened his mouth to say something but couldn't quite find his voice.

"We're going to a convention," Brandon said with a grin before he slid into the back seat beside his brother and slammed the door shut.

The man swallowed. "What kind of convention, exactly?"

Johnny opened the driver's door and shrugged. "The fun kind."

And I'll be invoicin' the Marine for every damn part of it.

The stares didn't stop as Johnny drove them into downtown Philadelphia, mostly because the Humvee swayed with every turn and hung way closer to the road than it should have. The valet at the hotel dropped the keys twice because he was too busy gaping at the cyborgs who emerged from the vehicle that should have been able to hold the weight if they'd weighed as much as regular humans or magicals.

"What?" June sneered at him as she passed. "You've never seen a woman before?"

"Huh?"

"She's messin' with ya." Johnny handed him a fifty and nodded. "Have a good one."

The borgs followed him toward the entrance of the hotel and gazed at the tall buildings around them with wide eyes.

"Where are we again?" Brandon asked.

"Where are—we've been talkin' about this for days. Philadelphia."

"Yeah, but...what is this?"

A woman wrapped in a huge puffy coat with mittens and gloves barreled out of the revolving front door and dragged a large rolling suitcase behind her. June crossed the opening of the door and hissed at her.

The woman shrieked and slapped a gloved hand to her chest as the handle of her suitcase clattered to the sidewalk. "What is wrong with you?"

"Jesus." Johnny caught June's upper arm and yanked her toward the regular front door. "It's only jet lag, darlin'. Nothin' to worry about."

Then the woman noticed the other three borgs heading into the hotel with the dwarf and her mouth fell open. The two men trying to exit the rotating door stumbled over her suitcase and snapped her out of her disbelief.

"You can't simply stand there, lady."

"You have to get out of the way."

Johnny heard the ensuing argument before the front door closed behind him and shook his head.

June jerked her arm out of his grasp. "Don't touch me."

"Then don't go full psycho-borg on innocent strangers. How about that?"

"She came right at me."

"No, she walked out a door. And you—hey. Uh-uh. What're you doin'?" He lurched toward Clint, who stood at the elevators and reached for the call button with the sparking tip of the metal rod on his finger extended. "Cut that out."

"It's a button," the usually silent borg whispered.

"Yeah, and it ain't for you. And put that away. You'll get us kicked out before we even get a room." He pulled Clint away from the elevator and gestured toward the front desk. "Christ, have none of y'all been in a hotel before?"

Brandon shrugged. June stared at the other guests in the lobby who stared at her. Leroy stood perfectly still and absorbed every detail. "I have. I think."

"You think, huh?"

"Yeah. I think I remember."

"Great. Come on. We gotta check in." Johnny corralled the borgs with grunts and the occasional tug away from the gift shop or an *Employees Only* door. He stopped at the front desk and nodded at the concierge.

"Are you checking in?" the woman asked with a broad smile.

"Yeah. Johnny Walker."

"A moment, please." As she typed his name in, a crowd grew in the lobby although they maintained a wide berth around the borgs gathered behind the dwarf.

"What is that?" someone muttered.

"Those are the best Halloween costumes I've ever seen."

"Yeah, and Halloween was two months ago."

June turned to glare at whoever had spoken and the onlookers shut up and returned to their business.

"Here you are, Mr. Walker."

"Call me Johnny, darlin'."

The concierge smiled coyly and studied him with interest as she bit her lower lip. "Okay. Johnny. You have adjoining suites, as requested. I see you're here for the Unified Tech Conference, correct?"

He raised his eyebrows. "Is that the one with all the weapons?"

"Uh…" She giggled. "As far as I know. The sign-in table is down the hall in front of Ballroom A. I suggest you put your name down now before the convention starts in the morning. It tends to get a little busy in here right before opening. And here are your attendee passes. For you and your…friends." When the woman's gaze settled on Leroy—who leaned over the far end of the front desk while his mechanical eye whirred and spun madly—she frowned. "These are your friends, correct?"

"Yeah, somethin' like that." He slapped his hand on the room keys and the convention passes and adjusted the strap of his duffel bag slung across his chest. "Do you need anythin' else from me, darlin'?"

"Not right now." Her smile returned. "But my shift's over at four. And the bar's open."

"That's good to know." He lifted the passes toward her in a salute and turned away from the counter. "Let's go. I have our room cards—dammit. Leroy, that computer ain't for you. Leave it."

The shifter borg scowled at the other computer behind the desk, then hurried after him. "We didn't, like…uh, go back in time or anything, right?"

Johnny snorted.

"I only mean that computer doesn't have much power—"

"It's a hotel. It ain't gotta be nothin' special." Johnny whistled at the other borgs and gestured for them to join him. "Let's go."

They headed down the hall that branched off the back of the lobby and stopped outside Ballroom A so he could sign them into the conference. A long banner hung over the door and the easels showcasing the convention's sponsors—*Welcome to Unified Tech. Where Reality Meets the Future.*

Unified Tech, huh? Sure. You can't expect 'em to say, "Buy your weapons of mass destruction here at low prices."

A group of men in business suits headed down the hall toward them and their conversation slowed and stopped when they saw the cyborgs and the dwarf hunched over the table to scribble their names in the large book.

One of the businessmen sniggered. "You look lost, friend."

Johnny froze in the middle of writing his name. "Nope. But thanks anyhow. Pal."

"This is the Unified Tech Convention," another man muttered and slid his hands into the pockets of his well-tailored suit pants.

"Uh-huh. It says that right there on the sign." The bounty hunter wrote in the rest of their names and dropped the pen on the open book.

"I'm not sure what you guys think you're signing up for but you have a team of funny-looking partners."

Johnny glanced at the ceiling before he turned away from the table to study the four businessmen who smirked at him and his companions. "Whatever you're sellin', we ain't interested."

Leroy somehow interpreted that as, "Put these assholes down," and aimed his segmented arm at the men. His metallic hand clicked and spun before it shifted into another gun barrel and a low hum filled the hallway as his arm powered up.

"Oh, I get it." The first businessman chuckled. "My niece goes to Comicon every single year. You guys missed it by a few months."

"Piss off." The bounty hunter stalked down the hall and snapped his fingers at Leroy. "You too, man. Put that shit away."

The shifter borg looked at him in surprise and lowered his arm slowly to follow him. The twins frowned at the businessmen, and June ignored everyone until one of the men passed them in the hall and sniggered. "What is it with chicks and the whole Terminator look?"

"It's the cosplaying, man. They're all weirdos, but she'd at least look better in a miniskirt and heels."

She twisted to look over her shoulder and caught two of them scrutinizing her. "And you'd look better with your brains splattered against the wall." She aimed her weaponized hand at them and snarled.

"Dammit, June," Johnny shouted from down the hall. "I said let's go!"

She didn't move until the businessmen stopped shooting her weird looks and finally left for wherever they were headed, which was probably the bar.

The bounty hunter punched the call button for the elevator to the fourth floor and scowled as the borgs joined him. "You know what? This is a bad idea. We're takin' the stairs."

Fortunately, the stairwell was empty so there was no one there to either stare or run screaming when the entire staircase rang and echoed with the metallic thump of borg feet on the steps and the occasional squealed crunch of the railing when June grasped it too hard.

"Y'all need to keep a low profile, understand?"

"I thought we were," Leroy muttered.

"Yeah, and that's the problem. We're goin' in undercover and y'all stand out like Yankee housewives on a damn airboat. I think I'll have to—"

The roar of June's propulsion boots echoed deafeningly in the stairwell and she rocketed through the center of the winding stairs before she landed on the fourth floor with a thump.

"And you gotta cut that shit out," he shouted at her. "No weapons at this shindig tomorrow, understand? No jetpacks. No...finger plugs. That's the rule."

"Then why are we here?" Brandon asked.

The dwarf turned the corner to climb from the third floor to the fourth and sighed in exasperation. "To be here. To keep your eyes open and your mouths shut and to back me up when we crash this deal. That's it."

When he reached the fourth-floor landing, June jerked the door open with a bang and disappeared into the hall. The door shut again and Johnny sighed at the new spiderwebbed crack in the glass pane. *This is what I get for takin' baby cyborgs in. Dammit, we should've started with a smaller job.*

They only passed an elderly couple in the hall, both of whom stared at the borgs and clutched each other's arms as they hurried toward the elevators. Johnny slid his room key into the door, shoved it open, and waited for his team to get inside and vanish from everyone else's prying eyes.

"Whoa." Brandon grinned as they entered the shared living area of the adjoining suites. "This is cool."

"This is home for the next couple of days, so try to not break any—"

The shriek of ripped metal cut him short and he whirled to where June stood with the handle of the door to one bedroom in her hand. Not surprisingly, it was now unattached. She tossed the handle onto the floor and disappeared into the room. The bedframe groaned and something snapped when she flung herself onto the mattress.

And folks call me reckless.

The bounty hunter clenched his fists and his nose twitched as he forced down an angry outburst. "Anythin' y'all break is getting' worked off to cover the cost when we get to Florida. Understand?"

"Doing what?" Brandon asked as he sat slowly on the couch. It groaned beneath his weight but held.

"I gotta think about it but I'll tell you right now, it ain't gonna be fun." He stalked across the living area past the kitchen and made a show of turning the handle of the opposite bedroom door gently. "See this? Y'all better learn real quick how to open a door without breakin' it or we'll be made the second we step into that conference."

Leroy stepped slowly along the kitchen counter and ran his regular hand along the granite countertop. "We can go scout the place now if you want."

"No, I don't want!" Johnny tossed his duffel bag on the bed, left the bedroom he'd claimed, and closed the door behind him. "Y'all are stayin' here until I come back."

"Where are you going?" Brandon asked.

"To see a guy about illusions. 'Cause right now, y'all look like you belong here about as much as I like watchin' the opera."

The twins exchanged a confused glance.

"Do you like—"

"No, dammit. I don't like the opera." Johnny swept his finger across the living area to point at the borgs and Leroy. "Now stay. It won't take me long. Your food is comin' up by special order, so don't go callin' for room service. And no TV."

"Why?"

"'Cause I don't trust y'all to not accidentally purchase somethin' I don't want on the damn bill. June, are you listenin'?"

The only reply he got was the sound of the TV in the other bedroom turning on and the two o'clock news blaring from the speakers.

Without another word, Johnny stormed toward the suite door and into the hall.

They are worse than the hounds and worse than the kid. I gotta get out.

CHAPTER TWELVE

The second he stepped out of the elevator and into the lobby again, Johnny pulled his phone out and made a call.

"Titus Hershen."

"It's Johnny."

"Johnny goddamn Walker. How the hell are ya?"

"Eh." The dwarf stepped through the growing crowd of people checking into the hotel in the early afternoon. They were probably those he'd see again tomorrow and the next day at the convention. "I need a favor."

"Yeah, that's the only reason you call me, isn't it?" Titus chuckled. "When did you get in?"

"I never said I'm in."

"Please. You don't call me unless you need a favor and you're already in Philadelphia. What's up?"

Without thinking about it, he almost walked into the revolving door. He managed to sidestep and shoved against the regular door instead to walk into the frigid Philly air. "Goddammit, I hate the cold."

"Yeah, you're in Philadelphia. Where are you? I'll come pick you up."

"All right, if you tell me you always pick me up, we have a problem. I'm comin' to you. I'm simply givin' you a heads up and makin' sure you're in the same place."

Titus cleared his throat. "I don't leave and you know that too."

"Uh-huh. I'll be there in twenty minutes."

When the valet caught sight of the dwarf, the guy searched the front of the hotel with wide eyes.

"Hey, I'm alone, all right?" Johnny pointed at the valet stand. "I need my car."

"Yes, sir." The man snatched the Humvee keys up and scuttled away to bring his vehicle.

The bounty hunter slid his phone into his pocket, folded his arms, and surveyed the street. Yeah, it was freezing, but he wasn't about to buy himself a winter jacket he'd never wear again after this job. And if the valet wanted another fifty-dollar bill, he'd bring the car around before he became a dwarf popsicle.

None of these folks are in their right minds choosin' to live here year-round. Maybe ever.

Twenty minutes later, he pulled up in front of a run-down house on the parkland of Philadelphia. The Humvee's engine sputtered to a stop when he turned the ignition off and he hopped out and hurried down the cement walkway to the front door. The frigid air made his face burn even beneath his beard before he knocked briskly. "It's Johnny."

"I know who it is," Titus called from inside. "I'll be a minute."

Yeah, sure. Make the dwarf stand outside in fifty below.

When the door creaked open, Titus Hershen held onto the edge with one hand and grinned at his old friend. "Johnny, it's like nineteen degrees out there right now. Did someone mug you for your coat?"

"I ain't wearin' a coat."

"Obviously. Jeez, come inside." The half-wizard limped away from the door and his wooden leg thumped on the floor beside the crutch fitted snugly around his forearm. He closed the door behind his visitor and shook his head. "Did you forget Philly gets cold in the winter or what?"

"Nope." He sniffed, folded his arms, and tucked both hands under his armpits for extra warmth. "All them extra layers get in the way."

Titus laughed as he headed through his house and his wooden leg and crutch thumped simultaneously. "Of what?"

"A knife. A gun. My belt. My pockets. Any movement at all."

"You know, I've heard Florida's like a completely different world, but it sounds like you guys have a warped idea of how jackets work."

With a smirk, the bounty hunter followed his friend through the house until they reached a room at the rear lit with black-lights, UV lamps, and a neon-green bar light along the top of the back wall. "You've been upgradin'."

"A little, yeah."

"And you're growin'… What's that there?" Johnny pointed at a terrarium connected to a collection of gear, tubes, lights, and some kind of humming fan.

"It's illegal and incredibly hard to grow so don't touch." Titus limped to a tall cabinet in the back. "So what is it this time, huh? A protection amulet? Oh, hey. I got these in from a guy in Colombia. They are made from the claws of some weird-ass Oriceran tiger-thing I've never heard of but they work. Stick one above each kidney and bam. You're completely immune to pain. Until you take them out again, obviously."

Johnny studied the five-inch needle that glowed a sickly brown-orange and shook his head with a grimace. "It's temptin'."

"I know. You want 'em?"

"Maybe another day. Listen, I'm fixin' to find some hardcore illusions for…" The dwarf puffed his cheeks out. "My team."

"Yeah, right." Titus laughed and returned the needle to the cabinet. "Johnny Walker with a team."

"I ain't messin' with ya."

The half-wizard hobbled around on his crutch and cocked his head. "Oh. Seriously? When did that happen?"

"Trust me, it's new. I'm still workin' the kinks out."

"Well, yeah, I can get you illusions. I don't know if they'll be much better than what your team could already cast themselves unless you have a group of shifters working with you."

"Naw, only the one."

Titus narrowed his eyes. "And the others are…"

"Cyborgs."

"Ha! For a guy with his particular screwed-up sense of humor, you get funnier every time I see you."

"They were experimented on by an ex-CIA nutjob who wiped most of their memories and their magic's on the…underwhelmin' side." Johnny spread his arms in a helpless gesture. "It ain't that funny when I'm the one who has to hide 'em in plain sight and keep 'em from blowin' this next job up."

"Wow. You're…still not joking. And cyborgs are real. Now I've heard everything. Okay. Tell me about these guys and I'll see what I can come up with."

"All right." The dwarf sniffed and scanned the neon-glowing room. "A Crystal woman who'd rather kill a fella than walk around him. The shifter has a robot eye and a gun hand. And the twins are…tech guys, I guess. Oh, but hey. Make those two different from each other. I can only tell 'em apart when one of 'em talks."

"Uh-huh." Titus stared at his friend, drew a sharp breath, and hobbled toward a workbench on the other side of the room. "Okay, Johnny. I'll take your word for it. Where are you going? I need to know how to make them all…blend in if possible."

"The weapons convention downtown."

The other magical laughed. "I know, I know. You're serious. But you have to admit, Johnny, the shit you get yourself into is pure gold sometimes. You know that, right?"

"And that's why I call you every time I come to Philadelphia."

"Yeah." Titus shook a finger at his friend, pulled the drawers of his workbench open, and rummaged around. "The only thing you're missing is a jacket."

Titus worked his magic in the next half hour. Johnny declined the half-wizard's invitation to stay for a cup of coffee or something hot if he insisted on not dressing appropriately for the middle of winter in Philly.

"Naw, I got heat in the car. And I ain't fixin' to leave the borgs alone in that hotel room any longer than I need to."

"The what?" The man handed him a thick black drawstring bag big enough to fit a shoebox. "Oh. Right. Cyborgs. Yeah, Johnny. Good luck. It's good to see you too, by the way."

"Thanks for this. Send me a bill, huh?"

"Nope. When a guy saves your life, you don't charge him for a few trinkets. It's all good."

"All right." He stopped in front of the front door and nodded at Titus' wooden leg. "Call me if you want an upgrade on that one too. I think I can put somethin' together that'll get you off that crutch in three days."

Titus reached out to shake his hand and chuckled. "I think you have enough cyborgs to deal with, honestly. But I appreciate it."

"I didn't mean—" He couldn't help but chuckle when the half-wizard laughed and pumped his hand enthusiastically. "Yeah, okay. You got me. Take care."

"You too. Hey, for chrissakes, at least put a hat on or something. You're making me cold just watching you."

As he raised a hand in the air and hurried down the walkway toward the Humvee, Johnny clenched his teeth against the frigid air. Titus' laughter cut off abruptly when the guy closed his front door.

This had better be the last time I gotta step foot outta that hotel. I ain't buyin' a coat.

CHAPTER THIRTEEN

The door to the hotel suite opened with a click, and Johnny trudged inside with the black bag of crafted illusions.

"All right. Y'all get over here and—" His boot came down on the edge of a jar lid and it careened across the room, which was littered with empty pickle jars and loose lids exactly like the one he'd kicked. "What the hell?"

"We had lunch." Brandon belched loudly and was instantly echoed by Clint. "Thanks for covering that, by the way."

"Y'all can thank me by cleanin' this place up. Who lives like this?"

"It's a hotel." Leroy sat on the couch with one arm flung over the back and one leg stretched fully out in front of him. "We don't have to clean up."

"You do if you wanna eat while we're here 'cause I ain't holin' up with four slobs who can't even screw a lid on the right way. Come on…"

"What's in the bag?" June asked from the doorway of her bedroom.

"Your new looks. And don't tell me y'all ain't in need of somethin' different. We won't make it through the doors of that ballroom otherwise."

"Huh." Leroy chuckled. "I wouldn't have pegged you as the fashion-forward type."

"Very funny." The dwarf sat in the armchair across from the couch and jerked the drawstring bag open. "I had a buddy of mine put together some illusions. Y'all can't be runnin' around this convention lookin' like you belong at a *Star Trek* con with all those capes and lightsabers or whatever."

"Um..." Brandon leaned forward on the couch. "I'm fairly sure that's *Star Wars*."

"Naw."

"No, I remember that."

He glared at the twins but Clint backed his brother up with a slow nod. "Anyhow, that ain't where we're goin' so y'all need to look like everyone else. My buddy has some serious skills in growin' illegal plants in his private pharmacy and occasionally puttin' together a little extra boost for me I can't get anywhere else."

June snorted. "You brought us drugs?"

"What the hell? No. Magical boost. 'Cause I don't—" He shook his head and pulled the first item out of Titus' black bag. "Never mind. Here. This one's for you."

The Crystal borg looked warily at him before she finally stepped out of her room and reached for the necklace that dangled from his outstretched hand. "I'd honestly rather have drugs."

"Well, you ain't gettin' any so jump off that train before it leaves the station. These are illusion artifacts—injected or covered or however he does it. If you can't cast your own illusion, Titus is the guy who can make it for ya. Make sure these stay on while we're in public and it'll be smooth sailin' the rest of the way."

It feels like I'm talkin' outta my ass with that last part.

He withdrew a navy-blue glasses case next and tossed it to Leroy. "Put those on."

The shifter borg opened the creaking case slowly and removed a pair of large, thick-rimmed black glasses. "Your friend knows I only have one real eye, right? And that I'm a shifter—"

"And shifters hardly ever have bad eyesight? Yeah. I told him." Johnny stuffed his hand into the bag again. "The guy thinks it's hilarious and ironic but you're wearin' 'em."

The last items to come out of the bag were two pairs of boxer shorts—one burnt-orange with forest-green stripes and the other green with orange stripes. He tossed these to the twins and shrugged. "It looks like y'all win the jackpot. You're least likely to have your illusion snatched off your body in a fight if crashin' this deal goes south."

"If?" Brandon held his green pair in front of his face and frowned as he stretched the waistband.

"Naw. It ain't gonna happen." After he tossed the bag on the coffee table, the bounty hunter leaned back in the armchair and raised an eyebrow. "Well, go on. See how they fit."

"You want us to put these on?" Brandon exchanged a glance with his brother and Clint shrugged before he stood to head to the bathroom near the front door. "Right now?"

"I gotta make sure y'all look like you could pass for literally anyone but who you are. We gotta do this right."

"Fine." With a sigh, Brandon stood and walked into Johnny's room to change.

"It had to be a necklace, huh?" June grumbled. "I don't even own a dress."

The dwarf snorted. "You sound like Amanda. Put it on."

Rolling her eyes, she undid the clasp of the delicate silver chain and fastened it again behind her neck. The second her hands fell away, all trace of her physical augmentations vanished.

Her ice-flecked hair gained another six inches of glistening blonde waves. The jetpacks built into her metal feet became gray-satin stilettos, and the maroon dress was better suited for a cocktail party than a weapons convention.

She spread her arms and glanced at her transformation. "What?"

Johnny leaned sideways against the armrest and stared at her. "Well. There ain't a chance in hell now that folks will think you have weapons hidden up your…outfit."

"I won't wear this."

"Technically, you aren't." Leroy raised the thick glasses slowly to his face. "Only the necklace."

She scoffed and whirled into her bedroom to storm into the connecting bathroom.

Good work, Titus. The heels even sound real.

When Johnny turned to look at Leroy, he saw nothing more than a regular-looking dude—albeit still dramatically broad in the shoulders—seated on the couch in a casual business suit. The shifter borg's mechanical eye was completely gone, as were all his metal pieces and whirring gears. Leroy lifted his segmented hand and wiggled his fingers slowly. "Shit. I have two hands again."

"Nope. It only looks like you do. I'd try to not grab anythin' with that hand anyway or you'll be called out for the kinda strength even a shifter ain't got."

"Fuck this!" June shouted from the bathroom.

Johnny leaned toward her room. "You can't change it now. Smile and nod and don't let folks draw you into conversation." *The crabby-ass Crystal's a damn bombshell until she opens her mouth.*

The doors to the half-bathroom at the front of the suite and to Johnny's adjoining room both opened and Brandon and Clint stepped out at the same time. They looked at each other and burst out laughing.

"Aw, come on." The dwarf slumped in his armchair.

Leroy laughed with the twins and glanced from one to the other a few times. "It looks like you two stepped out of a Sherlock Holmes movie—without the funny hat and the pipe, of course."

The twins were dressed almost identically, with slight variation in the colors and patterns of their dark tweed vests. Pocketwatch chains dangled from their breast pockets and their normally shaggy dark hair was now lighter, longer, and slicked back from their foreheads. Brandon touched his hair as he studied his brother. "We're redheads now?"

"Naw, that's only Clint." Johnny smirked. "You have more of an unidentifiable brown goin' on. And now I can finally tell y'all apart simply by lookin'."

Brandon readjusted the waistband of his crisp slacks and frowned at the shiny leather loafers on his feet. "I thought boxers were supposed to be comfortable but these suck."

The dwarf shrugged. "You get what you get, brother."

"What are you smiling at, you dapper asshole?" The wizard borg nodded at his brother across the room.

Clint grinned and spread his arms.

They stared at each other for thirty seconds before Brandon sighed. "You didn't put your clothes on, did you?"

His twin shook his head slowly.

"Dammit, don't stand here in your skivvies." Johnny pointed at the front bathroom. "It don't matter if I can see it or not. Now I know. Come on."

June's heels clacked across the floor of her room before she appeared in the living area and heaved a massively aggravated sigh. "I'm not doing this."

Brandon's eyes widened. "June?"

"See?" Johnny clapped his hands and stood. "It's perfect. Y'all can't even recognize each other."

"You look like a hooker."

She glared at the young cyborg and jerked the clasp of the necklace around to the front so she could get it off faster. The illusion faded instantly. "They look like trust-fund babies from Massachusetts. Leroy's...normal. And I have to look like I'm out working the streets?"

"It ain't that bad." Johnny rubbed his hands together and nodded. "All right, fellas. We have schematics to go over and a plan to get down as much as we can. It's time for y'all to hook up."

Clint snorted a laugh when Brandon scowled at the dwarf. "To do what?"

"Hook up. Christ, with your tech. Give Leroy the layout of the convention so he can project it from his eye hole. Do I need to spell it out more than that for y'all?"

"I'm only checking, jeez."

He shook his head as the twins converged on Leroy and the couch and took their seats on either side of the shifter borg. *Forget neurological damage to their magic. It's like I have a group of teenagers with their minds in the gutter all the damn time.* "Let's go."

The twins each placed a hand on one of Leroy's shoulders and curled their fingers around the metal bars along the shifter's collar bones that were now visible since he'd removed the illusion glasses.

"Ready?" Brandon asked.

Leroy tilted his head. "Load it up."

A pulsing energetic hum flared from both twins into the shifter, visible as a low crackle of blue light that raced across his shoulders and up both sides of his neck. His mechanical eye spun faster than ever and opened fully before a new projection spewed from the lens to fill the center of the hotel suite.

"Man, if that ain't a neat trick," Johnny muttered. "All right. So here's what's gonna happen, and the only excuse for not stickin' to the plan is if someone pulls a gun on you first. For real. Not as a demo. 'Cause, you know, weapons convention. Got it?"

The twins nodded. Leroy gave the dwarf a thumbs-up without moving his head an inch to keep the projection steady. June merely stormed across the room to lean against the kitchen counter and watch from afar.

"All right. Ballroom A. The front entrance is here and the emergency exits here and here. And there's an extra storage room or staff room or whatever between Ballroom A and Ballroom B. If you hear anythin' about private meetups or see anyone moving toward the back exits or the staff doors, let me know. My guess is it'll be in the staff room or close to it. These guys ain't fixin' to meet for a high-level deal like this in a back parking lot. They'll wanna get lost in the crowd on their way in and out of their little chat."

"So what do we do before the meeting?" Brandon asked.

"You listen and watch. That's it." Johnny ran a hand through his hair. *If Lisa were here to listen to me makin' a real plan, I'd never hear the end of it.* "Bartlett said we're lookin' for a fella by the name of Epsley. There isn't much to go on besides that, but he's the one their intel snatched up. He'll be makin' the deal with the guys tryin' to smuggle this shit overseas. Now Leroy ain't gonna draw attention with those glasses. He's more of a pencil-pusher type, and they're practically invisible. You'll be my right-hand man so stay with me. June, you can canvass the place all you want but try to stay in one place while you do it."

"Why?"

He looked up from the projection and sighed. "'Cause you'll be drawin' more than enough attention as it is. Trust me."

She scoffed. "You don't think I can handle it."

"No, that ain't it. Look, I know good-lookin' women with insane power can take care of themselves. I've learned a thing or two in the last eight months. But for the love of the Everglades, June, don't go takin' care of yourself by blowin' fellas up if they get a little forward. Which they will, understand? Try to act natural."

"Blowing assholes up for being assholes is natural."

"Then pretend to be normal." Johnny glared unblinkingly at her from across the suite. *Shit. Here I am, tellin' her something that would make me punch a guy's lights out for tellin' me.* "Listen, it ain't about what we want in the moment when we get in there, all right? If we screw this up, even bigger assholes are gonna roll into this country with weapons that ain't exactly approved—or stoppable once they're all set up and ready to be fired. We can all agree on that at least, right?"

"Yeah, weapons of mass destruction sound bad," Brandon muttered. Clint stared at him with wide eyes and nodded enthusiastically.

Leroy cleared his throat. "We're with you, boss."

Although the shifter borg didn't move so he could keep the projection steady, the twins looked over their shoulders at June and waited for her reply. She scowled at Johnny. "How come you don't have to put an illusion on?"

The dwarf spread his arms in what he hoped was a placatory gesture. "'Cause I can pass for a guy who showed up at a weapons convention to look at the weapons, not to be the weapons. And 'cause when folks recognize me, it tends to open doors. Sometimes."

She rolled her eyes in response but the fact that she didn't try to argue with him or storm into her room again like a moody teenager meant it was safe to assume she was still on board too.

"Good. Now, y'all go over the layout. If you have any other ideas that might help, let me know. We'll throw whatever around until it sticks. I gotta make a call."

"To who?" Brandon asked.

"None of your business." Johnny stepped into his room as he pulled his cell phone out. "Carry on."

With the door shut, he stalked toward the attached full bathroom and shut that door too before he made the call. Lisa answered after the first ring.

"That didn't take long."

"I'm callin' to check in, darlin'. How are the boys?"

She laughed. "Your dogs are fine, Johnny. Honestly, it's like they don't even notice you're gone."

"Hell. That ain't a thing you say to a guy missin' his hounds."

"No, that's what you say when someone's worried about how everyone else is doing. Meaning you don't have to worry."

He leaned against the bathroom counter and sniffed. "What about Amanda?"

"She's out running that obstacle course."

"Has she finished it yet?"

"Not yet, but almost. I can't believe the school has magical guns aimed at children. But at least she gets up again every time. You know, I've heard it's hard to keep kids off technology but I might have to set a time limit on this course. She's obsessed."

"Naw, she's only warming up."

After a slight pause, Lisa laughed lightly. "How's Philadelphia?"

"Freezing. I hate it."

"Johnny, I meant the job. Is everything going smoothly so far?"

"Sure. I have the borgs covered with illusions and we're headin' to the conference tomorrow. So, you know, if I can't get away tomorrow night at the right time to give you a call, Happy New Year. Early."

"Well, that's forward-thinking of you."

"I'm only tryin' to—"

"Happy Early New Year, Johnny." The laughter in her voice made him smirk. "I'll take Amanda to school and then your dogs and I will fly out to join you. Until then, don't do anything I wouldn't let you talk me into, okay?"

"Huh." He couldn't wipe the crooked smile off his lips, even when he tried to rub it off. "I guess this will be a fairly tame openin', all things considered."

"That doesn't sound like you, but okay. Talk to you soon."

"All right, darlin'." He ended the call and grimaced. *All that talkin' nonsense and I didn't even ask how she's doin'. I probably won't live that one down either.*

CHAPTER FOURTEEN

By the time the Unified Tech conference officially opened at 10:00 am the next day, Johnny was ready to get the hell out of their hotel suite. He made sure to leave the door hanger on their room door declining room service for the day—because the borgs hadn't yet cleaned up after their feast—and led his fully illusioned team to the first floor of the hotel.

The lobby was packed. Some of the guests were older couples trying to check in or out, but the rest were conference attendees who swarmed toward the back of the lobby and the entrance hall into Ballroom A. He scowled at all of them and glanced continually over his shoulder to make sure the borgs stayed close enough that he could keep an eye on them.

These are all carbon copies of the jackasses who tried to scare us off yesterday. Or whatever the hell they were goin' for.

Most of the conference attendees did, in fact, look exactly like the group of businessmen who'd accosted him and his team in front of the sign-in table. A handful of people looked like they'd stepped off a flight from the dwarf's neck of the woods with camo vests, duck-billed hats, and long beards. They were merely spectators.

All of these people were spectators, he realized. The bounty hunter knew the buyers with the real money who came to explore the latest in advanced weapons technology would be the most unassuming. His gaze settled briefly on a man who stood a few steps inside the doors to the ballroom, his hands in the pockets of his loose pants as he scanned the convention and waited for the demonstrations to begin. Close to him but not with him, a woman in jeans and a turtleneck with thick glasses didn't smile at anyone and seemed entirely focused on studying the room. Those, he decided, were the kind of people they would most likely have to look out for.

The yuppies doin' themselves up to look rich probably spent all their extra money on the suits and the fancy watches.

When he and his team reached the ballroom entrance in the long line of people who paused to sign in before they were allowed through with their attendee passes, Johnny snapped his fingers and waved the borgs closer.

"Keep an eye out for folks who don't look involved with what's happening here. Epsley ain't interested in the demos on the floor. He's meetin' the seller. And come to me first with anythin' you find before we act. Understand?"

The twins in their stylistically weird East Coast getups nodded. June glanced disdainfully at him before she slipped into the crowd again and disappeared deeper into the ballroom.

"Damn." The dwarf tugged his beard. "I should have fitted y'all with comms for this."

"Don't worry about it," Leroy muttered and scanned the attendees around them as they moved through the open double doors. "We don't need comms."

"For real? Why are you smirkin' like that?"

"I'll hear from June if she finds anything."

"Oh. So y'all have built-in comms."

"Nope. I never really believed in telepathy before waking up in that lab, boss. But I can tell you now it's a real thing."

Johnny snorted and stared at the huge guy beside him who would look otherwise unassuming if it wasn't for his sheer size. "Hell. I didn't believe in cyborgs until you woke up in that lab either. Nothin' surprises me anymore."

The shifter pushed the thick-framed glasses up the bridge of his nose and nodded. "It's time to get to work."

"Ha! You're seriously playin' the part, ain'tcha?"

"I'm only trying to act normal."

"Uh-huh. Let's go check it out." He nodded at the twins, who turned to head in the opposite direction across the ballroom, and rubbed his hands together. After he'd scanned the various booths and demo tables around them, he smacked his companion's arm with the back of his hand. A dull metallic thump rose from the contact, and he stepped away immediately. "Well, I know which arm is which now. Look at that over there—heat-seekin' game traps. Damn, I had no idea I needed one of those until two seconds ago."

Leroy slid his hands into the pockets of his tailored suit pants and strolled leisurely beside the dwarf. "I thought we were here for a different kind of weapon."

"We are. It don't mean we can't explore all the other great displays they have here. But keep your eyes open."

The Unified Tech convention seemed to have everything— even the weapons the bounty hunter hadn't thought of yet. The heat-seeking game traps were only in the prototype stage. There were others, however, that he had to force himself to not spend a fortune on simply to take them home with him so he could pick them apart—bio-signature handguns, thought-activated grenades, energy flares immune to the elements, and a surprisingly advanced application of weaponized nanotech.

As the first day of the conference kicked off, the ballroom filled with the sounds of video recordings of the new weapons testing, the conversations between vendors and onlookers asking questions, and the shout of a young intern begging some douchenozzle to not fire the weapon inside.

Johnny smirked at the booths they passed and made mental notes of all the new weapons either on the market, about to be available, or seeking big-wig investors to continue research and production.

I should have started comin' to this years ago.

Every so often, he turned to scan the ballroom for the twins and June's bright-blonde hair spilling over the shoulders of her tight-fitting maroon dress. The brothers gave him curt nods whenever they made eye contact. June merely rolled her eyes and turned away from him. After the fourth or fifth man approached her to ogle her dress and try to start a conversation but was met only with a defiant glare, her admirers eventually learned to stay away from the gorgeous woman who scowled at everyone and everything.

At least she looks like someone who ain't interested. There are a hell of a lot of gold-diggers here, I tell you what.

After making their rounds to the booths along the edges of the ballroom, Johnny and Leroy walked up and down the rows of exhibits that filled the center. The next thing to catch the bounty hunter's eye made him laugh. "Holy shit. Leroy. Do you see that wizard over there at the green table?"

"Two World Gear?"

"Yeah. I know him."

"As in we need to keep an eye on him for the job?"

He almost smacked the shifter borg's arm again but stopped himself and pointed at the table instead. "Naw, as in I worked a case with him. Kinda. I think I know exactly what he has on display. Come on."

They slipped around the milling crowds of weapons enthusiasts until they reached the green Two World Gear table and the half-wizard who stood behind it.

"You know, only a few months ago, y'all were tellin' me I couldn't get my hands on one of these."

The half-wizard turned away from an attendee who studied one of the weapons laid out on the table, startled when he saw the dwarf, and broke into a wide grin. "Johnny. I'd say I'm surprised to see you here but it makes way too much sense."

"I didn't think I'd see you here, though." He gestured at the array of weapons on offer and cleared his throat. "Y'all told me it was only for fun."

"Yeah, well, we expanded. Who's your friend?"

"Oh, shit. This is Leroy. He's takin' notes for me."

The shifter borg snorted but pushed the thick glasses up the bridge of his nose again and smiled.

"And this is Chiron," the bounty hunter added to finish the introductions. "I pulled him and a few of his buddies out the middle of the swamp a couple of months ago. It's where I got to see these babies put to use for the first time." He slapped a hand on one of the laser-bomb cannons the group of Philly magicals had invented and brought with them to Florida. Chiron winced at the dwarf's treatment of his demo weapon. "It don't look like much, but this will take down an immortal armored worm about the length of this ballroom."

Leroy raised an eyebrow behind the glasses. "That's a metaphor I haven't heard."

"It ain't a metaphor, man. It happened."

Chiron chuckled and stared at the laser-bomb cannon until Johnny finally removed his hand. "We've made a few upgrades since then."

"No shit. I didn't think these could get any better than they already were."

The half-wizard shrugged and looked more uncomfortable by the second. "Well, moving up from target practice to using them in a real fight put a different perspective on what we'd been missing."

"Excellent." The dwarf grinned and reached for the weapon again.

"Hands off, Johnny. Come on."

"What? I ain't gonna fire it in here. So y'all are doin' okay in Philly now?"

Chiron grimaced. "We are—those of us who made it back. All things considered, though, that was most of us. I guess we have you and Lisa to thank for that, right?"

"Well, if you wanna thank me, brother, I ain't gonna turn you down."

"Eddie's here too. He's out taking a look around. Have you seen him?"

"Nope." Johnny stared at the laser-bomb cannon. "Tell him I said hi, though."

"Sure, Johnny. Good to see you. I should get back to manning the table, you know?"

"Yeah, yeah. Hey, have you put a price tag on these cannons yet?"

The half-wizard exhaled a slow, heavy sigh and nodded at a woman who stood beside Johnny and waited to ask her questions. "I'll be right with you, ma'am. Yeah, Johnny. There's a price tag. Are you here to buy weapons?"

"That's one of the reasons, sure. How many of these babies did you bring with you?"

Chiron glanced at Leroy, who only stared at him with a blank expression and folded his arms. "Three."

"Great. I'll take all of 'em."

"I…" The man chuckled. "Are you screwing with me?"

"Not even a little. Y'all kept the best damn weapons I never made all to yourselves last time. I ain't passin' this opportunity up." The dwarf pulled his wallet from his back pocket and slid a credit card out. "Do you have a card reader?"

"Uh…yeah." The other magical fumbled under the table for

the card reader and frowned in utter confusion. "They aren't cheap."

"'Course they ain't. I imagine y'all could charge a hell of a lot more for 'em too. Go on."

Chiron took the dwarf's card like it was a bomb about to go off. "Don't you want to know how much—"

"Nope. Run the card, Chiron. Then pack the merchandise."

The half-wizard ran his card, asked him to sign electronically, and turned toward the stacked crates behind his table. He drew out three sleek metal cases with thin handles and Johnny grinned like a lunatic the whole time.

"Good luck with the convention, brother." The dwarf extended his hand for a quick, enthusiastic handshake. "And good to see ya."

"Yeah, you too." Chiron looked like he'd been mugged and hadn't quite processed it. He shook his head and turned slowly toward the man who now waited to learn about Two World Gear's array of weaponry. The woman had given up minutes before.

The bounty hunter stacked the cases of laser-bomb cannons, picked them up, and turned to head away from the table with an extra bounce in his step.

"Do you want me to carry those?" Leroy asked.

"Like hell I do. Get your own."

After his initial ten minutes of glee, however, Johnny recognized the importance of having his hands free for their actual purpose at the convention. He slipped out to ask the front desk to take them to his suite. The same concierge from the day before was on duty again and she scrutinized him with a pert smile as he clunked the cases onto the counter. "Did you buy weapons in there or something?"

"Yep." He grunted at her wide-eyed surprise. "But they're empty and there ain't no one to fire 'em so I'd appreciate you gettin' these up to my room for me." As an afterthought, he pulled another fifty out and slid it across the counter. "This goes to whoever does it without askin' questions. Thanks, darlin'."

The concierge stared blankly at the bill and the three sleek cases, but by the time she'd thought of a response, he was already inside Ballroom A and in search of his team.

He found the twins first, who'd finally caved to the excitement of so many weapons together in one place. They stood in front of a miniaturized heat-seeking missile booth, their human-looking fingers outstretched toward one of the demo weapons. Faint silver sparks illuminated at their fingertips before Johnny hauled them away with a fist clenched around the back of each twin's shirt. "Back the hell off, boys. And put the damn finger-guns away, huh? This ain't happy hour."

"You could've fooled me," Brandon muttered as he staggered to keep up with the dwarf.

"Get back to work. We're canvassin' for Epsley and a deal, not toys."

"Says the guy who bought three of his own," Leroy said behind him.

The bounty hunter spun and glared at him. "Quit sneakin' up on me like that. Damn. And none of y'all have the money to buy any toys, so if you break it, I buy it. I ain't fixin' to haul the whole damn conference home with me, either. Where's June?"

"Same place." Leroy nodded over his shoulder toward the far side of the ballroom. The Crystal borg stood with her arms folded over the skin-tight cocktail dress, scanned the attendees, and scowled at anyone who approached. "I think we might have something, though."

"Oh, yeah? Like what?"

Leroy leaned toward the dwarf's ear and muttered, "I did a visual scan of the staff room on the left side of the ballroom. Someone's been seated there for the last ten minutes."

"And you only thought to tell me about this now?"

"It could have been staff." The shifter shrugged. "And you went to ship your toys upstairs."

"Yeah, fine." Johnny frowned and nodded. "Keep up the visual scannin'. Let me know if anyone else steps foot in there."

"You got it, boss."

"You ain't gotta call me that, Leroy."

"Why? That's what you are." The shifter failed to mention the fact that he didn't pay them anything.

Naw. I merely let 'em tear my property up for free.

Leroy turned to meet June's gaze and nodded. She unfolded her arms and strolled across the ballroom toward the door to the staff room, where she settled into her new position. It was as conspicuous as hell but only because the damn illusion made her conspicuous.

"Telepathy." Johnny snorted. "All right, I'll bite."

CHAPTER FIFTEEN

After another half-hour of watching and waiting, the twins wandered through the maze of weapon exhibits to find Johnny beside the refreshments table. He jammed a prosciutto roll into his mouth, grimaced, and snatched a napkin up to spit it out again. "That ain't meat. It's meat-flavored paper. Have y'all ever had one of these?"

Clint shook his head as Johnny tossed the wadded napkin into the trash.

"We might have hit a homerun, Johnny," Brandon said. "We picked up some conversation."

"Uh-huh. Let's hear it."

"Um…" The wizard borg glanced around and lowered his head toward him. "Even if we could play it back without Margo, I don't think this is the right place—"

"No, tell me."

"Oh. Right." He glanced at his brother and elbowed him in the side.

With a frown, Clint raised a finger for them to wait. His eyelids fluttered and all expression disappeared from his face. "I know they jacked the price up but I still want to talk to these assholes and give them a piece of my mind. Then we'll get the hell out of here. The rest of this is like a toy store in comparison. Amateurs."

His eyelids fluttered again before he looked from Johnny to Leroy with a shrug.

"Yeah, that sounds about right." The bounty hunter tugged his beard thoughtfully. "Did you find out who said it?"

The twins shook their heads in unison. "We picked it up through the noise."

"Sure. Okay. We'll find 'em."

"I think we might have already." Leroy nodded to where June scowled at a man in dress slacks and a long black peacoat who leered at her with a hungry grin as he passed. She looked away from him and raised her chin as if she were objectified like this all the time and had simply become used to it. The man slipped into the staff room with two bulky-looking bodyguards at his side and the door closed behind them.

The Crystal turned her head slowly to look at Johnny and the others beside the refreshment table and raised an eyebrow.

"That's what we've been waitin' for." The bounty hunter nudged Leroy's other arm—which didn't emit a metallic thump beneath the illusion—and strode across the ballroom. "Tell her to not go bustin' in there on her own first, huh?"

"She knows." Leroy cast a sly glance at the food on the table, shook his head, and hurried after the others.

Everyone else ignored them as Johnny and his team of two East Coast gentlemen, the pencil-pusher, and the bombshell blonde moved toward the staff door.

"All right. Y'all let me do the talkin'. And keep the damn illusions on, huh? I ain't fixin' to get to the point where we gotta use force for this one but if it happens, it's best we don't give folks a way to recognize cyborgs blowin' up the Unified Tech Con. Got it?"

Leroy turned to scan the ballroom for anyone who might be

watching them—like a natural-born bodyguard—and the dwarf jerked the door open. The twins and June followed him quickly before Leroy slipped inside.

"…price you gave me and that's the price I expected." The man in the peacoat loomed over a table at the other side of the room where an unamused bald man sat alone. The hired muscle stood on either side of their principal with their arms folded and their muscles bulged in a show of at least physical power. Their boss didn't do a very good job of matching it with his intellect.

"Circumstances have changed," the bald man said and spread his arms as if everything was self-evident. "If you can't roll with the punches, you'll have to move on."

The hopeful buyer thumped a palm on the table. "We had an agreement!"

"To meet here for an in-person discussion." The other man's gaze slid behind his prospective customer and he raised an eyebrow. "It didn't include a finalized purchase price and it certainly didn't include a third party."

"What?" His visitor spun and sneered at the sight of Johnny Walker and his team, who stood only a few steps away from the door. "This is private. Get out."

The bounty hunter settled his fists on his hips and took a chance that Colonel Bartlett's intel wasn't a waste of his time. "Give it up, Epsley. Sometimes, you simply can't run with the big dogs."

"And you would consider yourself a big dog?" the bald man asked and finally looked at least partially amused instead of bored. "Mr.…."

"We'll get to my name later." He pointed at Epsley. "I think your time's run out. Unless you got the what he's askin' for right now."

"How do you—" The snorted and gestured in exasperation. "I don't even know you."

"Oh, don't worry. I ain't easily insulted."

"You can't barge in here and interrupt a private meeting I arranged."

The bounty hunter smirked. "Watch me."

"He's right," the bald man interjected, still seated casually behind the table. "If you can't meet the price, Mr. Epsley, I can't meet the demand. If this…gentleman doesn't follow through in the way you couldn't, I'll contact you again to see if you've reconsidered."

"This isn't how—"

"Leave."

Epsley seethed and stalked across the room toward Johnny, his hired thugs close on his heels. "You have no idea who you're messing with, asshole."

"Yeah, you too."

"Seriously? You think your accountant and these two… professors can handle my guys?" The man turned his attention to June and scrutinized her again with a laugh. "You're so out of place here, sweetheart. What were you planning to do? Seduce the man into a better deal?"

"On second thought, I have no shortage of interested parties, Mr. Epsley," the bald man called from the table. "If you can't control yourself and get out of here, your name's off the list."

"Yeah, I heard you." With a sneer, the man pointed at Johnny and inclined his head. "Whoever you are, I'll find you. Then we'll see how much you can pay. I'll destroy you."

"Whatever helps you sleep at night." He didn't move. *He'd better move on outta here. If his backup bozos make a move, my borgs are out in the open.*

Epsley sighed heavily and turned toward June. "I'm in room 872—the Elegance Suite—if you're interested. Whatever this dwarf thinks he's giving you, it's nothing compared to what I can."

Aw, shit.

The man extended his hand toward her long, shimmering,

completely fake blonde hair while his gaze remained fixed on the low cut of her dress. Before his fingers even reached her face, she stepped back and in the blink of an eye, pulled the necklace free with a quick jerk. The sparking barrel of the silver rod in her arm flared to life and aimed directly at the man's crotch before her illusion necklace landed on the floor. The tiny swiveling sight of the personal missile launcher embedded in her left shoulder locked onto Epsley's face.

"Holy fuck." The man leapt back and squawked in alarm, while his guards slid their hands toward the butts of their pistols strapped to their hips.

Leroy chuckled. "I wouldn't, guys. Hers are bigger."

"W-w-what the hell is this freak doing here?" Epsley shrieked. "Fuck. You...shit. Get that thing out of my face!" His bodyguards exchanged a glance, removed their hands from their weapons, and raised them in surrender.

"Here. Allow me." Johnny turned to open the door of the staff room, which immediately filled with the deafening background noise of the convention in full swing on the other side. "You might find better luck with what's out there."

Epsley shoved one of his guys in front of himself to use as a heavily muscled shield as he staggered toward the door. "I'll ruin you, see if I don't. You'll pay for this."

"Uh-huh. And what he's sellin'. Good luck."

As soon as the second bodyguard scurried through the door, The bounty hunter pulled it shut and the staff room fell mostly silent again. "Now. If you have the time..."

He turned again to find the bald man standing in front of the table, his eyes wide above an eager smile as studied June intently. "I always have time for a man with friends like this. Although I don't believe I caught your name."

Johnny nodded at the Crystal. "You can stand down now."

For once, she chose to listen and powered all her weapons down in a second. Her metal feet clinked on the floor when she squared her stance and folded her arms. Brandon stooped to retrieve her necklace and she snatched it from him with a scowl but didn't bother to put it on.

The dwarf was already halfway across the staff room with his hand outstretched. "You can call me Johnny."

"Blake." They shook briefly before the arms dealer straightened the front of his suit jacket as he walked around the table again. "Please. Take a seat."

"Thanks." Johnny settled into a chair and studied the man's eager interest in June—for her built-in weapons and clicking mechanical parts rather than the nightlife outfit she'd worn previously. *At least now we have somethin' he's interested in.*

The man sat silently for a moment, his eyes narrowed intently on the Crystal before he turned his full attention to the bounty hunter. "You're already aware of what my client's bringing to the table."

"Your client. Yeah." *It makes sense they'd only send the mouthpiece.* "And I'm here so y'all are aware of what I'm bringin'."

"Quite. No offense intended, Johnny, but I can't help being a little more curious than usual. You're not an independent dealer on your own, are you?"

"No." He folded his arms. "I'm the guy they send out to make deals they ain't fixin' to dirty their hands with."

"Ah." Blake smirked. "Then you and I already have much more in common than I expected. And I'm sure you understand that I also have to ask who your employer is."

"The US Marines."

The man leaned back in his chair and stared at him with hard eyes. "I find that hard to believe."

"No, you don't. The military in this country has been doin' it for a long time. Buyin'. Sellin'. Settin' the stage, if you catch my meanin'."

With another glance toward the cyborg woman and the other three gentlemen who still looked wildly out of place, Blake nodded. "And the US Marine Corps is prepared to offer what my client's asking?"

"That's right." He sniffed and lowered his head. "Major Dorn specifically. I expect your client will recognize the name."

"Why would you think that?"

The dwarf shrugged. "'Cause Dorn's been doin' this for a long time too. Feel free to check in with whoever you need to check in with. When they clear it, you let me know. I assume the next time we see each other, we'll be exchangin' more than only words and a handshake."

"Indeed." Blake still couldn't stop his gaze from trailing toward June. "Two-point-five billion. Which I'm sure you were already aware of, but I'd rather not let anything else get lost in translation."

It took everything Johnny had to not burst out laughing. *Bartlett's gonna shit himself.*

"That's fine. Like I said, we're prepared."

"Yes, I can see that. Let me ask you something, Johnny." The man barely lifted his finger to point at June. "Is that the only one?"

"The cyborg? Naw."

"I assume these are under military contract as well."

The bounty hunter let himself smirk a little at that. "Nope. Only mine. I like to dabble."

"Excellent." His focus still fixed on June, Blake removed a small notepad and pen from the inside pocket of his suit jacket. "There's no need to bring your offer to my client. As long as these...cyborgs, did you say?"

"Yeah."

"As long as these cyborgs of yours are on the table for contracting as well, I'm confident we can all come to an agreement that leaves every party much more satisfied than we expected." He scribbled something on the notepad, tore the sheet off, and slid it across the table toward Johnny. "Usually, I like to remind prospective buyers of how highly we value punctuality for these things but with you, I don't think there's a need. Your timing was impeccable."

He nodded. "I'm lookin' forward to it."

"Yes. So am I." With a curt nod and a hard smile, the man stood and buttoned his suit jacket. "Enjoy your weekend."

With that, he walked toward the opposite door of the staff room and disappeared through it.

Johnny slapped a hand down on the notepaper and studied the message there.

Our Lady Point Ranch. Tuesday. 4:00 pm.

"Well, shit." He stood and pocketed the note before he turned to face the borgs. "That went well."

June scoffed. "It would've been better if you'd let me shoot the bastard in the—"

"Yeah, well, he learned his lesson. And we have our ticket to these weapons." Johnny stood and pushed his chair in before he strode across the room. "We're gonna be in Philadelphia for a while longer and I have some calls to make."

"Not to your girlfriend again, right?"

Johnny pointed at Brandon as Leroy opened the door. "No, smartass. To the Colonel and the name I dropped to get us in."

If he's even still a major and if he ain't dead by now.

The borgs wanted to stay at the convention. All he wanted was to kick back in the hotel room alone with a celebratory drink or five but his team was persistent.

"They have items here even we could use," Brandon said. "The kind that doesn't have to be...uh, you know. Surgically implanted."

"Uh-huh. I already found what I'm interested in, though. There ain't no point in stickin' around."

"I will not spend the next week locked in that hotel room," June all but snarled.

"Well, hell, I didn't say you had to." Johnny glanced at the necklace she'd managed to repair with the help of Clint's quick finger-welder—another cyborg surprise—and turned away again to avoid staring at the low-cut front of her illusion. "And I gotta call Titus about that necklace. There ain't no tellin' how long that illusion will hold now that you broke it."

"I made a point."

"You didn't stick to the plan." He ran a hand through his hair and scanned the next row of exhibit tables he hadn't yet seen. "Granted, the sight of that bigass cannon on your shoulder might be what got us in with no questions asked."

"He asked questions," Brandon interjected.

"Not the kind that matter."

"I want to stay," Leroy said and pushed his glasses up his nose. "At the very least, we can get some good ideas for making equipment of our own, right?"

"Are you readin' my mind too?" The bounty hunter looked sharply at him.

The shifter borg frowned. "No."

"You'd better not be. Come on. We gotta get back. I can't make these calls with all this damn noise—"

"Come on, Johnny." Brandon spread his arms and stepped in front of the dwarf to cut him off. "Only another hour. Maybe two. We won't touch anything."

"I know. 'Cause we ain't stayin'."

"You can go back to the room, boss," Leroy added. "Give us a time and we'll come up when we're done."

"There is no way in hell will I leave y'all down here alone to mess with everyone else's weapons, illusions or not."

"And there is no way in hell I'll go to that hotel room right now." June pivoted sharply and headed toward a large booth with a tent proclaiming the newest technology from AeroMark. "So deal with it."

"Aw, come on. Y'all can't gang up on me like that. This ain't—"

"Ladies and gentlemen." The voice boomed through the sound

system and only dampened the noise by a fraction. "It's now twelve o'clock and I would like to direct your attention to the scheduled demonstration by our special guest, exhibitor, and one of our esteemed sponsors, Mr. Clayton Zen with the ZenOptics Corporation. In only a moment, I'll hand the mic to Mr. Zen. But I'd like those of you who would like to see the first official public glimpse of the ZenOptics Corporation's new molecular disassembler prototype to please join us at the back of the ballroom at the north windows. I can't tell you more right now but this is not something you want to miss."

The mic bumped against something with a shuffle of static and a second speaker cleared his throat. "Thank you, Daniel. Let's give our host a warm round of applause, shall we? And one for the entire event staff of this incredible hotel and of Unified Tech for putting together such a spectacular array of cutting-edge innovations in the realm of weapons technology."

Some of the attendees turned to give their applause, but those in the back couldn't see who they were listening to and therefore didn't care.

"Johnny." Brandon gave the dwarf a pointed stare. "Come on. Molecular disassembler? We have to see that."

"Naw. It can't be nothin' special." Despite his words, he craned to try to peer over the heads of the crowd in front of him.

"Now," Mr. Zen continued, "it gives me the utmost pleasure to finally reveal to all of you what we at the ZenOptics Corporation have worked on for the last five years. An entire generation of advanced technology and sophisticated weapons applications is right here in one place for you to see—the Scrambler."

The crowd toward the back of the ballroom went wild. They cheered, whistled, and clapped as the sound of a mechanized system droned in the background.

"It could be something awesome," Leroy muttered. "If it's not, we'll go back."

"How does it work?" a man near the front of the stage shouted.

"Ah, yes. That is what everyone's here to see, isn't it?" Mr. Zen chuckled into the microphone and the crowd laughed with him. "Let me show you."

The heavy click and low whine that rose quickly in pitch sounded like it came from a weapon as big as Margo. A brilliant flash of buzzing green light issued from the back of the ballroom and glass shattered, followed by another uproarious cheer from the crowd.

"Shit. Let's have a better look." Johnny stomped through the crowd and didn't bother to turn to see if the borgs were following. He knew they were.

CHAPTER SIXTEEN

Lisa walked into Johnny's house which was now officially and entirely empty. With a heavy sigh, she dropped her car keys on the worktable and headed into the kitchen. Her gaze found the half-empty bottle of whiskey on the counter and she raised an eyebrow.

Yeah, I'm starting to get why Johnny drinks all the time.

It hadn't exactly been rough to drop Amanda off at the Academy to start her second semester, but the kid had an uncanny habit of acting completely oblivious about everything one minute, then turning and saying something that made the agent question her sanity. Among other things, this had specifically included the half-Light Elf's relationship with Johnny.

At the very least, that kind of skill would go a long way in the girl's future career as a bounty hunter. If that was what she wanted.

Right now, it's too early to tell. But it's not too early for a drink, though.

She narrowed her eyes at the whiskey bottle as she deliberated, then stepped slowly toward the cabinet and reached for a rocks glass. She'd have only a little drink. It would help her to stop worrying about all the cryptic comments Johnny had made about this job and the weapons deal and everything they still had to do. If he could drink like a fish and no one cared, she could have one alone at three o'clock in the afternoon with no one around to judge her.

Right?

"Right." The rocks glass clinked on the counter and she was about to pull the lid off the bottle of Johnny Walker Black when the hounds exploded into bloodcurdling bays in the back yard. She jumped in surprise and tightened her hold on the bottle. "Peace and quiet. Is that too much to ask?"

The dog door clicked open and shut, followed by a yelp and a thump before both hounds raced into the kitchen. They wouldn't stop barking, however.

"Okay, whoa." Lisa stepped away from the counter and raised her hands to her ears. "I don't get it."

Luther raced in a tight circle and Rex inched toward her as the effort of his harsh barks lifted his front paws off the linoleum floors.

"Stop. It's too loud in the house. Come on. Go outside if you want to do that." She brushed past them and opened the back door. "There. Go on."

Both hounds raced outside again and bounded from the back porch but they immediately resumed their howls as they spun and jumped and became even more uncontrollable.

Lisa left the door open and frowned at them. *I can't even imagine what Johnny would hear them say right now if he were here. It can't be anything lucid when they act like that.*

Once she returned to the counter and the whiskey, she poured herself a little less than Johnny usually poured her and took a tentative sip. "Yeah. This'll get the job done."

Taking small sips, she headed into the living room and settled on the couch. Honestly, she liked the fact that he didn't have a TV, a computer, or any other kind of brain-numbing device she could let herself be sucked into for hours on end. But now that she was there alone, she wondered what she was supposed to do with the time.

Since he had finished Margo's upgrades, there was Internet at the house, though.

Her gaze slid to her tablet where it rested on the couch beside her.

Hey, if my hardest choice today is whether to read or binge-watch something on Netflix, I'd say things are going well.

She picked the device up and took another sip of whiskey.

The hounds' harsh barking rose again and grew closer. Their claws scrabbled across the floor as they raced through the house and howled, barked, and made some other kind of choking sound she had no idea how to identify.

Luther darted out of the workshop first, his head thrown back to release a piercing bay until he slid chest-first into the opposite wall of the hallway. As the dog snorted and shook his head, Rex raced out after him and somehow avoided collision with any walls before he found her seated on the couch.

They raced toward her again, as frenzied as they had been before, and Lisa tossed her tablet onto the couch. "What is going on? Come on. You guys were great until five minutes ago—hey! Rex, down!"

The larger hound's paw knocked against her drink as he bounded onto the couch and spilled whiskey over the upholstery and her lap. She stood abruptly and sighed. "Great. I haven't even had a whole drink and I now smell like a bar. Go outside."

He leapt off the couch again and darted down the hall, then stopped and turned to stare at her, panting.

"I don't know what you want. You've already eaten. Twice—and don't tell Johnny. And I know fetch isn't a thing you normally do—"

She jumped when Luther howled wildly and darted around her. He began to paw her legs from behind.

Lisa stumbled forward with a grunt. "Ow. Hey!"

Rex barked and wouldn't let up.

"Luther! Get off!" She swatted at the smaller hound and he backed away with a low growl. "Oh, come on. Don't tell me Johnny's gone for a few days and you guys turn into demon dogs. I don't buy it."

She strode down the hall and Rex backed away quickly but he barked and crouched lower with his tail between his legs. He glanced constantly from her to the back door in the kitchen.

"Wait." Lisa studied Luther, who spun in circles again in the living room but had replaced the incessant barking with a desperate, high-pitched whine. "Crap. Okay, we did this once before, right?"

Both hounds barked once in unison.

"Yeah. Right. Bark once for yes?"

They barked again, and Rex uttered a high-pitched whine this time.

"Okay, okay. If there's something wrong, bark—"

One bark each issued from the hounds, then Luther darted toward her and growled.

"So what is it?" Lisa shouted. She couldn't understand a damn thing the dogs said, and the fact that they resumed their mad barking again as their claws clicked and scrabbled on the floor didn't make it any easier at all. "Screw it."

She ran into the bedroom and skidded to a stop in front of the nightstand on her side of what was now their bed. The drawer opened with a bang, and she rifled frantically through it for the joke of a black box he'd given her.

One of the hounds howled continuously in the hall.

"I'm working on it!" Finally, her fingers found her prize and it toppled onto the mattress before she could open it. Suddenly all thumbs, she managed to get it open with a click of the tight hinge and pulled the silver bullet-shaped canister out.

One hound yowled endlessly in the hall and the other chuffed and grunted fiercely in the open bedroom doorway.

"Yeah, okay. I'm...okay." She puffed her cheeks with a quick exhale, pressed the business end of the canister against the side of her neck, and smacked the other side. It hissed and thumped and entered her skin with a sharp sting before a wave of dizziness overwhelmed her. She stumbled against the bed. The canister toppled to the floor and spun to a stop. She smacked her lips and grimaced. "Is that...onions?"

"Holy shit, it worked!" Luther shouted in the hall.

"Yeah, that's what Johnny said too his first time." Rex sniggered and trotted into the bedroom. "You'll get used to it, lady, but right now, we gotta—"

"Oh, my God." Lisa stared at Rex and her legs wobbled enough to make her sag onto the mattress. "I can hear you."

"Freakin' finally," Luther called. "Let's go!"

"Wow." Fighting to catch her breath, Lisa regarded them with a shocked expression. "You guys don't sound anything like I imagined."

"Lady, if you don't get your head out your ass and come with us right now, we won't sound like anything. We'll be dead."

"What?"

Rex closed his jaws around her limp wrist and gave her a gentle tug. "Right now. Come on."

"It's a freakin' bomb, lady!" Luther howled.

"What?" That pushed her to her feet and she raced through the house after the hounds. "Where?"

"Outside. Come on."

The hounds scuttled through the kitchen and out the back door and bounded off the porch to race across the yard. Lisa's hip knocked against the edge of the kitchen counter when she stopped to redirect herself toward the doorway. With a grimace, she rubbed her hip and ran down the stairs.

"Where did it come from?"

"How the hell should we know?" Luther stopped at the edge of the lawn to shoot her a scathing glance. "It wasn't us it was them."

"Come on. Come on." Rex doubled back to her as she followed them to the edge of the swamp. "Hey, you can swim, right?"

"What?"

Luther sniggered. "She seemed less clueless before she could hear us, right?"

He splashed into the water and swam through the swamp toward the houseboat.

Lisa shook her head. "I'm not the right magical to handle an underwater bomb—"

"Well, it's a good thing it's in the houseboat. Come on." Rex followed his brother and they scrambled through the shallows before they had to doggy-paddle across the much deeper expanse of the river to reach the houseboat.

"Oh, shit." Lisa stared at the metal behemoth in front of her and jerked her casual blazer off. "Are you sure it's a bomb?"

"Very sure," Luther replied as he paddled in a zigzag path toward it. "Like ninety percent."

She kicked her shoes off, tossed her phone into the grass, and hurried after them.

By the time she reached the houseboat, the hounds were nowhere in sight. She reached the ladder at the stern and hauled herself up, dripping wet and pumped with adrenaline. "Rex! Luther!"

"Hey, look. You made it." Luther trotted around the corner on the narrow walkway surrounding the multiple stories of the mansion on the water and shook himself vigorously from head to tail. Water sprayed everywhere and he licked his chops. "And you can swim."

"Wait, how'd you guys get—"

"There's a ramp on the other side," Rex said and paused to shake himself too. "And the stairs are over here."

"It's upstairs?"

"Okay, lady, I know you can climb stairs. Come on!"

Lisa threw the stern-facing door open, and the hounds surged in front of her. Their barks echoed deafeningly in the narrow metal stairwell. "Hey! I can hear you now so keep it down. Please."

"Telling a couple of hounds not to bark." Luther trotted to the second-story landing and disappeared through the open doorway. "I can tell you've never been on the hunt for a magical bomb before."

But at least the hounds were quiet after that.

When she reached the top of the stairs, she paused to catch her breath and take a look around. The place was a mess. Empty pickle jars had been discarded everywhere and charred holes marred the walls. The wet bar that had come with the houseboat had been ripped out of its position and hurled against the far wall. On the right, the wall had probably been used as target practice and DIY cyborg art all at once. Two giant smiley faces were blasted into it. One of the eyes had been punched out altogether and offered a direct view to Johnny's back yard.

"Let me guess. June did this."

"Yeah, probably. It's her floor, after all."

"Her floor?"

Rex licked his muzzle and trotted through the debris. "Duh. No way can all four of them share a room."

Her stomach turned. *And Johnny's holed up in a hotel suite with them right now.*

"Okay, so where's this…bomb?"

"Yeah, yeah. It's back here, lady." Luther barked, skittered sideways, and lowered his head. "Right. No barking. Sorry."

"You'll see. Hurry." Rex followed his brother into the adjoining room, which also had its door knocked off its hinges.

The frame hung slightly askew and with a massive dent on one side. "There. Right there. In the closet."

"There's a bomb in the closet. Great. These cyborgs—" The second Lisa stepped through the doorway, the force of powerfully concentrated magic struck her like...well, like an actual bomb. Goosebumps raced across her skin, and she balled her hands into fists. "I know what this is."

"Yeah. The same thing that killed that CIA lady, right?" Rex whined and sat in front of the long, narrow closet, also without its doors.

"Wow, you guys truly do pay attention."

"No, that's only Rex," Luther replied as he sniffed the floor. "I listen and mostly forget everything that—hey. Rex. It's the same kinda bomb that—"

"We know!" Lisa and Rex shouted at the same time. The half-Light Elf stepped cautiously toward the closet as a flare of energy prickled across her skin.

The bomb was the only thing in there—a small, round ball of what looked like swirling silver fluid mixed with the same kind of sludge they'd seen from the rogue Cyborg in Pittsburgh. It thrummed and emitted a radioactive-looking golden glow. Bright white sparks flickered across its surface.

"When did this start?"

"Uh...like ten minutes ago. So we came and got you."

"Okay. Right." Her teeth gritted, Lisa flexed her hands and clenched her fists again before she studied the bomb about to detonate in front of her. "I'm very sure I can—"

The ball squealed before it cut off abruptly like the first piercing shriek of a boiling kettle and a blast of white light burst from it in all directions. The closet sustained most of the damage and wooden panels shattered and splintered and rained on top of the glowing orb.

"If you can, you better do it now, lady," Rex said with a low whine. "Or we're toast."

"Toast? Where?" Luther sniffed around. "Yeah, I smell something burning."

"Be quiet!" Lisa shouted. "Please."

The hounds shut up and sat simultaneously.

She rubbed her hands together and thought of the way Johnny had pushed her and her magic to power his living-memory reader. *There's no way I'm not more pissed off now at the thought of being blown up on a ridiculously large houseboat.*

The bomb sparked again.

With a deep breath, the half-Light Elf raised both hands and focused on the insanely concentrated blast of her energy-shield magic that launched from her palms. The golden column of light struck the bomb with a deafening crack and a growing roar and the floor shuddered beneath her. The hounds barked wildly and skittered back, and she shouted with the effort required.

In two seconds, the white sparks surrounding the bomb combined into one giant energy flare and grew larger and brighter faster than her magic could quell it. She took one more step forward, made one final push with the only bomb-diffusion method she knew, and the white light exploded.

In the next moment, she was catapulted away and couldn't see a thing.

"Lady! Hey, lady!"

Luther's voice sounded incredibly far away.

"Come on. You gotta wake up. If you're tired, we get it. But maybe we should get out of here too. Right?"

Something warm and wet licked her cheek. Lisa groaned and turned sideways to stop the corner of something hard from pressing into her back. She scowled around the fuzziness and her vision gradually returned enough that she could tell she now stared at the same level of the houseboat but from the opposite side of it.

"Did it work?" she muttered and grimaced at the ache in her arms.

"Well, we're not dead. So probably."

"Unless this is what it's like on the other side of the rainbow bridge," Luther mumbled and looked slowly around them.

"I'm very sure being dead doesn't hurt this much." She propped herself against the pile of rubble behind her and rose slowly to her feet. Once she could stand without wobbling, she glanced at her hands, turned them to check for damage, and nodded. *So far so good. It merely feels like I burned them off.* "Is it gone?"

"Is what gone?"

"The bomb, Rex."

"Uh…no. It's still there."

"It doesn't have a light, though." Luther pranced across the room toward the closet and his tail wagged enthusiastically. "So that's probably good."

"Yeah, probably." Lisa staggered across the wreckage toward the closet and found the bomb still there, exactly where she'd left it. Or where whoever else had left it there for her to find.

Or for me to not find and simply get blown up. But at least it doesn't look live anymore.

"Can you guys tell who this belongs to?"

"Yeah. It's June's."

"Seriously?" She turned to glare at the hounds, who stood and looked at her with happy dogs' smiles as they panted.

"She probably put it down and forgot about it," Rex suggested. "It's no big deal."

"Yeah, it happens all the time," Luther added.

Lisa snorted. "I don't think so."

"Yeah, well, agree to disagree. Good thing you were here to blow it up first, though, right?"

"Uh-huh." She knelt in front of the diffused bomb and brushed her fingers gingerly against it. No hum of energy and no sparks issued from the now dormant device. "Shit. That was a close one."

"And we saved the day!" Luther threw his head and bugled a howl.

"Luther."

It cut off abruptly and the hound sat on his haunches. "Right. Noise. Sorry."

The half-Light Elf retrieved what now appeared to be nothing more than a round ball of metal parts with some kind of weird, slightly sticky organic membrane and stood. Still, she wasn't a magical bomb specialist. It could simply have blown the excess energy and was simply waiting to accumulate more. "I think I'd better keep an eye on this."

"Good idea."

"Yeah, we'll help you."

"Hey, Rex. How cool is it that she can hear us now?"

"I know, right? Hey, lady. You gonna tell Johnny what you did?"

She smiled as she tucked the gooey cyborg bomb under one arm and headed across the houseboat's second floor toward the stairs. "I'll think about it."

He sure kept me in the dark for long enough.

Luther snorted. "Wait. What did you imagine we sounded like?"

CHAPTER SEVENTEEN

It had taken a few days for Johnny to get through to Colonel Bartlett about the meeting he'd had with Blake. When he finally did, the colonel sounded exactly as he'd expected when he dropped the price-bomb on him.

"Do you think we have that kind of money lying around to throw at these guys?"

"You do if you wanna keep these weapons outta the wrong hands. Besides, if this next meetin' with them goes the way I expect it to, y'all won't have to spend a dime of your precious military fundin'. But now, I need to speak to Major Dorn. If he's still around, of course."

Bartlett fumed into the phone. "You dropped a name you weren't cleared to use."

"Hey, it ain't your name. But at least the one I gave has actual real ties to mine goin' decades back. So is he still around or not?"

"Yeah." The colonel snorted fractiously. "I'll bring him in on it. Next time, run it through command first."

"Piss off, Bartlett. I ain't in the chain. That's why you sent me on this job in the first place." The dwarf hung up without letting the colonel respond and felt better for having done so. With a smirk, he pulled Lisa's number up to move them to the next stage.

"Johnny. Hi."

"Hey, darlin'. How you doin'?"

"Oh, you know. I'm simply keeping everything running down here. I'm fine."

"Are you sure? You sound a little...off."

She sighed into the phone. "This probably isn't the best conversation to have over the phone but we need to talk."

"Shit." Johnny jerked the phone away from his ear, scowled at the closed door of his hotel bedroom, and lifted the device again. "We might as well get it over with now, darlin'. I'll find someone else to watch the hounds until I get back. You can pack your stuff—"

"What? No—"

"Well, I ain't flyin' you here so you can break things off to my face."

"Johnny? Shut up. It has nothing to do with you, not specifically."

He inclined his head and narrowed his eyes at the carpeted floor at the foot of the bed. "Folks don't say, 'We need to talk,' if the talk ain't about...you know."

She chuckled. "I'd never have a relationship talk like that over the phone. Although I'm flattered to hear you weren't surprised at all when you thought that's what I was doing."

"I wasn't...not..." He cleared his throat. "Forget it. We're okay? You and me?"

"Of course. Unless something happened in Philadelphia I should know about."

"Nope. It don't mean the hotel lady doesn't try every day."

"What?"

"Nothin'." He snorted and shook his head. "So we'll have this talk about whatever when you're here. Do you feel like givin' me a heads-up?"

"Yeah, we can—Luther. Stop." She snapped her fingers and a yelp came over the line. "I said stop. Get out of the trash. Are you kidding me right now?"

"Lisa?"

"Yeah."

"Are the boys givin' you trouble?"

"No. Not any more than usual—out! Jeez." The sound of a slamming door made him jerk his head away from the phone. "Sorry. What were we talking about?"

"This talk."

"Oh, right. Yeah. We need to talk to the borgs, Johnny."

"You're talkin' about the same ones I had to barricade out of my bedroom to keep 'em from sneakin' in at night to sleep on the floor, right?"

"Well, I don't know any other cyborgs, so—wait. They're trying to sleep on your floor?"

"It doesn't matter."

"Okay, fine. But we need to sit them down and go over the rules again about not leaving their bombs all over the houseboat."

"Huh."

Lisa made a growling sound. "Of course that's your only reaction."

"Well hell, darlin'. It ain't like I knew they had bombs."

"I don't think it's intentional, but still. That's where we're at."

"And y'all are okay?"

"We both know I can handle a few cyborg explosives."

Johnny grinned. "You used the energy shield, didn't you?"

"Yes. Now, I need a shower and I'm a little on-edge about the whole hidden-bomb scenario. So… How are things for you?"

"About the same. Listen, I got the okay to move forward with what we're doin'. I might need a little extra support for an in-person meetin' with Bartlett and another guy. And Felix called this mornin'. He said the jet's ready to fly again, so I'll send him there to pick y'all up."

"What happened to the jet?"

"Meh. It ain't a big deal. Somethin' about strainin' the load limit with four cyborgs onboard or somethin'."

"Oh, my God." Despite the slight edge of stress to her tone, Lisa laughed.

"But Felix said she's good to go. So I was callin' in the first place to say you and the boys should meet him tomorrow mornin' at six. Then, you get to join us."

"I hope you don't expect me to try sneaking into your room at night to sleep on the floor."

"Very funny. I think it's safer to see if another room close by has opened in the last few days. I'm fixin' to hand this whole damn suite to these overgrown kindergarteners so I can hear myself think again."

"You've made it this far. What's another few days, right?"

"You and your ever-lovin' bright side." he chuckled. "See you tomorrow, darlin'."

"Bye, Johnny."

He tossed his phone onto the mattress and gave himself a moment to think about seeing Lisa tomorrow. *We've been doin' this all-day-every-day thing for only two months, and I'm already missin' her. You got it bad, Johnny.*

A crooked smile spread across his lips until a loud crash, the shatter of glass, and the twins' braying, honking laughter came from the other side of the door. "Y'all keep it the hell down out there!"

"Sorry, Johnny," Brandon called out sheepishly.

"But you should come see this," Leroy added. "She—"

"I ain't comin' out until mornin'. Quit blastin' holes in the damn walls!" The bounty hunter slipped off the bed and headed to the minibar stored beneath the huge dresser. He could easily barricade himself in his room for the next twelve hours because he'd had the foresight on their first night there to stock the minibar with everything he needed.

The borgs were still asleep and snoring like thunder when he emerged at 8:30 am. Fortunately for the dwarf with heavy boot-steps, his team were even heavier sleepers. No one stirred as he snuck out of his hotel suite and headed downstairs to the Humvee.

The jet landed earlier than he'd expected and by the time he pulled up in the giant growling vehicle, Lisa and the hounds had already debarked from the aircraft and now descended the rolling staircase onto the tarmac. He left the engine running and stepped out with a grin.

It's weird to see her steppin' outta my jet all on her lonesome with my hounds. I kinda like it.

"Hey, Johnny," the pilot called from the top of the stairs.

"Felix." He nodded. "How's she flyin' now?"

"Like a dream. I made sure to have the mechanics add those extra upgrades you mentioned. They had to run the numbers three times before they believed me when I said you know what you're talking about."

"Good man. I appreciate it."

The pilot waved again and propped himself against the doorway of the jet to watch Lisa's slow progress.

Johnny headed toward her and had to lower his sunglasses on the unusually sunny winter day to be sure he wasn't seeing things. Her hair was a tangled mess. Dark circles were visible under her eyes, which were perpetually wide, and her gaze flicked from side to side as she approached him. She looked like she hadn't had a wink of sleep in days.

"Johnny!" The hounds darted toward him and barked happily while their tails wagged like crazy. "Oh, man, Johnny. We thought we'd never see you again!"

"Yeah, you're not dead!" Luther threw himself at his master when the dwarf dropped to one knee to greet them.

"I have no idea why y'all would think that."

"'Cause we haven't seen you in, like, ten years." Rex butted his brother out of the way so he could get in a good lick across his master's wiry beard. "Yeah, you sure taste like Johnny."

"All right. Cut it out." He scratched each hound's head vigorously before he stood and hurried toward Lisa. "Hey, darlin'. Do you want me to take your bag?"

"No." She shuffled forward across the tarmac. "I want to go somewhere quiet. With a drink. And…I don't know. Nothing else."

"She's had a rough time, Johnny," Luther added.

"Yeah, did she tell you about the bomb? You know, it looked like an egg."

The hounds sniggered. "If giant robot chickens laid eggs."

Lisa's eyelids fluttered as the hounds sniffed the area and exchanged an endless flow of jokes. She stared blankly at the side of the Humvee and jumped when Johnny cleared his throat.

"Whoa. I ain't see you like this in…ever, to be honest." The bounty hunter stepped slowly toward her and reached gently for her bag anyway. "You sounded fine on the phone. A little shook up, maybe, but not like this."

"I'm fine. Truly."

"She was only pissed at us because we kept getting into the trash," Rex confessed. "After she told us not to, like, ten times."

"Yeah, even though we told her you weren't around, Johnny. So it didn't matter if she fed us more than twice a day or let us have a little fun—"

With a snarl, Rex lunged at his brother and gave him a warning nip in the face. "Shut up, bro. You weren't supposed to tell him that, remember?"

"No, we're not supposed to tell him about the lady two-legs sticking that weird bullet against her neck and being able to hear us." Luther whipped his head up to look at Lisa and both hounds sat together with matching whines. "Whoops."

Johnny widened his eyes at her. She exhaled a massive sigh and shrugged.

The dwarf threw his head back and roared with laughter. It made her jump again and she staggered back two steps with an uncertain chuckle.

"Hey, he's not mad."

"Bro, I know it looks like he's laughing, but this could be a whole new level of pissed-off-Johnny we haven't seen yet."

He stumbled toward the Humvee and slapped a hand against the driver's door, shook his head, and continued to laugh unabated.

Lisa looked slowly at the hounds. "I think we broke him."

"I'm sure we broke you first. Hey, Johnny!"

Luther barked with his brother and ignored her wince at each sharp noise. "Johnny, you okay?"

"You dyin'? I heard two-legs can do that, you know. Die from laughing too much."

"I only—" Johnny slapped the car again, exploded with another belly laugh, and tried to suck it all in again as he straightened and faced them. "They—ha!"

"It's not that funny," Lisa muttered.

"Aw, hell." He wiped the tears from the corners of his eyes with the back of his hand and dropped her suitcase before he approached her again. "Okay, I guess it's been a shock."

"Not so much. I used that canister on purpose."

He rubbed both her arms and chuckled as he blinked away the last of the tears. "Still. Why didn't you say anythin'?"

She leaned away from him, stared at the side of the airport building, and a small smile brightened her weary face. "I thought it would be a fun surprise."

"Ha! Well, you sure managed that. I ain't laughin' at you, darlin'. I didn't expect that one, is all."

"And I didn't expect to have to inject myself with that…whatever it was so I could hear your dogs and keep the houseboat and your entire property from blowing up. So...you know. Surprises for both of us."

The dwarf glanced at the hounds, who now stood again, panted, and wagged their tails enthusiastically. "That's why you did it?"

"Honestly, I thought they were possessed until I used the canister." A wry, exhausted laugh burst out of her. "And we were almost too late."

"Not true, Johnny," Rex said.

"Yeah, we had at least ten more seconds."

"Damn." He wrapped his arm around Lisa's shoulders and pecked her on the cheek. "At least it was for a good cause, right?"

"Ha. Sure." She let him lead her around the front of the Humvee and help her into the passenger seat. "Johnny?"

"Yeah." It took everything he had to not erupt into laughter again.

"I know it's only two coonhounds I've been able to hear for a few days, but I feel like I've babysat a dozen toddlers for a week straight. Please tell me there's an off-switch for this."

"Uh..." He scratched the back of his head. "Well, not yet. I suppose I should have thought of that before I put it all together, but hey. You'll get used to it."

A renewed fire of strength and determination flared behind her previously glassy eyes and she shook her head slowly. "Fuck that. I can handle it for now but when we're done with this job, you're making an off-switch."

"Yes, ma'am." Johnny closed the passenger door gently and managed to keep a straight face until he retrieved her bag. The sight of the hounds made him snort with another barely restrained laugh. "Have y'all been givin' her hell simply for fun?"

"Come on, Johnny. You know we're good hounds."

"Yeah, and it's not like we did anything bad. Except for the trash."

"Luther, shut up."

"It's not like he doesn't already know."

"Huh." He scowled at his reflection in the tinted window. "I don't remember losin' that much sleep when I got the collars workin'."

"Oh, that." Luther sat to scratch behind his ear. "Yeah, that might have been us."

"We missed you, Johnny." Rex trotted toward his master and his tongue lolled from his mouth. "And we couldn't sleep so we stayed up all night telling jokes."

"Yeah, twice."

"We slept on the plane, though."

"Uh-huh." The bounty hunter shook his head, opened the back door, and slid Lisa's suitcase onto the floor, then gestured for the hounds to hop inside. "And now that y'all are with me, I don't wanna hear a peep outta either one of y'all the whole way to the hotel. Understand?"

"Yeah, Johnny. You got it."

"Anything you want. We missed you. This is great."

They bounded into the back seat and he shut the door behind them before he slid behind the wheel. Lisa's head rested against the passenger window, her hands placed palms-down on her thighs and her eyes closed. He patted the back of her hand gently and muttered, "Thanks for keepin' the place from blowin' up, darlin'."

She moaned with exhaustion and wobbled her head in an attempt to nod. "I only want quiet."

"I know. I told them not to make a—"

"Peep," Luther said in a high-pitched squeak before both hounds sniggered in the back.

Johnny snapped his fingers and lifted a finger without turning.

"Sorry, Johnny."

"Sorry."

Both hounds lowered themselves onto their bellies and curled side by side on the back seat.

The dwarf looked at them in the rearview mirror and pressed his finger to his lips before he turned the vehicle away from the private runway.

Lisa had already passed out.

CHAPTER EIGHTEEN

Johnny drove around the city for an extra hour to give Lisa more time for her nap. When he couldn't continue to ignore the fact that he'd left four maturity-stunted cyborgs alone in the suite, his conscience finally got the better of him.

She was almost impossible to wake, but the hounds finally whispered at her for long enough from the back seat that it pulled her out of her desperate sleep. He carried her bag in one hand and supported her in her zombie-like shuffle with the other as they headed into the hotel lobby. When the concierge who'd been hitting on him for almost a week saw him enter with a tall brunette half-Light Elf on his arm, she was too busy glaring at the couple to notice the two coonhounds following their master, unleashed and unconcerned.

At least without the borgs, they could all use the elevator.

The noise from their hotel suite filled the hall the second the elevator doors opened. Lisa started to perk up a little more and withdrew her arm from his tightening grip on it.

"Jesus. I can't leave 'em alone for even a few hours."

Raucous laughter came from the room, followed by two loud thumps and an underlying buzz.

"What are they doing?"

"We're about to find out." He flashed his room key at the lock and threw the door open. "What in the ever-lovin'—"

"Hey, Johnny." Brandon tossed a pillow onto the couch, although the evidence still floated around the room as hundreds of tiny white feathers. Clint whisked his hands behind his back and tried to blow a wayward feather off his nose.

"Pinch me, darlin'."

"What?" Lisa stared at the destroyed suite with wide eyes.

"I said pinch me. 'Cause there ain't no way four grown-ass adults spent the last few hours havin' a goddamn pillow fight in the hotel—ow!"

"You told me to pinch you." With a heavy sigh, he rubbed his arm and stormed into the room. "Y'all gotta be kiddin' me with this crap."

"It wasn't technically a pillow fight," Brandon said and raised his finger in protest.

"I don't technically give a shit." The bounty hunter continued his determined progress as the hounds sniffed and snorted more feathers into the air.

"Whoa, did you guys have a goose in here?"

"Tons of feathers, bro. Hey, borgs don't have feathers, right?"

"They probably have all kinds of stuff we don't know about."

After placing Lisa's suitcase inside his room, Johnny slammed the door shut behind him and froze. "What the hell?"

The twins and Leroy turned in the direction of his stare and Leroy sniggered. "Oh, yeah. That was part of the...uh, not pillow fight."

"Why is there a damn smiley face burned into the damn door?" He thrust a hand toward the door to the room June had claimed.

"I don't know." Brandon shrugged. "It makes her happy?"

Clint honked a laugh and tossed two rogue pickle-jar lids onto the couch.

"Don't worry about it, boss." The shifter passed his hands through the air like it was no big deal. "We were merely passing the time. It'll get cleaned up."

"Uh-huh. With a bill twice as big as stayin' here for a week 'cause y'all can't keep your damn weapons holstered. Christ."

The door to his room creaked open again and he whirled around as Lisa slipped inside. "What are you doin', darlin'?"

"Getting us a drink."

He snorted and turned to the borgs. "Sit down. June!"

"Bite me," she shouted from her room.

"Did somethin' happen I need to know about?"

The twins shrugged. Leroy plucked a surprisingly large handful of feathers from the barrel of his hand-cannon. "I don't think she likes sharing space."

"Well, I don't either and you don't see me burnin' the doors and rippin' pillows up. June! We're goin' over the next steps so I'd get out here if I were you."

"Or what? You'll ground me?"

The dwarf's eyes widened so much, his temples ached. "I don't get it. I can't. This ain't a base of operations on a job. It's a goddamn daycare."

The sound of a glass smacking onto the dresser in his room made him turn. Lisa hissed a sigh before she stormed out of the bedroom again with a small shoebox tucked under one arm and a glass of whiskey sloshing in the other hand. "I'll handle it."

He blinked in surprise when she barely slowed to hand him the glass. "Where's yours?"

"I drank it."

The hounds skittered out of her way when she blasted through the pile of feathers on the floor and reached the door to June's adjoining room.

"Uh-oh..." Luther lowered himself into a crouch and tucked his ears against his head.

Rex whined, sat, and licked his muzzle. "She'd better be careful."

Leroy clicked his tongue. "June won't hurt her. She might shoot a laser an inch above her head but that's not fatal."

The hounds turned to look at the shifter borg. "We're not talking about June."

"You haven't seen Lisa pissed, have you?"

Johnny snorted into his drink.

The half-Light Elf pounded on the bedroom door branded with a wobbly smiley face. "June! I'm giving you one chance to open this on your own before I come in."

"If you're looking for girl-talk so we can cry on each other's shoulders, you can kiss my ass."

Lisa drew a deep breath, opened the shoebox, tossed the lid behind her, and burst into the Crystal borg's room.

"Hey, what the hell—" That was all June said and the other woman said nothing at all.

"What's happening?" Brandon whispered.

Leroy rubbed the back of his neck and leaned sideways in an attempt to get a better view inside the room. "Girl-talk?"

"Oh, I get it." Luther sat and cocked his head, panting. "Johnny, that's what you meant by two-leg bitches speaking a different language, right?"

The dwarf forced a cough and backed toward his bedroom door in case he needed to be within easy range of the whiskey in the minibar. *Now she can hear every damn word they say and I still can't respond without puttin' my ass on the line.*

The door to June's room creaked open slowly. The Crystal borg stepped out with her arms folded and scowled at the floor. Lisa followed closely behind her with drooping eyelids still heavy with sleep and nodded at Johnny. "I think it's time for that talk now."

Leroy winced at the heavy warning in such a simple sentence. "Should we go?"

"No." Johnny pointed at him. "The talk's for y'all. Sit down."

The guys sat on the furniture in various stages of destruction, but June stayed where she was. *Yeah, I ain't gonna push that one.*

"All right, listen up. Lisa found a little problem—"

"Big problem, Johnny," she interrupted. "An explosive problem."

"Right. 'Course." He cleared his throat. "An explosive problem at the property. Now as far as we can deduce 'cause we've seen it before, cyborgs have some kinda…energy runoff. We get it. But y'all can't go leavin' these energy bombs in the damn houseboat before we take off for a job."

"Um…Johnny?" Brandon's hand inched hesitantly into the air.

"You ain't gotta raise your hand, man. Say it."

"We don't."

The dwarf raised his eyebrows. "Don't what?"

"Leave the bombs in the houseboat."

Clint shook his head vehemently.

"We might have a hard time with many other…normal things," Leroy added, "but we're not stupid. We shoot them out into the swamp because there's—"

"One time, okay?" June shouted. "It was one time! I put it in the closet because Johnny called us out for another stupid, boring meeting for no reason and then I forgot. I can make a mistake. The rest of you screw up all the time. I get to every once in a while too. So please. Back off!"

Everyone in the now-crowded living area stared at the Crystal borg, who tossed her ice-crusted bangs out of her eyes and sighed although she didn't meet anyone's gaze.

"All right…" Johnny downed the rest of his drink and set the glass on the kitchen counter. "Well, now you know. So this is a warnin'. No more cyborg bombs in the houseboat." No one else said a word and he nodded at Lisa. "What's in the box?"

"The bomb that almost turned your property into a crater." She approached and handed it to him.

The dwarf grinned like she'd given him the only gift he'd ever wanted. "Darlin'. I can't believe I'm sayin' this but I am so glad you went through my things."

"What else was I supposed to do with it?" She smirked, looked at the borgs, and saw only confusion on their faces. Her smile faded and she shrugged. "I hope you don't mind that I made a few adjustments. As it turned out, the bomb was only…uh, resting."

"You turned the livin'-memory reader into an explosion-proof cage for an energy bomb that still ain't detonated." He looked at her and swallowed thickly. "It's beautiful."

"Are you…" She pressed her lips together and brushed her hair away from her face. "Are you crying?"

"No." Johnny sniffed and blinked away the mist that had formed in his eyes. He focused his attention on the bomb-cage instead, removed it from the box, and turned it to examine it. "How'd you think of that?"

"It was a lucky guess, honestly."

With a cough of surprise, He replaced the device in the box and caught her hand. "You're one of a kind, darlin'. And I know exactly how we can use this to our advantage. If you need to get some shuteye, we'll stay quiet out here." He glared at the borgs and the hounds all watching what had to be the weirdest display of affection any of them had seen. "Won't we?"

"I'm very sure I'm wide awake now." Lisa squeezed his hand. "But I could do with another drink."

He set the box on the kitchen counter and cleared his throat. *She's runnin' on fumes and somehow knows how to push all my buttons. The good ones.* "Yeah. There's a bar downstairs. I ain't tried it yet."

"That sounds good."

"Y'all stay here. Order up more pickles if you need 'em."

"And what about the job?" Leroy asked.

"We're back on it tomorrow. But I ain't seen this woman in a week so we have some catchin' up to do. Y'all mind your own."

Lisa laughed when he tugged her gently behind him toward the front door.

"Hey, Rex. Do bars have private rooms?"

"I don't think so."

"There's no way they're going downstairs for a drink."

Leroy's smothered laughter cut off abruptly when the door closed behind the couple and they moved quickly down the hall together.

"Bar first, if you want. But then I aim to check if there's another room open, 'cause no way in hell am I spendin' another night with only one wall between me and the damn borgs." He rested his hand gently on the small of her back until they reached the elevators. "You have no idea how good it is to have you here, I tell you what."

She grinned. "Now that is something I'm very sure you don't tell all your lady friends."

"I only have the one now, darlin'." Johnny pulled her in for a long kiss.

A door across the hall opened and closed and the warbling voice of an elderly lady came from behind them. "Aren't you two the cutest thing? Good for you."

They ignored her and for the first time in a long time, Johnny didn't give two shits about who saw him doing what with a woman, especially Lisa Breyer.

When they finally released each other, they had to call the elevator from the lobby floor again because the little old lady had taken the trip down without them.

CHAPTER NINETEEN

Late-afternoon the next day, the entire crew—Johnny, Lisa, all four borgs, and the hounds—pulled up at the checkpoint gate of the Marine Barracks in Washington for their in-person meeting with Colonel Bartlett and his team. It seemed the man didn't want Johnny and his team walking through his personal space in Beaufort. The drive from Philly to the base was only two hours but it was cramped and hot and felt way too long.

The guard at the gate took one look inside the crowded, low-hanging Humvee and nodded for them to pass. But once they reached the first parking lot, a second guard raised a hand for them to stop. Johnny rolled his window down and draped his arm over the edge. "We're here to see Colonel Bartlett."

"Yes, Mr. Walker. I'm aware."

"So what's the problem?"

"I need everyone not in the front of the vehicle to step out."

"Nice try."

The guard put a hand on his service weapon and took a step back. "I have my orders, sir. The, uh...cyborgs don't have clearance."

Johnny snorted. "Why the hell not? Bartlett cleared them as my team before we left Florida."

A short silence followed before the man squinted through the open window and wrinkled his nose. "Can they remove their weapons and leave them here with us before entry?"

The inside of the Humvee was silent except for Rex and Luther panting in the back seat, where they'd gotten super cozy curled beside Clint.

"Shit. All right. Everyone with a gun built into them, get on out."

Both back doors opened before Leroy and June slid out first. Brandon had to scooch across the seat to exit from the middle seat, and the entire Humvee wobbled and lifted six inches to its regular height. The guard stepped back again when June scowled at him and nudged the door shut. Finally, the back gate opened and Luther and Rex leapt out. Brandon gave Clint a hand out of the very back and Johnny turned the engine off. He and Lisa stepped out as well and the dwarf spread his arms at their guard. "Are you happy now?"

"My feelings about the matter are irrelevant, sir."

"Yeah, yeah. Keep spoutin' what they feed ya. Come on, boys. We have ourselves a sit-down."

The hounds sniffed the parking lot as they followed their master and Lisa toward the building ahead. "Weird kinda smell out here, Johnny."

"Yeah, like...big trucks and lots of guns. Kinda smells like home."

"Without all the swamp and dwarf."

"Or whiskey."

Lisa snorted and immediately wiped her smile off when Johnny glanced at her. He turned toward the borgs and pointed at them. "Y'all don't give 'em any trouble, understand?"

Leroy nodded. "We're good, boss."

"Naw, I was talkin' to the guards."

When they reached the front door of the plain squat building, another Marine posted on guard duty stepped in front of them and pointed at the hounds. "I'm sorry, sir. No pets inside the building."

"Well, it's a good thing I didn't bring pets."

"Sir, I can't let you—"

"Take it up with Colonel Bartlett if you're so twisted up about it," Johnny growled. "I agreed to not bring 'em with me to that convention last week, but I'll be damned if I'm leavin' these hounds outside on a military base."

"It hasn't been—"

"Well, I'm clearin' it right now, son. Unless you wanna risk these two takin' out all your MPs in two minutes flat. They've done it before."

The Marine darted a glance over his shoulder at another man who stood behind a counter and a glass pane. The second soldier shrugged and the one standing in the visitor's way stepped aside.

"Smart move but give it time. Long enough in the military will pull all the free thinkin' outta you eventually."

The man glanced at the ceiling and shook his head as the dwarf and his partner headed down the hall. The hounds sniffed the floor but didn't seem to think anything was worth commenting on unnecessarily.

"Did they truly do that?" Lisa whispered as they turned the corner into a narrower hallway. "Take out military police in two minutes?"

"It's theoretical, darlin'. You simply replace 'Boneblade' or 'Red Boar' or 'Crazik' with MP, and it's the same damn thing."

"Huh."

Colonel Bartlett waited for them beside the open door to his office. The man glanced at the hounds and his nostrils flared. "You threatened my men in the lobby, didn't you?"

"And you're shorter than I expected." Johnny brushed past the man and entered the office. The hounds trotted after him and sniffed the walls and the baseboards.

"Agent Breyer." Bartlett extended his hand toward Lisa.

"Colonel."

"You know, as much of a public figure as this guy's become over the last few decades, it was far easier to find information on you."

"Well." She offered him a small smile as he released her hand. "Johnny hasn't quite caught up with the rest of us when it comes to technology. The social kind, I mean."

"Either way, I'm impressed by what I've seen. You have some serious wins under your belt, even for a magical."

The only thing she could do was smile and nod and slip past the man into his office.

"He's blowing smoke, lady," Luther said as he sniffed the right-hand wall and the base of the bookshelf.

Rex sniggered. "Yeah, up his own ass and he has no clue."

Being able to hear that from them brought a real smile to Lisa's face.

Johnny snapped his fingers and pointed at the floor beside him. The hounds dutifully made their way to their master's side, then another door opened at the other side of Bartlett's office, and their second military liaison entered the room.

An old man in full dress uniform studded with stripes and pins shuffled through the doorway and closed it gently behind him with a weak nudge. The head of the cane clutched tightly in his hand was molded in the shape of a duck's head, and the narrow end thumped along the carpeted floor as the man hobbled forward.

Bartlett passed his visitors to pull the chair out from behind his desk as the feeble officer made his way toward it.

Johnny studied the old guy carefully as he lowered himself in the executive desk chair. The wooden frame and probably his bones creaked at the same time. "Who's this?"

The aged officer grunted and kept his hand on the head of the cane. "You mean you don't recognize me?"

"Nope."

Bartlett took a side chair from the small table beside the bookshelf and placed it beside his desk, having given it up for the older officer to use. "You asked for him, Johnny. Here he is."

The dwarf's mouth dropped open. "Dorn?"

The old man smiled to reveal a uniform line of slightly stained dentures. "That's Major General Dorn, Johnny. You never stuck around to see it happen."

The bounty hunter approached one of the chairs for guests on the visitors' side of the desk, stared at the old man, and sank slowly into the chair. "You aged like shit."

Dorn wheezed a chuckle and pointed at him with a crooked finger. "And you aged like your old man."

Johnny clenched the wooden armrests of his chair with both hands and leaned back. "It runs in the family."

"For me too, isn't that right?" The officer coughed and glanced at Bartlett. "Let's get this over with, Colonel. I don't have all day."

He looks like he doesn't even have two hours.

Lisa sat in the chair beside Johnny's and the Major General's eyes lit up when he saw her.

"And who is this beautiful little thing?"

"Special Agent Lisa Breyer," she said and leaned over the desk to take the old man's hand when he reached toward her.

Dorn lifted her palm in his and finally released his cane so he could pat the back of her hand at the same time. "Very special."

"My partner," Johnny added. Lisa darted him a glance when the old man finally released her, and the dwarf inclined his head at her. *We might as well call it what it is at this point. It's not like the old geezer has a leg to stand on anyway.*

Rex sniffed the floor beside Johnny's chair. "What is that smell?"

"Smells like death, bro."

"No one's dead in here. Yet."

Lisa cleared her throat, smiled politely, and hoped the hounds didn't keep up the commentary through this meeting.

Johnny gave her a sidelong glance and hoped very much the same thing.

"You be careful with this one, Johnny." Dorn shook a crooked finger at Lisa as he shifted in his chair. "Get too close and there's trouble headed your way."

"We ain't here to talk about my trouble." The bounty hunter sniffed and glanced at Bartlett. "Only yours."

"So then let's talk." Bartlett folded his arms and leaned back in his chair.

"Johnny doesn't talk," Dorn said with a crooked smile. "He breaks things and runs away."

"And you line your pockets with blood money," the dwarf snapped. "Look where it got you. Are you feelin' good about your life, Dorn?"

"I have everything I need and the full support of my brothers. You, on the other hand, are nothing more than a hired gun at this point." The old man uttered a hacking cough mixed with another laugh. "Do you feel good about your life?"

"I wouldn't trade it for both goddamn worlds."

"We're here to discuss the arms deal," Bartlett interjected and frowned at the nonstop animosity between the dwarf and the Major General. "So let's move to—"

"No, this is good." Dorn lifted a gnarled hand toward the colonel beside him. "It's been...what, Johnny? Sixty years?"

"Sixty-three." The bounty hunter's mustache bristled when his upper lip twitched in a sneer. "I could have waited twice that before seein' your ugly mug again."

"Well, we both know I won't make it that long so you're off the hook."

"Yeah, no shit," Rex muttered as he lowered himself to his belly at Johnny's side.

Luther turned in a quick circle before he joined his brother. "Oh, that death smell's coming from him. What happens if he drops dead while we're still here?"

"Someone's gotta get rid of the body, right? Hey, Johnny. You need someone to get rid of a body, we're your hounds—"

Johnny snapped his fingers and the boys shut up.

Lisa sighed quietly but managed to keep a straight face.

"Still snapping to get everyone else's attention, I see." Dorn glanced at the dwarf's fist clenched around the armrest again. "It looks like you still haven't outgrown a few things."

"It's a warnin' for my hounds," he responded. "They don't like you."

"Oh, too bad."

"Major General," Bartlett started, "with all due respect, sir, I'd like to turn to the matter at hand—"

"Do you know why Johnny never made it as a Marine?" Dorn asked and smiled at Lisa. "He didn't tell you that, did he?"

She pressed her lips together and glanced at Bartlett. The colonel shook his head and shrugged.

"It don't matter," Johnny said. "And the colonel wants to talk about—"

"Sure it does." The old officer wheezed another laugh. "History never disappears, Johnny. You know that. It's why you dropped my name at your little meet-and-greet with the arms dealers' mouthpiece. Lucky for you, I'm not dead yet so I still get to clean up your mess."

"I'm merely workin' with what you set up for yourself a long time ago, Dorn."

"And you've carried this grudge around with you the whole time. To be perfectly honest, I'd completely forgotten about you until Colonel Bartlett brought your name to my attention again."

The bounty hunter cleared his throat. "I ain't bitin' your bait,

Major General, so let's get down to the business we came here for and we'll be on our way."

"We can bite, Johnny," Rex muttered.

"Yeah, say the word and we're on him like two hounds on a dead guy."

"Bro, that's what it would be."

Lisa forced a cough to keep from chuckling. She stared directly at the edge of the desk in front of her and didn't move.

"Sir?" Bartlett glanced at Dorn, who finally stopped sneering at Johnny and waved his hand in flippant consent. The colonel shifted in his seat. "So your meeting with this Blake character now has Major General Dorn's name all over it. And his approval."

"Which I can revoke at any time," the old man added. "So don't fuck this up. I'm not shelling out two and a half billion for shit. Not when you can get it for us for free."

"I don't work for free," Johnny muttered.

"I bet you do for her." Dorn nodded at Lisa. "Am I right, sweetheart?"

"This Tuesday at four o'clock," she said and ignored the old man's leering gaze, "at Our Lady Point Ranch. That's the info Blake gave us and we plan to be there."

"Without any money?" Dorn clicked his tongue. "That's walking a fine line."

"Oh, I have the money." The dwarf shrugged. "But then I'd have to invoice y'all for it. With interest."

She gave him a wide-eyed look but he ignored her. *Playin' hardball with this asshole's fun enough without havin' to explain what I'm doin'.*

"Hmm." the major general leaned back in the creaking chair and adjusted his grip on the head of his cane.

"No money changes hands," Bartlett said. "We've received new intel, Johnny. The weapons have made it Stateside. We picked this up via satellite imagery but by the time we sent our people out there, the drop site was empty."

Johnny raised an eyebrow at the colonel. "Y'all missed the weapons of mass destruction makin' it into the US and now, they're bein' shipped around to who the hell knows where and you're still sittin' on your asses?"

"I prefer it that way. It's why we brought you in." Bartlett nodded firmly. "We have reason to believe those weapons will be at that ranch when you arrive to make the exchange. You need to ensure they don't go anywhere else, understand?"

"Yeah. I understand." He gritted his teeth and glared at the Marine officers in front of him. *They knew the whole damn time and they think I'm dumb enough to do what I'm told. Dorn hasn't changed.*

"Good. Now tell me about this team of yours." Bartlett nodded toward the office door. "The ones detained outside."

"Cyborgs." He shrugged. "It wasn't part of the plan at first, but it turns out they got us a better in than anythin' else."

"Cyborgs." The decrepit officer sniggered. "Is that some kind of code?"

Bartlett removed his phone from his pocket, flipped through it, and slid it across the desk toward the major general. "Actual cyborgs, sir."

"Well, that's…" Dorn squinted at the device and slid it toward the colonel. "It's unnatural. And you expect these people to let you walk into this meeting with those freaks beside you?"

Johnny shook his head. "This Blake fella seemed especially interested in 'em so we're goin' in with the cyborgs as bait and will try to manufacture a deal. He believes they're nothin' more than soldiers turned into livin' weapons and asked if I could contract a sale so that's our leg up. I let my team give them a demonstration, and we're that much farther in the door."

Bartlett grimaced at his phone before he returned it to his pocket. "Are you sure they can be controlled?"

The dwarf snorted. "Sure. About as much as I can be controlled."

"That's disappointing," Dorn muttered.

"But when it counts? Yeah, they'll do what needs doin'."

"You realize we only have one shot at this, right?" Bartlett glanced from Johnny to Lisa. "If you screw this up—"

"We won't. Now I ain't got fancy medals and a big office and a base of soldiers waitin' on me, but I reckon I been doin' this kinda thing a hell of a lot longer than either of y'all." Johnny jerked his chin at Bartlett. "And I know I'm older than you."

"Fine." The colonel stood from his chair and went to the bookshelf, where he opened a cigar box and withdrew two long silver pens. "Then take these and you and your team are cleared to get this done. We won't get in your way. Contact us again when it's finished."

The man handed a pen to each of them, and they frowned at the odd parting gift.

"Nice pen." Johnny pointed at Bartlett with his. "I ain't signin' a contract. That leaves a trail."

"I'm well aware of your distaste for leaving a trail, Johnny." The man slipped one hand into his pocket and nodded. "Which is what the pens are for."

Both pens emitted a short hiss. Lisa dropped hers with a sharp breath. When the pinprick of Johnny's stung his palm, he stood and hurled it across the room. It clattered against the far wall and the hounds leapt to their feet to scramble out of the way.

"Are you outta your goddamn mind?" the dwarf roared.

"No." Bartlett shook his head. "I'm merely ensuring that you don't do anything stupid. Ninety-six hours. That's how long the tracking lasts before it will flush out of your system. We'll know where you are every step of the way."

Lisa stared at the tiny bead of blood in her hand. "You can't do this."

"I just did, Agent Breyer. Feel free to take it up with whoever you like but by then, the evidence will be gone. Johnny Walker Investigations took on a military contract. This is part of that contract."

Major General Dorn broke into a wheezing cackle, threw his head back against the chair, and bounced his legs up and down. "You think—ha! You think you're so smart. Johnny Walker and his team!"

"Yeah. Keep laughin'." The dwarf glared at him. *He ain't got much longer in this world to laugh anyhow.*

The old man tapped his cane against the desk as his laughter consumed him. A moment later, he stopped, his smile gone as his eyes widened within the wrinkled folds of his face. "This..." He cleared his throat. "This meeting's over."

"Sir?" Bartlett frowned at him in concern.

"Get them out! We're done here."

Luther and Rex raised their heads to sniff at the air. "You smell that, bro?"

"Oh, yeah. We should get out of here, Johnny."

"The dead guy crapped himself."

Lisa leapt from her chair and managed to force her laughter down only enough that it came out as a shrieked grunt.

Bartlett frowned at her. "Are you feeling okay, Agent Breyer?"

"Mm-hmm. It's, uh...jet lag." She nodded furiously at the colonel, turned quickly, and headed to the door without another word.

Johnny approached the desk and leaned toward Major General Dorn with a grin. The man glared at him, all traces of amusement completely gone. "Who needs help cleanin' up their messes now, Major General?"

The old man trembled with rage but said nothing as the dwarf turned to walk after Lisa. He snapped his fingers and both hounds trotted out quickly behind him.

"Hey, Johnny, you think he knows?"

"I heard two-legs do that when they die. They shit everywhere."

"What's he gonna do with it?"

Johnny joined Lisa in the hall and felt a hell of a lot better after this meeting than he had beforehand. *He made his bed and can damn well sit in it.*

CHAPTER TWENTY

When they returned to the hotel in Philadelphia to gather the rest of their belongings and prepare for their illegal arms deal, Johnny and Lisa made sure all four borgs stepped into the hotel suite before he opened the second hotel room two doors down. The hounds trotted in after him and headed to the giant bowl of water on the floor.

The dwarf poured himself a drink the second he reached the kitchen counter and knocked it all back before he poured a second. Lisa leaned against the wall inside the door and watched him silently until he went to sit on the couch. "Well, that was interesting."

"You've seen me drink before, darlin'."

"You know what I'm talking about."

"Yep." He sighed and took another slow sip. "Sorry I roped you into a military-grade tracker injected into your hand."

She laughed and joined him on the couch. "Yeah, that seemed weirdly high-tech for something a colonel would keep around in his office."

"They must've upped their game."

"Don't beat yourself up about it, okay? I don't blame you."

"Oh, I know. We'll work around it and we'll get this job done one way or another. The trackers ain't gonna set us back."

"Hmm." Lisa stole his drink, took a sip, and handed it back. "So why are you upset?"

"Naw, I ain't."

"Okay, we've been through this way more times than I can count. I ask what's wrong. You say nothing. I tell you you're the worst liar I've ever seen, you laugh because it's true, and then you tell me anyway. So let's skip to that last part."

He leaned back against the couch and studied her from the corner of his eye. "You have this all worked out."

"That's why I'm still here. How about this? I'll give you a little push." She nudged him with her shoulder and the dwarf finally cracked a crooked smile. "How do you and an asshole like Dorn know each other?"

"He was my drill sergeant."

"In...bounty-hunter school?"

He snorted and raised his glass to his lips again. "Boot camp."

"Oh. When he mentioned you not making it as a Marine, I assumed he meant you never tried."

"No, darlin'. I tried. Then I gave up 'cause the kinda tryin' they wanted of me wasn't worth it."

She leaned against him even more and he raised his arm to drape it around her shoulders. "What did you do?"

A short laugh burst out of him. "Why is it that everyone always thinks I'm the one who did somethin'?"

"I don't know. I'm imagining you as... Wait, how old were you?"

"Eighteen."

"Wow. Dorn's that old and he's still on base?"

"There's no way in hell he's still on active duty. Or has a command." Johnny pulled her closer and drank more whiskey. "Bartlett called him in 'cause I stepped in it when I dropped his name. I didn't think about how much time had passed."

"Well, at least he had a good laugh out of it, I guess."

Luther sniggered. "And a good shit."

Johnny snapped his fingers. "That's enough."

Lisa wrinkled her nose and stifled a laugh. "I almost completely lost it in there. Those hounds…"

"Always stickin' their noses where they don't belong, ain't they?"

"Hey, it's not our fault, Johnny."

Rex heaved a sigh that ended in a snort. "We didn't stick our noses anywhere. That was all the dead guy."

"Anyway…" Lisa nestled against his side and waited. "What happened between you two?"

"Boot camp. Drill Sergeant Dorn. Simple as that, ain't it?"

"No, there's more or you wouldn't be deflecting."

"Hell, darlin'. I ain't gone down that road in a long time."

She reached for his hand where it dangled over her shoulder and laced her fingers through his. "You went down it again today in that meeting and I can see it still bothers you."

"And this is the part where you tell me I'll feel better after talkin' about it."

Lisa shrugged.

"All right. Dorn was a good drill sergeant as far as they go. He smoked our platoon until we couldn't see straight and I loved every damn minute of it."

"Huh. No surprise there."

He snorted. "I didn't even make it through entry-level 'cause I found out he was fuckin' around with some shit he wasn't supposed to."

"Like what?"

"Naw, it don't matter. I did what I believed had to be done."

"You turned him in?"

"Hell no. I beat his ass to a bloody pulp. It earned me an unclassified discharge and that was it."

"Hmm." Lisa frowned at him. "And that's why you hate the military?"

"Naw, that's how it started. I've seen so much other shit along the way. Friends of friends knowin' someone who knows somethin'. But Dorn's the kinda guy who uses the power he has to his advantage all the time, no matter who gets hurt. There's a reason I dropped his name to Blake at the convention."

"You think they know each other."

"I think Major General Dorn's name gets tossed around more than he realizes in those circles. Hell, he probably does realize it and don't care. The man's responsible for buying more illegal weapons from overseas than anyone I ever heard of and only some of it for the military. Most of it is for himself."

"Wow."

"I can't touch him 'cause he's a goddamn major general now." With a wry chuckle, Johnny downed the rest of his whiskey and sighed heavily. "The bastard will be dead soon and I still ain't reached the halfway mark."

"If you're careful."

"Very funny, darlin'."

They sat together on the couch for a moment longer before Lisa drew a sharp breath. "Was he as grossly misogynist way back then?"

"Probably. Or it's old age and he can't keep it in."

Rex and Luther laughed uproariously. "He couldn't keep a lot of things in, Johnny."

"Yeah, like his—"

"Stop!" the couple shouted together.

The hounds stared at them and Luther lowered his head slowly onto his paws with a heavy sigh. "I thought both of you being able to hear us would be fun."

"I didn't make those collars for fun, boys." When Lisa laughed, the dwarf pulled her closer against him and chuckled. "All right, maybe a little. But y'all do a damn fine job on a hunt and out in the field when I know what the hell you're tryin' to say. It saved our asses more'n once."

"And sniffed out June's forgotten bomb." Lisa leaned her head on Johnny's shoulder again. "You said you knew exactly what to do with that. Now, I'm curious."

"We're gonna take it outta that box and let it blow, darlin'. Merely a little extra show of what the borgs can do. The way Blake was droolin' all over himself when he saw June, I reckon he'll lose it completely when he sees all four of 'em and a bomb."

"Great. So we do have to blow up a horde of things to stop someone else from blowing up even more."

"That's the only way I work, darlin'."

CHAPTER TWENTY-ONE

When it came time for the entire crew to pack up and head out of Philadelphia—now with zero evidence that the Unified Tech Convention had even existed—Johnny stormed into the suite the borgs had completely taken over, fully prepared to demand that they get to work and clean the hell out of the suite. It had already been done, however, and his mouth snapped shut on the unspoken tirade he'd prepared.

"What the—" He looked around and dropped into a squat to check under the couch. "Did y'all call the maid up here? I told y'all I wasn't payin' for—"

"See?" June stepped out of her bedroom and her emotionally vented smiley face burn had somehow miraculously been removed from the door. "He doesn't think we can do anything for ourselves."

"No maid, Johnny." Brandon gave him two thumbs-up, and Clint copied his brother perfectly. "We can clean."

"How the hell did y'all pull that off?"

June shook her head. "He forgets we're magicals. You know, with magic."

"Can dwarves do magic?" Leroy asked. "'Cause I know I can't."

"That ain't got nothin' to do with it."

"Maybe he never learned," Brandon muttered. Clint shrugged and headed to the front door.

"Next stop in the plan—right, boss?" Leroy clapped his non-metal hand on Johnny's shoulder. "We'd better get a move on."

The dwarf ran a hand through his hair as the borgs filed out to join Lisa and the hounds in the hallway. *If they've been screwin' with me this whole time, I ain't givin' 'em enough credit.*

In the hallway, all four borgs donned their illusion trinkets from Titus to instantly become their completely ungenuine selves. With a shared smirk, the twins pulled their illusion boxers out of their pockets and tugged them on over their pants. Brandon stretched the waistband of his and let it go with a snap before his entire appearance changed. Clint sniggered.

"This is what you guys rolled around the convention looking like?" Lisa studied Leroy curiously and raised her eyebrows. "Well, I guess it works."

"It was a fun conference, yeah." The shifter pushed his glasses up the bridge of his nose.

"June. You look—"

"Like a hooker. I know. I heard."

"No, that's not—" Lisa smothered a laugh. "You look very nice."

"Well, it's not me."

"No, I know. I only... Okay."

"Y'all couldn't have done all that inside the room?"

"You burst in like you were in a hurry, boss." Leroy brushed invisible lint off his fake shirtsleeve. "So we hurried."

"Well let's get goin', then." Johnny strode toward the stairs. "We have work to do."

"This is so weird," Luther muttered as he and Rex moved beside Lisa. "They look like regular two-legs, but they smell like...not."

"Like magicals but not," Rex added.

"Bro, it's like that shifter CIA lady."

"Yeah, except she was brainwashed. Those guys are...brain-wired?"

"Brain-fried."

"Brain-farted. Oh, wait. No. That was me."

"Hey, just because we've all finally had a good night's sleep doesn't mean you two can start all over again," Lisa told them through the side of her mouth. "I love you both but this is way too much."

"Hey, you're the one who stuck that pokey in your neck."

"Because there was a bomb."

Rex sniggered. "We love you too, lady. Don't tell Johnny. He might get jealous."

Fortunately for the dwarf and his refusal to buy a winter jacket, Our Lady Point Ranch was an hour southwest of Corpus Christi and almost at the southern tip of Texas. Which, of course, they had to take another trip in the jet to reach. Felix looked especially pleased to see Lisa looking much better than she had on her flight a few days before. "We're all ready to get up and out, Johnny. And no stops along the way this time."

"Fine job, Felix."

June slumped into her seat and folded her arms. "I could have gone myself and waited for you there."

"And do what?" Brandon turned in his chair to frown at her. "You're already bored by everything."

"Well, at least I'd be bored alone."

When his brother looked at him in confusion, Clint shrugged and exaggerated a grumpy face.

"Wait." Johnny turned in his seat and pointed at the Crystal borg at the back of the cabin. "Do you honestly think you can fly all that way?"

She raised an eyebrow. "I could get across the country twice without having to stop."

"That's good to know."

"What are you planning now?" Lisa muttered as the jet turned to taxi down the runway.

"An escape route. Kinda. Don't worry about it."

"Johnny, do you honestly think an entire cache of WMDs from outside the US at an asking price of two-point-five billion is simply hanging out at a ranch in Texas?"

"I have no idea, darlin'. The only thing I'm bettin' on is that somethin' we need is there. If it ain't the weapons, it's our ticket to findin' 'em."

They decided to rent two large SUVs when they landed. The Humvee rental in Philadelphia hadn't fared well after the abuse of four extra-metal cyborgs piled into the seats. Lisa let Johnny take the lead and followed him to the airport with the twins both seated in the back seat because neither one of them had wanted to sit up front. Instead, Luther sat in the passenger seat beside her.

"Hey, this is cool, right?" The hound sat erect on his haunches and whipped his head from side to side as they pulled onto the highway and headed toward the southern coast. His tongue lolled from his mouth and long strands of hound slobber splattered across the dash and the center console. "I don't think I've ever sat up front. You should split us up more often, lady."

Lisa darted him a sidelong glance. "This is probably a one-time thing."

"Aw, come on. How come? I love it."

Because we thought splitting you two up might make you shut up a little longer.

"Why would we ever do this again?" Brandon asked from the back. "That doesn't make sense."

She looked at the twins through the rearview mirror and shook her head. "No, I was talking to Luther."

"Oh…" Brandon nodded slowly. "I thought only Johnny did that. Yeah, the guy's a little weird and he has issues."

Clint honked his donkey-like laughter.

"But you? I don't know. I simply thought you were less crazy."

"I'm not. And neither is Johnny." It took a second for the entire thought to sink in and she couldn't help but laugh. "Although now that I'm in his shoes, so many more things make sense."

Luther giggled. "That's ridiculous. His feet are way bigger than yours."

"It's a figure of speech."

"What, being crazy?" Brandon asked.

"Okay. Everyone stop talking." She punched the radio's power button and flipped through the stations for anything that wasn't half-static. The first song they landed on was "Roar" by Katy Perry.

"Oh, yes!" The twins high-fived each other. "We love this one."

Lisa stared at the back of Johnny's SUV in front of her and tightened her grasp on the steering wheel. *I can listen to one cyborg singing way off-key to Katy Perry. Sure I can.*

Brandon spread his arms wide with a final shrieking note at the end of the chorus and smacked one hand against the window and the other against Clint's face. His brother burst out laughing and shoved him to his side of the rear seat.

Her teeth gritted, Lisa drew a deep breath. *I'm not so sure this is any better.*

When the two-hour drive that felt like three days finally ended, both vehicles pulled up at the gated entrance of Rio Pacific Railway. The guard in the gate tower waved them in and Lisa leaned forward to get a better view through the windshield. "Wow. I had no idea there was this kind of space out here."

"Hey, hey. Roll the window down, huh?" Luther smashed his nose against the window. "I smell hamburgers."

"It looks like this is a cattle ranch. Or at least it was."

"Plenty of space to blow stuff up, right?" Brandon muttered and peered through his window. "And the weapons are here?"

"I don't know. That's what we're about to find out."

A huge utility vehicle barreled down the dirt road toward them and skidded to a stop in front of Johnny's SUV. The driver waved for them to follow, turned on the road again, and accelerated away.

Lisa squinted at the dust cloud that rose in front of her. *They had to send someone to say, 'Follow me down the only road there is.' Or they're trying to make this look more legit.*

The dirt road branched into three after another half-mile, with not a single building in sight. Or livestock, for that matter. The utility vehicle made a sharp left turn down the steep hill and they went off-road toward the river that ran through the property. Once they climbed the next gentle slope and descended the other side, the welcome wagon set up for them came into view.

Lisa slowed to a stop beside Johnny's SUV and squinted at the three utility vehicles parked half a mile from the river and the huge live oaks growing on its banks. A giant table had been set up on the other side of the vehicles, with heavy-looking cases stacked beneath it.

A dozen men stood around them with bullet-proof vests and armed with assault rifles held casually at their sides.

"This looks…interesting," she muttered.

"It looks like an ambush," Brandon replied. "Except that we knew they'd be here."

"Yeah, I know. Okay, keep quiet and follow Johnny's— What are you doing?"

The twins, still dressed as debonair gentlemen, slumped in their seats and fidgeted with their pants.

"We're supposed to be weaponized idiots." Brandon grunted and finally pulled the illusion boxers down his hips before he kicked them off onto the floor. "We can't pull that off looking like…well, not us."

"Okay. Hurry, though." Lisa cut the engine and slid out as Johnny, June, and Leroy emerged from the second SUV.

Rex bounded out after the Crystal woman and ran toward

Lisa's open car door. "Luther! You made it! I thought you were a goner!"

"Dude, I got to sit in the front!" Luther skittered across the center console and hopped out Lisa's door. The hounds spun and sniffed each other's backsides. "Yeah, it's you, all right."

"You too. Had to make sure."

Lisa closed the door and snapped her fingers. Both hounds sat immediately and stared at her with wide eyes.

Luther licked his muzzle. "Whoa."

"Yeah, that worked. Do we, like, listen to her now?"

"Quiet." She raised an eyebrow at them and walked toward the strip of brown grass between their rented SUVs and the utility vehicles where the armed men waited for them.

Yeah. I think they do listen to me now.

The thought brought a small smile to her lips but she forced it back and focused on business.

The twins finally scrambled out of the back and Johnny's entire team converged in front of the cars.

"Johnny." Blake stood in front of the huge table with his arms spread wide and the sun glinted off his bald head. "Here we are."

"Here we are." The dwarf met him in the middle and they shook hands briefly. "You brought a hell of a welcome with you."

"It's merely a precaution. Nothing over the top." Blake nodded at the four borgs who stood motionlessly in front of the SUVs. "And I'd be willing to bet you're packing far more heat than my guys."

"Let's get to it."

"Of course. I thought we could start with a little demonstration of what you're bringing to the table then let you peek at what my client's offering. How does that sound?"

Johnny shrugged. "Fair enough."

"Excellent. Bring them down." Blake waved the borgs forward but didn't seem to expect them to move on their own.

The bounty hunter turned to direct what he hoped was a

warning glance at his team, snapped his fingers, and pointed at the open area beside the table.

The hounds stood from where Lisa had left them but stopped when the borgs walked forward instead.

"Oh, wait." Luther's head whipped from side to side as he looked from the borgs to his master. "Wait, that wasn't for us?"

Rex sat, then stood, then sat again. "This is getting weird, bro. All this snapping and talking and not talking. How are we supposed to know anything anymore?"

"Johnny?" Luther called with a whine.

The dwarf pointed at his hounds. "Stay."

"Oh, okay."

"Yeah, that was easy enough."

Blake turned away from the table with a tablet in his hand and his smile widened as he scanned each of the borgs. He walked down the line they'd formed beside the table and paused in front of each one to take a closer look.

Johnny hooked his thumbs through his belt loops and gave the man another minute. *Yeah, he likes that. Standin' there in a row like good little soldiers. They'd better stick to the plan this time.*

"I've been looking forward to this since our first meeting," Blake said as he stepped away from them. "I was most excited to see the female in action, but now I think I'd like to watch the big one first."

Johnny nodded and headed toward the borgs. "Good choice. You're up, Leroy. The rest of y'all, step back."

June gave him a glance that almost broke through her planned veneer of no expression whatsoever, but the bald man didn't seem to notice. He was too busy studying the different gears and gadgets and segmented pieces of Leroy hungrily as she and the twins stepped back.

"You named them?"

"Well, I had to call 'em somethin'." The bounty hunter shrugged. "What do you wanna see?"

"A demonstration, obviously." Blake's smile flickered in and out. "Something big."

"You heard the guy." He clapped Leroy on the back and stepped away with the bald man. "Make it big."

The shifter raised his arm and the pieces of his metallic hand whirred and clicked and morphed into the massive barrel of his rocket launcher. The borg's internal mechanisms sparked and flared with blue and silver light as the low hum rose quickly into a deadly wine. He pulled back and fired.

A massive ball of blue energy erupted from his hand cannon and launched across the empty field. There was nothing out there to use for target practice but the end result would have been the same. The ground exploded in a massive cloud to rain dust and brown grass and overturned stones in all directions. Smaller pebbles pelted the utility vehicles parked around the table. They pinged off the metal cases stacked beneath the table and Blake and his men ducked to avoid being hit.

When it was over, the crater in the ground fifty yards away was bigger than one of the utility vehicles. Smoke curled from it in thick waves and the man laughed. "I'm very sure I caught all that."

"Are you're filmin' this?" Johnny frowned at the tablet in the man's hand.

"My client will want to see this, I assure you."

Leroy stepped back and turned toward them. Blake's armed men seized their rifles and swung them to aim toward the shifter borg.

"Y'all don't gotta do that." Johnny gestured for them to relax. "This is how he stands down."

"What else can he do?" Blake approached Leroy and held the tablet up so he could catch a good shot of the cyborg's mechanical eye spinning as the shutter swirled wider and narrower. "This is incredible. Where did you say you got these again?"

"I didn't." The dwarf sniffed. "And I ain't sellin' that information, so don't try to put it on the table."

"No, of course. Sure. Are all this one's…abilities somewhat the same?"

"Uh-huh. Big guy, big guns."

"I have no difficulty believing that, Johnny. We'll cycle, then. Now, I'd like to see the female."

The female. Like she's a goddamn science experiment. Well, not anymore, at least.

Johnny nodded for Leroy to step back. "June."

She strode forward to take the shifter's place and looked straight ahead.

"Yes. I was surprisingly impressed by this one's little display for Mr. Epsley." Blake scanned the Crystal borg with his tablet. "She's a…what are they called? The icy magicals."

"Crystal." The dwarf stepped back and hoped the guy wouldn't get too close to June and end up as a puddle of guts in the field. *He ain't got a clue about magicals. I assume I can use that too.* "Leroy's a shifter. Or was, at any rate. I ain't seen him shift from how he is now. On account of all the…gear."

"That would be a feat, wouldn't it?" The bald man stepped away from June. "Is he stable?"

"It ain't the weapon has to be stable. It's the hand holdin' it."

"Right." The man darted him a wary glance. "I was referring to the nature of shifters specifically."

"He ain't gonna wolf out on ya, I know that much." He nodded at Leroy, who caught the gesture from the corner of his one good eye. The other one probably saw way more than that. "They'll do what they're told."

"Excellent. She's next, then." Grinning in anticipation, Blake backed away until he bumped against the table and focused the tablet's camera on June.

"Have at it," Johnny told her.

For a moment, it seemed she wouldn't move at all. She stood

completely motionless and stared directly ahead, and even her mechanical parts remained still and silent.

"What's wrong with it?" the man muttered.

"Nothin'. She sometimes takes a minute to—"

The tiny cannon mounted on her shoulder clicked, spun forty-five degrees to the right, and fired. Bright-orange light erupted from the narrow cylinder of her weapon, whizzed past the arms dealer's head, and missed him by a mere six inches. He ducked and had enough presence of mind to whirl and try to catch the whole thing on his tablet.

The closest tree growing on the riverbank blazed with orange light before it erupted in a spray of cracked branches, wooden splinters, and a shower of leaves. What remained of it after that had already caught fire by the time the debris cleared.

The security team at the utility vehicles whistled and shouted encouragement at the destruction and nodded like they'd be next for a shot at the shoulder cannon.

Blake cleared his throat. "Does she need to be recalibrated or something?"

"Huh?"

"That shot almost took my head off."

"Naw, she's fine. She does much better with an actual target. I should've been more specific with the command."

"Ah. June?"

The Crystal borg's hand hidden from him by her body clenched into a fist with a metallic shriek.

Johnny gritted his teeth and waited. *Stick to the plan. For the love of not gettin' killed right here and now.*

"She don't talk much," he muttered.

"Of course. Only when someone gets too close for comfort, right? Hey." Blake snapped his fingers at his men and pointed into the field. "Go set a target up for this one out there. I need a better shot."

Two guys pulled a giant crate out of one of the vehicles and carried it onto the open ground.

"How's that?" the man asked.

He glanced at June's extended index finger. "She can go farther."

The bald man waved his men farther.

"Yeah...you have 'em keep goin'." The second the dwarf saw her finger vanish into her fist again, he raised his hand. "That's good! Right there, fellas!"

The men dropped the crate and jogged to safety.

"You can't be serious." Blake chuckled. "Have they all been tested for range?"

"For the most part. I'm sure there are a few things I ain't discovered yet, but that's all part of the fun, huh?"

"Ha. Fun. Yes. Fire away, J—"

June raised her right arm with astounding speed—even faster than she'd raised it to level it at Mr. Epsley's crotch—and fired. The high-pitched whine hadn't even risen around her before the crate two hundred yards away exploded. The shockwave of whatever force she'd unleashed from her hand ruffled through her hair and a harsh, hot wind blasted back into Johnny and Blake.

The arms dealer man stepped back, his mouth open. "What was that?"

"Well." He scratched the back of his head. "One of those things I ain't discovered yet. Some kinda propelled force, maybe. Telekinetic energy. It's hard to tell unless you pick 'em apart."

"Have you?"

"No. And I don't recommend it. If you break the merchandise, I ain't doin' a return exchange and I don't know how to fix 'em."

"Fair enough. Let's see the other...are they twins?" Blake narrowed his eyes at Brandon and Clint, who both stood perfectly still as per the plan.

"It sure looks like it."

"Well, get them up here."

Still standing in front of the SUVs, Lisa watched the entire fake demonstration with her arms folded and a perpetual scowl on her face. *Real demonstration. Fake purchase in his future. They're doing better than I thought.*

The hounds inched toward her and sat. Rex licked his muzzle. "This is weird, right?"

"Yep."

Luther nipped at an itch on his back. "It feels wrong, you know? Like... Hey, Rex. It's like those dog shows. You know, where they get out there in that ring and run their masters around like dumb little puppets."

"Yeah. Poor bastards. We'd never do that to Johnny."

"Or you, lady. Don't worry."

She nodded and kept her gaze on the twins who stepped forward for their demonstration. If she looked at the hounds, she didn't think she could stop herself from laughing.

CHAPTER TWENTY-TWO

Blake ran each of the borgs through two more rounds of demonstration. After the last one, Johnny thought June would break and throttle the guy simply to watch his head pop off his shoulders in her hand. Fortunately, she controlled herself.

The grand finale arrived when the bounty hunter asked Lisa to get the box out of his car. She returned with the stabilized bomb in her arms and he offered it to Blake for a closer look.

"I'm not interested in that type of gadget, Johnny." The man turned his nose up at the box and began to swipe through the video segments he'd taken of the borgs.

"It's included in the price."

The bald man stopped and took a second glance at the box. "Why?"

"'Cause I ain't found a way to stop the cyborgs from makin' 'em. It's some kind of energy runoff. They have a helluva lot of power coursin' through 'em all the time. What they don't use has to go somewhere."

"They...produce these?"

"Uh-huh. They gotta be handled the right way and within a certain timeframe. Otherwise, you have unpredictable detonations on your hands. This case keeps 'em inactive. I'd be happy to sell you patent rights on it too if you want."

"My client isn't interested in patents or gadgets or small-level explosives."

"Yeah, I know." Johnny thrust the box into June's arms and nodded at the field. "Go on."

She stared at Johnny, pulled the case from the shoebox, and ripped the hinges off as well as the gelatinous membrane around the bomb she'd made. Without a word, she stalked into the field. The dwarf grimaced at the destroyed pieces of his tech and sighed. *It's for the long game, Johnny. That's all it is.*

The Crystal borg went farther out into the field than any of the other targets by almost twice the distance. She dropped the bomb in the browning grass and pointed at it. A zap of white light burst from her finger, and her biochemical explosive was reactivated.

Blake clicked his tongue in annoyance. "How long does it take to—"

Her propulsion boots roared to life with an orange flare and she launched skyward as the bomb glowed with a golden light. The armed men shouted and aimed their rifles at the cyborg woman who soared in a high arc overhead. With a deafening crack, the bomb detonated and threw up a massive mushroom cloud of dirt and crackling magical energy.

Two seconds later, June landed beside Johnny with a dull thump and gave him a deadpan stare.

"That..." Blake finished filming with his tablet as the smoke and golden light of the explosion still rippled through the air before it faded with the debris. "That sweetened the deal considerably, Johnny."

"Yeah, I thought you might like it."

"Okay." The arms dealer turned toward Johnny and scanned the borgs again briefly before he smiled. "My client is prepared to offer five million for all four. And he'll take another fifty off the final purchase price of his weapons."

The bounty hunter snorted. "No offense, but I'd rather make the actual deal with him in person. And I think I earned a little taste of what I'll be gettin' in return at the very least."

Blake typed something on his tablet, turned the screen off, and placed the device on the table. "Of course. That's only fair and we expected it. I'm afraid my client isn't available to meet you face to face until tomorrow evening. I hope you don't mind that I've already booked a suite for you at the Port Royal Ocean Resort in Corpus Christi."

"That's a hell of a gesture."

"It's nothing, truly. But it'll give you a chance to consider my client's offer in the meantime. I'll call the room when he's available to let you know where you can meet him."

"All right."

The man extended his hand with a smirk, his eyes wide. "It's a pleasure doing business with you, Johnny."

"The business ain't over yet but at least you enjoyed yourself."

"Oh, more than you know." With a final greedy glance at the borgs, Blake folded his arms and watched the team return to the SUVs.

No one said a word as they climbed into the vehicles. Blake's armed men stood their ground, their rifles held casually now that the threat of having their heads blasted off by hand cannons was behind them.

Johnny and Lisa shared a glance before each slid behind the wheel of their prospective rentals. *We have so much to work through in the next twenty-four hours. The resort's as good a place as any to do it.*

The suite reserved in his name—only Johnny and nothing else —was much nicer than he'd expected. It was also massive.

"We might as well call this a penthouse," Lisa said as she walked through the immense living room furnished with tasteful pieces that wouldn't hold up to a borg's weight for longer than half a second.

"They're pullin' out all the stops." Johnny folded his arms. "When the money's this big, you get whatever suite you want."

The hounds raced across the living room and their claws clicked madly on the floor. "Johnny! We call that one!"

"How did they know?" They pounced onto a large beige divan on the other side of the living room. Luther rooted around with his snout and inched the side of his face across the upholstery. Rex spun before he settled on his belly and stretched his hind legs out far behind him.

"Giant dog bed, Johnny. It's perfect."

"It's ours."

"Enjoy it while it lasts, boys."

"Hey, boss?" Leroy stepped out of the hallway that connected this living room to a second living area beyond. "Are there supposed to be this many rooms? It feels like we walked into someone's house."

"I guess that's the point. Do you think y'all can find a way to divide the space without breakin' anythin'?"

"I get this room." June strode past Leroy and pointed into the second living area.

"The whole room?"

"No, the whole side."

He rolled his eyes and followed her so they could discuss the actual arrangement. The twins walked through slowly in a daze.

"This feels familiar," Brandon muttered.

Clint nodded and turned in wide, slow circles.

"Lisa." Johnny stopped beside a narrow staircase leading to the second floor of the suite above the kitchen. "I think this one's for us."

"Are you sure that's not the laundry room?"

"It wouldn't matter anyhow. It's above the rest of this mess."

With a smirk, she pointed at the stack of laser-bomb cases

he'd set on the island countertop that wasn't even part of the kitchen. "I feel we should put these away somewhere."

"Yep." He hurried toward her to haul all the cases away, then moved to the stairs. "The top floor's far enough away from sticky fingers down here."

She looked at the hounds on the huge divan. Rex had rested his head between his paws. Luther lay on his back, his hind legs splayed wide and his front paws dangling at his face. Both of them were already snoring.

"Don't break anything," she shouted as she followed Johnny up the stairs.

"We'll clean it up!" Leroy called in response.

The bounty hunter was right. The top of the stairs opened into an overly opulent master bedroom with a giant jacuzzi sunk into the tiles at the far end and not a door in sight. He placed the laser-bomb cannons on the floor against the wall, slung his duffel bag beside them, and kicked his shoes off before he moved to the bed in the center of the room. "it ain't my style but there's somethin' to be said for all this room."

"Johnny, it's the size of your entire house."

"Naw. Not quite. Come here." He patted the mattress beside him, which was lower than normal hotel beds on a platform frame with drawers beneath.

"There's no way that's an actual King. Not even California King."

"Sometimes, there's too much of a thing and it don't even have a name." Her laugh made him grin as she looked around the giant bedroom and walked slowly toward him.

"Is that an allusion to something else?"

"Nope. Exactly what I said."

She sat beside him and they both flopped back onto the bed to look at the ceiling. "Oh, wow."

"Huh." Johnny tilted his head and his reflection in the mirror mounted on the ceiling tilted its head too. "I wasn't expectin' that."

"That's not normal, is it?"

"Darlin', I'd have to spend much more time in joints like this to have any clue how to answer that." He caught her hand and laced their fingers together. "I'm not sure I'm a fan."

"Yeah, it's a little…gratuitous?"

With a snort, he turned his head to study her profile. "Have you noticed how the longer we been doin' this together, the fancier our hotel rooms get?"

"Oh, I've noticed. But don't try to claim the credit. You haven't booked half of these rooms. Or paid for them."

"Uh-huh. I think you might be somethin' of a lucky charm for me."

Lisa finally looked away from their reflection in the ceiling and met his gaze. "Is that right?"

"I ain't tellin' you somethin' you don't already know."

"Maybe." She squeezed his hand. "This whole situation, though…I don't know."

"What d'ya mean?" He propped himself on his elbows, and Lisa sat fully and ran a hand through her hair.

"Doesn't it feel a little weird to you that Blake or his client or whoever they are would set us up in a suite like this, no questions asked, and tell us to wait until tomorrow?"

He regarded her with his crooked smile. "Darlin', I'm sharin' this suite with four boneheaded cyborgs, three laser-bomb guns I bought from a friend, and two coonhounds I can hear in my head. If shit don't feel a little funny by now, there's somethin' wrong with me."

Lisa laughed and pulled her legs onto the bed to cross them beneath her. "You're forgetting something in that countdown."

"Yeah." He reached out and stroked her arm. "And you, of course. You're one of a kind."

She clicked her tongue and grinned at him. "That was a good one."

"You like that?"

"Yeah. Johnny Walker throwing out a pickup line that doesn't sound like he's choking on it. Well done."

"We'll handle whatever happens tomorrow the way we always do. Funny business or not, understand?"

"Do I understand? Please. I wasn't looking for reassurance."

"I know." He rolled off the bed and headed to his duffel bag with the embroidered skull and crossbones. "It don't mean we can't enjoy the night and tomorrow the best we can."

She shook her head slowly and couldn't help but smile when he returned with a bottle of whiskey and snagged the water glasses on the dresser. "You brought a bottle with you on the job."

"Three." The stopper popped off the bottle and bounced across the gigantic mattress. "I did spend a week in a much smaller suite with the aforementioned companions."

"Please tell me this isn't the last one."

"Oh." He paused in front of the bed, the open bottle poised over the glasses nestled next to each other in his palm, and raised an eyebrow at her. "Are you fixin' on downin' all this tonight?"

"Yeah, right. Pour me a drink."

CHAPTER TWENTY-THREE

They received the call on the hotel line from Blake at almost 7:00 the next night. With all this space for the borgs, the hounds, and Johnny and Lisa to spread out like they had for slightly over twenty-four hours, he'd almost forgotten this wasn't a real vacation. But all the space and quiet he'd had upstairs for most of that time had put a perpetual smirk on his face, and he answered the phone in a particularly good mood.

"This Blake?"

"Johnny. Rio Pacific Railway yard in two hours. My client's very much looking forward to meeting you and examining everything in person. If it looks good to both of you, I imagine tonight will be the last time you and I have to deal with each other."

"Naw, I ain't gettin' outta the game anytime soon."

"But my client may no longer need a middleman. See you soon." Blake hung up and the dwarf raised an eyebrow at the receiver before he dropped it into the cradle.

"Huh. The guy sounds damn confident about this. They ain't gonna like the way it turns out."

"Was that Blake?" Lisa asked.

"Yep. Rio Pacific Railway. How long a drive you think that is?"

Seated at the bar stool in the giant kitchen at the back of the penthouse suite, she pulled her phone out and ran a quick search. "Two hours. Ninety minutes with you driving."

"And you keepin' up. All right." He stuck two fingers in his mouth and whistled shrilly. "Everyone in the kitchen!"

The borgs streamed in from various sides of the room. Clint held an open pickle jar under one arm and stabbed the contents with the metal extension on his middle finger.

"We're headin' out to finally make this damn exchange."

"You're not buying the weapons, though." Leroy folded his arms. "Right, boss?"

"No. I ain't. But they don't know it and that's how it's gonna stay until we're outta options. So y'all be ready for anythin' that might go down, understand?"

June held her hand out toward Clint, who casually slapped a pickle into it before she bit half off with a loud crunch. "Like a fight?"

Johnny sighed. "Yeah, like a fight. That's what it means when somethin's goin' down. At least in this context. These guys wantin' to buy y'all think I'm the one in control of you—that y'all ain't nothin' but weapons. We played that off damn nicely yesterday at the ranch, so y'all keep it up tonight. I think it will play to our advantage more than not. Right. It's time to move out."

With a sigh, Clint put his pickle jar on the counter. Leroy and Brandon each snagged the last two spears and munched them on the way across the gigantic suite.

The hounds trotted after Johnny as the dwarf headed to the stairs to the master bedroom. "Hey, Johnny. You're going the wrong way."

"Yeah, the door's over here. It's easy to get lost in this place."

"But we'll help you find it."

Their master's voice echoed down the staircase. "I ain't

headin' to an arms deal without any arms of my own, boys. I'll be down in a minute."

Lisa's estimate of an hour and a half to reach the Rio Pacific Railway wasn't very far off at all. The train yard was completely dark when they pulled up to the gravel parking lot at 8:55 pm. The second both SUV engines cut off, the floodlight over the station building clicked on to cover them with its blinding glare.

Johnny stepped out of his vehicle with Leroy and June in tow. Lisa slid out with the hounds and the twins and everyone but the animals raised their hands to shield against the bright light.

A door clicked open and shut before Blake's shadowy outline waved them forward. "Come on back. He's waiting for you."

"Does this client of yours have a name?"

"He prefers to give it himself." When they rounded the small square building, the floodlight at the front was still bright enough to see a line of outdoor tents stretched down the length of the train yard beside the silent tracks. The canvas whipped in the wind, and another bright light from a utility vehicle parked forty feet away lit the way for Johnny and his crew to follow their guide.

This don't seem like the best place to throw a party, but okay.

"Johnson," Blake called and waved a man toward him. "Go tell him they're here."

Johnson nodded and hurried down the line of tents.

"This way first if you don't mind." The dealer led them toward a separate set of tracks, this one holding a rusted train that looked like it hadn't moved in years. He gestured toward one of the open metal cars.

"It don't look like anyone's in there," Johnny muttered.

"Not yet. My client prefers to leave the merchandise out of the way while he conducts negotiations. It's only temporary, but..." Blake shrugged. "It has to be done."

"You want me to lock 'em in the train car?"

"Temporarily."

Johnny turned to study the borgs in the low light and grimaced. *They're already too weird about tight spaces as it is. Now I gotta ask 'em to be locked up again on purpose.*

"All right. You heard the man."

Without showing any reaction whatsoever, all four borgs marched across the alley between tracks and headed to the car. June launched herself through the open door and turned her boots off to land with a clang. Leroy jumped up in one swift motion, and the twins took slightly longer to climb up the ladder.

"Excellent." Blake nodded at two more armed men who'd come to join them, and one of them trained his rifle on the borgs while the other hauled the sliding metal door of the train car shut. The heavy steel latch clicked into place and that was that. Blake nodded. "Now for the fun part."

The hounds sniffed the loose gravel between the railroad tracks. Luther snorted. "Smells weird out here, Johnny."

"Yeah, if lies had a smell, I'd say this is probably it."

"My client's waiting here in the last tent," their guide continued. "He was particularly impressed by the videos I sent him yesterday. I have no doubt you'll get exactly what you're looking for after this."

"It sounds good to me." The bounty hunter scanned the darkness around the line of tents, where dark forms moved between train cars and behind parked vehicles.

"Johnny, there are more guys here than last time," Rex muttered.

"They're everywhere," Luther agreed. "And I don't think they want us here."

Yeah, I see 'em. Johnny glanced at the hounds and snapped his fingers. They looked sharply up at him and sat when he raised his index finger. An open hand commanded them wordlessly to stay.

"Why aren't you saying anything, Johnny?"

"Yeah, you know we can hear you, right?"

He left his hand up for another two seconds, then nodded and turned to follow Blake.

"Oh… Luther, he doesn't want anyone to hear him talking to us."

"Hey, Johnny. If you don't want anyone to hear us, scratch the back of your head."

The dwarf scratched the back of his head vigorously and darted Lisa a sidelong glance as they walked farther away from the floodlights.

"Hey, good one. Rex, we can figure this out."

"Yeah, hey, Johnny! Cough once if you're trying to tell us to standby 'cause there's about to be trouble—"

Lisa beat him to it and coughed loudly into her fist.

"Hey, they're both in on it. Heard you loud and clear, Johnny!"

"Well…not clear. But we'll stay."

Johnny and Lisa exchanged a hasty look. *Maybe the borgs have telepathy, but I think this is as close as we're gonna get to the same thing.*

"Here." Blake stopped at the very last tent, clapped briskly, and gestured toward the tent flap that was drawn aside by another armed guard. "Enjoy yourselves."

As soon as the bald man backed away, half a dozen men closed in on Johnny and Lisa, their weapons drawn.

"Hey!" Lisa twisted and jerked her wrist out of a man's tight grasp before she slapped him in the face. "Hands off!"

"Whoa, whoa, whoa." Johnny raised both hands and glared at the assholes who pushed closer. "Hold the fuck up now. We came in quietly and unarmed to—" Someone rammed the butt of a rifle into his back between his shoulder blades. With a grunt, he stumbled forward and dropped to his knees.

"What is this?" Lisa spat. "We had a meeting!"

"No, you don't." A giant man in coveralls stalked toward them. "You're merely two morons who thought they'd get rich playing the wrong guy." He bent over to swing a vicious right hook at Johnny's face.

The dwarf whipped sideways and swayed on his knees but didn't fall.

"Johnny!" His partner struggled against the three men who now attempted to drag her away. She kicked and twisted but was unable to get her hands free for long enough to fire any fireballs or energy magic. And as per Johnny's request, she hadn't brought her service pistol. "Let go of me! Johnny!"

"It's all right, darlin'." He spat a glob of blood onto the gravel. "It's only a misunderstandin'. I'll get it cleared up in a minute."

The man in the coveralls sneered and shook his head. Lisa's shouts faded as the men dragged her into one of the other tents. The hounds barreled down the lane between the railroad tracks and howled frantically.

"Johnny!"

"We're coming, Johnny!"

"Wait." The dwarf widened his eyes at his attacker, who had drawn his arm back in preparation for another blow.

The man finally realized two coonhounds were on the loose and snarled at the other guys who surrounded the dwarf. "Shut those dogs up, huh? That's the last thing we need."

The closest man spun and opened fire on the animals.

"Holy shit!" Luther darted under the train and belly-crawled beneath the car to safety.

"Johnny, what do you want us to—"

"I said wait!" the dwarf shouted. The sudden outburst made the mad dog-shooter pause and he turned to look at his boss for direction.

"Are those your dogs?"

"Yeah. And I'm sayin' wait. Listen to what I have to say, huh?"

The man sniggered. "I think you've already had enough time."

"If anyone else hears about this, you're all going down," Johnny warned. "At the right time, understand?"

"Luther!" Rex shouted as he skittered between two train cars to join his brother. "I think he's talking to us."

"Johnny, are you talking to—"

The dwarf uttered a loud, hacking cough and spat more blood.

"That's a yes. We told him to cough for yes."

"Okay, then shut up and listen like he said."

In response to the dwarf's glared challenge, the man raised an eyebrow and punched him in the face again before he crouched to deliver a hard uppercut into his gut. The bounty hunter grunted and swayed again. "You're done. The guys you're working for are done. Everything you have is ours." He nodded at two of his guys. "Get him in the tent. He wanted a talk so we'll have a talk."

Johnny saw the rifle butt swing toward his temple and didn't even try to duck out of the way. He didn't feel his face and shoulder hit the gravel when he blacked out either.

CHAPTER TWENTY-FOUR

The slow, rhythmic slap of something heavy striking flesh was the first thing Johnny heard when he came to. His back and shoulders ached, not to mention the throbbing pain in his temple and his quickly swelling bottom lip. He tried to stand but was tied securely to the chair beneath him, his wrists bound painfully by what he assumed were zip-ties.

When he finally managed to open his eyes and clear his blurry vision, the overhead light hanging from the center of the tent was too bright. It lit up every massive pore on his adversary's ugly face, including the stains in his crazy-looking grin. The man thumped the end of a crowbar into his open hand in a slow, steady rhythm. "There you are."

The bounty hunter grunted and tried to blink the dizziness away. "Here I am."

"You realize what this means, right?" The man stepped forward.

"That you've been standin' there slappin' yourself with a piece of metal for fun? How long was I out? If it was more than five minutes, you must be feelin' a little sting by now."

"Ralston must have hit you harder than I thought. Oh, well. That means this'll be a fun conversation."

"Well, it was supposed to be." Johnny sniffed and raised his head slowly to scan the giant man with open disdain. "But then you got in the way and I got lied to."

His captor didn't give any warning before he swung his fist into his face again. The dwarf's head snapped to the side and blood splattered along the tent wall. "Like you lied to Blake, you mean?"

Johnny chuckled through the pain that flared through his cheek. "I ain't told a lie in my life."

This time, the man swung the thick end of the crowbar at Johnny's shoulder. He gritted his teeth against the dull crunch of something—maybe cartilage, maybe not—but uttered no sound other than a low grunt. "You said you were the middleman for a buyer. A mouthpiece who's survived long enough to stay being a mouthpiece doesn't make deals for himself on the side." The crowbar whacked against the side of his calf and he grunted again. "If anyone knows that, it's Blake. He made you the first time you met."

"Then why am I here?"

"Because we like to play games too. Marcel likes to play games. That's who you thought you were meeting tonight, by the way." The man drove his fist into Johnny's gut again, then turned and walked away to enjoy the moment. "And I like games. Sure, I could've killed you already, but this is fun. Do you think we don't know who you are?"

"I can't read minds." Johnny coughed for real this time and spat another glob of blood. "Sorry."

"Johnny Walker. We've heard of him here and there. And we know exactly who you're working for." The crowbar came down again on his other shoulder and this time, he growled through his clenched teeth when the heavy thrust of pain streaked into his already bruised temple.

Outside, the hounds raced silently along the lines of tents, sniffing furiously and staying away from the crazy two-legs with guns who liked to shoot dogs.

"Hey, Luther," Rex whispered and stopped two tents down from where Johnny was being beaten by a guy in overalls for fun. "She's in here."

"Lisa?" Luther sniffed at the bottom edge of the tent. "Hey, lady. You in there?"

She groaned as she came to. "What?"

"Hey, if you can still hear us, cough once."

"Dude, we already did that one—"

Lisa coughed once and sucked in a harsh breath. "What's going on?"

A man chuckled inside the tent. "You and that dwarf are done. That's what's going on." The click of a pistol hammer being pulled back rose from inside. "I wouldn't try anything. If you're good, maybe you and I can have a little fun before we kill you."

"Lisa, listen," Rex said quickly. "Johnny's fine. He's getting the shit kicked out of him but he's fine."

"Yeah, and he told us to wait and listen. So that's what we're doing," Luther added. "We haven't figured out what for yet, though."

"Where are the cyborgs?" Lisa asked, her voice raspy and dry.

"The guns on legs?" The man inside sniggered. "They'll stay right where you left them until we're finished with you and the damn dwarf. That could take anywhere from five to thirty minutes, depending on Milton's mood."

"You won't get away with this."

"That already happened, sweetheart. But you're not getting away. I can tell you that much."

"Rex, the borgs!"

"Yeah, yeah. We'll go tell them." The hounds scuttled away but Rex stopped short. "If Johnny has a plan, we'll work it out. But... don't die, okay?"

Lisa heaved a sigh.

"I'll take that as a yes."

They raced down the train yard and darted beneath cars to avoid the other thugs with rifles patrolling the area. "Man, how many guys do they need?"

"I know, right? Johnny could do the same thing by himself and he doesn't look nearly as stupid doing it."

"Oh, hey. The borgs."

They stopped at the train car and sniffed the bottom of the sliding door.

"Leroy. Hey." Rex's front paws scraped against the iron door when he leapt up. "It's us."

"We know you can hear us, robowolf, so don't even try to play dumb."

Seated inside the car, Leroy pulled his legs away from the edge of the door and leaned toward the crack. "Shouldn't talk," he whispered.

"Then listen, okay? Johnny and Lisa know we're still out here. We'll tell him you're ready for a message. If he's still alive to give it."

"Bro, shut up." Rex snorted and leapt away from the car. "Keep your ears open, okay? We'll be back."

Leroy's mechanical eye spun madly when he looked at June seated on the other side of the car. They all knew to keep quiet. They were supposed to be dumb soldiers with built-in weapons, after all. But he relayed the hounds' message to her anyway without having to say a word, and with the night-vision imaging activated in his eye, he saw her nod.

They'd wait.

"Johnny!" Luther snorted and ducked around a parked car when two more gun-dudes walked past. "Jeez. I had no idea it would be so weird to yell and not bark at the same time."

"Don't bark. Come on."

They padded swiftly past a group of men talking in a circle on the other side of another vehicle.

"Yeah, as soon as we take care of these idiots, we'll load those robot freaks into the truck out front."

"How? They're in a train car."

"I don't know. I'm not the one making the plans. Christ. It's not like they can think for themselves."

"Then we take them to Marcel?"

"Yeah, genius. He gets his weirdo team and I guess the actual buyer of the other weapons is meeting him later."

"You know, I thought that dwarf was supposed to be, like...smart."

"Obviously not."

The men chuckled, someone lit a smoke, and Luther crouched to utter a low growl. Rex cut it off instantly with a nip on his brother's face. "Stop it."

"Ow. You heard what they said—"

"Who cares? None of it's gonna happen if we hurry and—"

"Oh, right. Tell Johnny. Come on!"

"Luther!" Rex chuffed and slunk past the vehicle after his brother. "Moron."

"You realize this is bad for business, right?" Johnny mumbled through his swollen lip.

"Bad for you all around, bud." The crowbar clattered to the ground and his captor landed another blow to his face. The bounty hunter sat and took it, even when the guy bunched a fist around his shirt collar and yanked him forward again to hold him steady. "We're taking everything you brought tonight and you're not getting a single dollar."

"You know, I was holdin' out hope there on that one—" The guy's fist cracked against the side of his head this time. He slumped forward and blood dripped from his split lip and everything else from the shoulders up that had started to bleed.

"You're a real smartass." His attacker stepped back. "I heard that about you, but I didn't know you were so stupid that you couldn't learn when to keep your mouth shut."

"Funny." Johnny breathed heavily simply to get through the pain that swamped him from everywhere at once. "I heard the same about you."

"Asshole." The man who used him as a punching bag sniggered as he rolled his shirtsleeves up. "You inserted yourself where no one wanted you to be in the first place. You know that, right? There's a price for that with guys like Marcel. And guys like me are the ones who get to come collect."

"You'd get a piece of me a hell of a lot faster if you cut a finger off or somethin'. I don't break easy, brother."

"Yeah, but you're getting there." The enforcer cracked the knuckles of each hand one after the other. "I can always tell. Too bad your superiors in Washington won't be able to send you reinforcements, huh? Or did they not brief you about how completely fucked you were gonna be when you got here?"

The bounty hunter cleared his throat. *This idiot still thinks I'm workin' for the military. I must've hit a nerve by cryin' Dorn.*

"Johnny!" Rex shouted from outside the tent. "We found them all."

"Yeah, Lisa's okay. She knows what we're doing. So do the borgs. So you give us the signal, Johnny."

"We'll handle the rest."

Well, now we're gettin' somewhere.

"It don't matter...if they briefed me or not," he said. His gruff voice gave out halfway through and he resumed after he cleared his throat.

"You don't ever shut up, do you?"

"Nope. The thing is, I ain't one to follow orders either. I never have been."

"I'm done listenin' to this shit." The man pulled a knife from his belt and grimaced as he nodded. "You're done making any noise at all."

"Any minute now, Johnny," Rex muttered.

"Yeah, we're waiting."

"You know who else ain't cut out for chain of command?"

The man stalked toward him with the knife.

"Those cyborgs." Johnny sneered at the blade that glinted under the light as it moved closer. "One wrong move, and they'll *blow the whole thing!*"

"That's it!" Luther shouted. "That's the signal!"

"Blow it up! Blow it up!" Rex howled and his brother picked the call up with him right outside the tent.

"Those fucking dogs." The man turned away from his captive and strode to the closed flap of the tent. Before he reached it, a massive explosion with a tinny undertone wracked the train yard. Steel groaned and crashed, train wheels squealed on the tracks, and two more quick explosions followed immediately after.

"What the—" He ducked instinctively at the noise and ripped the tent flap aside to see the blossoming mushroom cloud of blue-and-white sparks and thick yellow smoke that billowed from the train car. "Nice try. You're done."

He spun and lunged at Johnny, but the hounds barreled through the tent flap and targeted his legs without hesitation.

"You stupid asshole!" Luther shouted and clamped his jaws tightly around his shin. The man grunted and tried to kick him away, but Rex leapt up and caught a mouthful of his hairy wrist.

"Ah! Fuck!" He dropped the knife and tried to yank Rex free of his arm.

"No one stabs Johnny." Luther backed away, took a flying leap at the man's broad chest, and struck him squarely. He didn't see it coming and had no time to react before he staggered back with a fifty-five-pound coonhound snarling madly and attempting to bite his face.

Rapid gunfire rose outside, accompanied by shouts of alarm

and only the occasional thump and hiss of one of the borgs unleashing a seriously powerful shot.

"Rex! Knife!" Johnny shouted.

"Yeah, yeah."

The man blundered into the table at the side of the tent and toppled onto it. It broke beneath his weight, and Luther vaulted off his chest before he could swipe the hound aside.

Rex snatched the knife handle in his jaws and brought it to Johnny. "Here."

"My hands are tied behind my back, Rex," the dwarf said through clenched teeth.

"Shit. Right." Once the hound had deposited the knife in his master's bound hands instead of his lap, the dwarf managed to slip the edge of the blade between his wrists and cut through the zip-ties with one quick but awkward flick and his hands were free. "Huh. It's damn sharp."

"Get off me!" His captor kicked out at Luther, who dodged the foot and scrambled back as the huge man snatched the crowbar up. He swung wildly and missed the hound every time.

Luther snarled and barked as he darted forward and retreated.

I can't even reach the damn ropes. With the way his arms had been tied behind his back and secured to the chair, Johnny couldn't get the short knife anywhere near the ropes. "Luther."

"I got him, Johnny. Don't worry." The hound backed away even more toward the chair.

Rex darted around the other side of the man and snapped at his heels. The crowbar came down and narrowly missed the hound's nose when he leapt away.

"Luther, there's a—"

"Hey, asshole!" Luther barked nonstop. "I'm over here!"

With a roar, the huge man brought the crowbar up in a sweeping cross-swing. Luther darted behind Johnny's chair at the last second, and the dwarf rocked onto his feet to stand and bent forward. The crowbar splintered the thick wood of the chair's seat instead, shattered the back, and loosened the ropes around his arms.

For a split second, the dwarf and the man who tried to kill him and his hounds stared at each other in surprise. Then, Johnny lunged forward, dragged the broken chair behind him, and plunged the knife into the man's gut.

His opponent roared, staggered back, and unskewered himself in the process.

"Oh, shit! You sure got him, Johnny!"

"Yeah, get him again!"

With a growl like a bear, the man swung the crowbar at him again as the dwarf shucked off the last of the loose rope. Johnny ducked into the swing and sliced the blade across the man's wrist. The crowbar thumped against his shoulder before it toppled to the ground, but he kept moving. He landed another quick jab into his captor's kidney, and when the man staggered forward, his head thrown back in surprise and by the sheer force of the blow, he reached around his shoulder to grab him under the chin.

The knife did the rest on his throat.

"Whoa, whoa." Luther skittered around the heavy man as he fell to his knees. Blood sprayed everywhere as he clamped his hands around his throat to no avail.

"Let's go, boys." The bounty hunter ran through the tent and clenched his teeth at the sound of his opponent's body landing heavily. *I would've killed him faster if I had a gun on me. It ain't the right way to let a guy go.*

"Johnny, that was awesome," Rex said, hurried after his master, and completely ignored the man dying inside the tent. "How did you time it like that with the chair? Can you see the future?"

"Nope." He whipped the tent flap open and scanned the chaos the borgs had made of the train yard. "I was tryin' to keep Luther from gettin' his head bashed in."

"Oh, hey. Hey, yeah. I appreciate that, Johnny." Luther caught up to them with a low whine.

The dwarf glanced at the smaller hound and smirked. "But you already knew what you were doin'."

"Thanks. Wait, I did?"

"Come on. We gotta get Lisa."

They slipped out of the tent, ducked behind the next one in line to stay out of sight, and waited for the next group of Marcel's men with guns to race past toward the cyborgs who set magical fire to everything that moved.

"Um, Johnny? Why are you sneaking around?"

"Yeah, we do that. But not you. Usually."

"I don't like it any more'n you do, but I ain't got a gun—"

"Watch out!" Rex barked.

A man who stood on the other side of the tents had trained his rifle on the bounty hunter and his hounds. Johnny threw without having to think first, and before the killer's trigger finger could squeeze, the knife streaked into his neck and he fell.

"Bullseye!"

"Come on, Johnny. You don't need a gun."

"Yeah, but now I got shit." The dwarf waited for an opening and took advantage of the next whistling explosion at the front of the train yard to dart across the narrow avenue toward the guy with his boss' knife in his throat. He grasped the rifle and struggled to free the strap from around the body's shoulder before he turned toward the tents again. "Where's Lisa?"

"This one right here, Johnny. She's—wait." Luther sniffed at the canvas. "Nope. Sorry."

"Next one!" Rex darted past them both and skidded across the gravel with a yelp when someone opened fire from behind a parked vehicle.

Johnny swung the rifle and returned three quick shots. Two more bodies dropped. A second later, a massive sheet of steel plummeted and clanged in a noisy landing in front of the dwarf.

Pebbles sprayed everywhere, and he glanced at the dark sky before he moved on. *The borgs are rippin' train cars apart by hand now. It looks like they're learnin'.*

"This one, Johnny." Rex stopped beside the next tent. "Right here."

He pulled the tent flap aside and swung the rifle toward the first sign of movement as he strode inside. "Back the fuck up."

Lisa was on the ground and a skinny guy lay in her lap as his legs kicked violently against the dirt. One of her forearms was hooked around his throat and the other pulled up under his armpit and clamped around her wrist to add the extra pressure. "I'm a little busy for that, Johnny," she grunted.

He stepped fully into the tent and spun the rifle to aim at the other side. There was no one else there.

Finally, her captor stopped fighting the chokehold and he went limp. She shoved him off her and pushed to her feet. "I'm so glad I decided to use that canister."

"Right." Johnny snorted. "'Cause you can hear the hounds."

"Good work, boys." She jerked her captor's pistol out of his belt, checked the magazine, and nodded. "Time to go, right?"

"Well, unless you had somethin' else planned..."

She rolled her eyes, hurried past him, and headed outside into the slowly dying firefight.

She can take care of herself. That's the last time I doubt it.

CHAPTER TWENTY-FIVE

It took less than five minutes before the borgs had destroyed the last of Marcel's men who'd tried to kill Johnny and his team and steal what had turned out to be incredible assets.

"Is that it?" Lisa turned to walk backward as they headed down the avenue toward the front of the train yard.

"It looks like it."

"Wait. Johnny. Hang on." Luther raced between two shredded train cars and two seconds later, a shriek of pain and surprise rose from the other side. It wasn't a hound's shriek, either.

The dwarf darted after him, his rifle at the ready as Rex raced past him to get a head start.

"Get—ah! Get off!" Blake lay on his back with his arm in Luther's jaws. The hound shook it furiously, ripped both fabric and flesh, and dragged him sideways across the gravel.

"Well, look at this." Johnny lowered his rifle and cocked his head to watch Rex join his brother in a game of Chew-the-Two-Timin'-Bastard.

"We'll get him, Johnny." Rex latched on to the man's upper thigh and he yelled in pain.

"Yeah. He wanted to rip you apart. We'll rip him apart."

"All right, that's enough." The bounty hunter snapped his fingers and the hounds instantly dropped their play-toy. They backed away, still snarling, but waited for their master's next command. "Now it makes sense."

Blake clutched his arm and tried to stand, but his mangled leg wouldn't hold his weight. "You...you won't get away with this."

"Yeah, that's what they all say."

"Who's your client, Blake?" Lisa asked, her stolen pistol trained on the man who slobbered in pain.

"I already have a name, darlin'," Johnny muttered.

"You do?"

"Marcel."

The bald man uttered a nervous giggle. "If that's all you have, you're still screwed. He knows you're here. He'll find you."

"Here's the thing." He approached the panting man, squatted beside him, and rested the rifle across his thighs. "Your boss deals in weapons and that's about it. I deal in findin' people. Which means I'll be findin' him first."

"And do what? The whole place is surrounded by security. You'll never get in. And then what?"

"Huh. It sounds like you're sayin' I need to keep you alive, huh?"

"Well, that—" Blake winced and finally managed to control his sniveling. "That would be the smart thing to do because you won't get close to Marcel without me."

Johnny clicked his tongue. "That took you all of...what? Twenty seconds to switch sides?"

"He's a client. That's it." The arms dealer tried to shove himself back with the use of only one leg. "What he pays me is worthless if I'm dead."

"It's worthless in a prison cell, too." He snatched the man's good arm and hauled him to his feet. "You have a long time ahead of you in there."

The bald man's chest heaved as he limped on his good leg and tried to keep up with the dwarf, who dragged him toward the central avenue. "I-I have the plans. Right here."

The bounty hunter released his arm and turned slowly with an unamused stare. "Plans to what?"

"Marcel's place. In my pocket. I'll..." Blake reached behind his waist and whipped out not a folded set of plans but a pistol.

"Gun!" Lisa shouted and fired. Nothing but a click resulted.

Blake looked completely surprised by the fact that he wasn't dead but recovered and swung the pistol toward Johnny's face.

A loud crack echoed behind them and Marcel's bald middleman exploded from the shoulders up in a burst of red mist.

"Aw, what the fuck?" Johnny stepped back and wiped his face as the body fell. "Come on."

"Whoa! What?" Luther shouted.

"Oh, man!" Rex backed away, his tail sticking straight up in the air. "His head exploded!"

Lisa turned with wide eyes to where June stood on top of the train car behind them, her arms folded as the shoulder cannon powered down and sputtered out with a soft click. "Thanks."

"It wasn't for either of you." The Crystal borg turned and leapt off the other side of the car.

"Are you okay?" Lisa approached Johnny, who scowled as he flicked off globs of bone, brain matter, and a considerable amount of blood.

"I've had better days, darlin', but at least this ain't the last of 'em." He held his shoulder to try to feel the damage. "Did that guy use you as a livin' piñata too?"

"Yeah, with a crowbar?" Rex added as they all slipped through the train cars.

She tossed the defective pistol behind her and shook her head. "Nope, not like that."

"Good."

They returned to the borgs, who stood on this side of the front building on the property. Half of their faces were illuminated by the glow of the floodlights on the other side.

"I think we got 'em all, boss," Leroy said as his gun hand shifted into a regular mechanical hand.

"We gotta be sure."

Brandon shook his head as he and Clint scanned the train yard. "Yeah, I don't think anyone's coming after us now, Johnny."

"Right." The dwarf spat a final glob of thicker blood this time and sniffed. "So now we gotta decide how the hell we get the real weapons. Not that I don't appreciate the rescue, June, but Blake was the only one left who knew how to get in and what was bein' done."

The Crystal borg shrugged. "So?"

"So now we need a new plan."

"Hey, hey, Johnny." Luther stopped in front of his master, sat, and looked at him with huge puppy-dog eyes. Pebbles scattered beneath his wagging tail. "We know how to get in."

"Oh, right." Rex sat to scratch behind his ear and snorted. "We heard some dumbags talking about the rest of the plan tonight. You know, after they murdered all of you and left us alone to fend for ourselves."

"Yeah, jeez. In Texas. Those monsters."

"Spit it out, boys. We ain't got all night."

The twins and June stared at the dwarf having a one-sided conversation with his coonhounds. Leroy smirked.

"Yeah, we heard them right over...over there. By that car."

"It wasn't that one, bro." Rex stood and trotted toward the front lot where they'd parked the SUVs. "They said the borgs were going into the back of a truck out front and driving into Marcel's place so he could get what he wanted."

"Yeah, and that the real buyer would be there later to pick up the bad weapons."

Johnny and Lisa exchanged a wide-eyed glance.

"We still don't know how to get there, Johnny."

"That don't mean there ain't a way." He nodded toward the front, then turned to follow the hounds.

Lisa sighed and glanced at the borgs, who all stared at her now. "You heard him. Let's go."

CHAPTER TWENTY-SIX

Marcel Calloway stood at the wall-length window stretched across the northern-facing wall. From this view on the third story of the warehouse he owned north of Edinburg, Texas, he could see for miles. All that meant nothing, however, when he was pissed.

With his hands clasped behind his back, he turned from the window and paced across his office to pour himself a brandy at the wet bar. "I think you put too much faith in him, Wesley."

The older man seated on his couch smoking a cigar turned to drape his arm over the back. "He's never let either of us down before."

"He's never been late either. Until tonight." Marcel sipped his brandy, then lifted it to study the amber liquid in the low overhead lighting "Either something's wrong or he's finally grown sick of this life. Either way, he's made the wrong choice."

"Blake's fine." Wesley puffed on the cigar. "If anything, I bet those cyborgs gave him a little trouble at first. It's nothing he can't handle."

"That's not the point."

A burst of static came from the guard standing inside the door to Marcel's office. "They're here."

The man thumbed his shoulder radio and muttered, "Got it. Sir—"

"Yes, I heard." Marcel returned to the window, where the headlights of two semis turned off the frontage road to light up the road leading onto the property. "And he chose to ride in the transport vehicles."

"What?" the other man snorted. "That doesn't sound like him."

"I'm aware."

"Maybe he didn't want to deal with your accusations for one night and went home instead. He said he trusted the guys he contracted. Given how much he's paying them, I'd say he trusted them implicitly."

"We'll see." After he'd downed the rest of his brandy, Marcel left the crystal glass on the high side table and headed toward the door of his office. "Are you coming?"

"I'd rather finish my cigar. But bring them up if you want. I'm anxious to see these cyborgs in person despite the ridiculous name we're using. Let's think of something better."

"Be my guest." He reached the door, which his guard opened for him before he followed his employer into the hall. They took the elevator to the first floor and emerged in the open warehouse with the raised bay doors as the two semis pulled slowly into the front lot.

The brakes squealed and hissed as the trucks rolled to a stop. Marcel tugged the front of his suit jacket down and snapped his fingers at his men who waited in the warehouse before he pointed at the lot. "Let's get this done."

They drew their weapons—which was standard practice when anyone arrived on Marcel Calloway's doorstep these days —and fanned out around their boss to greet the new shipment.

He stepped out beneath the brilliant glow of the floodlights above the large doors and spread his arms. "Finally."

Three of his men went around the back of the first truck and opened the rolling door in under a minute. After a short scuffle, the thunk of metallic feet headed down the extended ramp.

Yes, he had heard about the female cyborg's metal feet. That had to be her.

His men returned from the back of the truck, each of them with a hand on the arm of a cyborg. "Sir. There were only three."

"Really." He studied his new acquisitions. The female, the overly large, hulking male with the incredible firearm—his actual arm—and only one of the smaller ones. "Check the other truck, then."

The three cyborgs stood perfectly still where the men had left them and stared blankly ahead into the warehouse.

Marcel pursed his lips and pulled his cell phone slowly from the inside pocket of his suit jacket. *Blake had better have a good explanation for the change of plans.*

Before his men could round the back of the second semi, the driver's door opened and the driver climbed out slowly. The men drew their weapons and aimed them at him. He was dressed like a British golfer and had slicked his bright-red hair away from his forehead in a flowing wave. He raised his hands, his eyes wide.

"What is he doing?" Marcel nodded at another man stationed beside him. "He has no business here except driving the truck."

His guard strode toward the driver, who honestly looked terrified. There seemed no logical reason why in the world would he have gotten out.

"Hey. Get back in the truck. You're not staying here."

The driver shook his head but stayed where he was.

"Are you stupid?" The newest man sent by Marcel drew his weapon too and approached the redhead to grasp a fistful of the man's shirt. "Get back in the truck." He shoved the barrel of his pistol toward the man's ribs. "Or are you trying to get yourself—"

The gun clinked against a metal torso.

"What the—"

The driver stabbed his finger against the side of the other man's neck, and the guard choked in surprise before he sagged and landed heavily.

"What's going on?" Marcel shouted as his other men backed away from the redhead with their weapons raised. "Get rid of him."

Four of the men opened fire on the driver. It was overkill, of course, but after five seconds, he realized it wasn't. The bullets pinged off his tweed vest and punched holes in the sides of both semi-trailers. When the men finally stopped firing, he spread his arms with a sheepish shrug and grinned.

"Blake!" Marcel roared. "If you're in there, get out here and explain to me what the hell is going on. Blake!"

The driver's door of the first truck swung open and a short man with a thick red beard swung out of the cab, holding onto the door with one hand. In the other, he lifted what looked like a black blunderbuss and aimed it at the center of the warehouse. "You have the wrong guy."

A blue glow brightened in the stocky barrel, and Marcel darted away from the center of the warehouse as the weapon fired and launched a churning blue ball of intensified energy through the garage.

Johnny roared with laughter as he hopped out of the semi's cab and blasted away with the laser-bomb cannon. "Eat my laser, assholes!"

Marcel's men opened fire but they had all of two seconds to do so before June, Leroy, and Brandon returned fire. And of course, their guns were way bigger.

Boxes, crates, and pallets of both avalanched from orderly piles inside the warehouse. The hounds leapt through the open door of the truck Clint had driven and joined the attack. Lisa hauled the second laser-bomb gun out of the first truck and surprised herself by laughing as she fired it at Marcel's men.

The night echoed with gunfire and explosions and the growing hum of the borgs' weapons powering up before they blasted anyone and anything that moved.

One of the enemy somehow managed to bypass Leroy's clicking, booming shots from his cannon arm and charged at Johnny. The dwarf lowered the laser gun, only to swing it up with both hands at the idiot's face. The man fell with a grunt and Johnny pressed forward to light the warehouse up with his gleeful destruction.

"Johnny!" Luther howled. "Hey, he's getting away!"

"The guy giving orders!" Rex added as he pounced on a gunman from the side and ripped a good chunk out of the guy's flesh.

"Where?" Johnny shouted.

"The door in the back! Come on!" Rex spat out a wad of the dead gunman, shook his head, and raced with Luther toward the door.

The dwarf didn't even need to ask the borgs if they could handle things outside as another wave of Marcel's hired guns streamed toward them from an outbuilding beside the warehouse. "Lisa."

"Yeah?" She fired another laser bomb that eliminated two gunmen and blew a massive hole in the steel wall of the warehouse. "Man, I didn't think I'd like this so much."

With a sigh, Johnny nodded toward the door the hounds had raced to after Marcel. "You can talk dirty to me after we bag this guy."

She laughed, fired another round at the oncoming thugs who retaliated with nothing but bullets, and hurried after him.

"Take a right, then a left, Johnny!" Luther shouted from somewhere up ahead.

"Yeah, the stairs," Rex added. "He took the elevator like a dummy."

"This way." The dwarf shoved the door out of the warehouse open and turned right down the hall. The stairs were on the left and he sprinted up them two at a time.

Lisa followed, cleared the area with a swing of the laser gun, and smirked. "Are we seriously going after the guy with these?"

"Do you have anythin' else on ya, darlin'?"

"No."

"Then these will do." Johnny paused at the second-floor landing, but the lights were off and it was completely silent so they raced up to the third floor instead. As soon as they reached the hallway, the door across from the stairwell slammed shut. Several deadbolts clicked into place and he laughed. "Yeah, right."

He fired another laser bomb and the churning blue sphere of raw energy demolished the door and two feet of wall on either side. Shouts came from inside the next room before the two partners stalked through the hole in the wall and scanned the well-decorated office awaiting them.

"Marcel!" Johnny shouted. "We were supposed to chat tonight—"

He ducked as something hard and heavy sailed toward him from the other side of the room. The ashtray cracked against the wall behind the dwarf, and Johnny stared at it. "Seriously? You're gonna throw—"

A crystal-ball bookend followed and shattered behind Lisa.

The bounty hunter raised the laser gun in both hands and aimed it at not one but two men who backed against the bookshelf along the far wall. "Y'all cut that out."

The shorter man in a gray formal vest snatched an intricately carved wooden box from the shelf and drew back to throw that too.

"Wesley," Marcel snapped and caught the man's arm. "Not that."

The man set the box down, stared at his colleague in confusion, and raised both hands in full surrender.

"So you're the guy, huh?" Johnny pointed at Marcel with the laser gun and clicked his tongue. "You know, for a heavy-hittin' weapons dealer, you sure ain't got the stones to use 'em."

"Which is why I sell them, you idiot." The man rolled his shoulders back and raised his chin. "Who are you?"

"Aw. Now see, if you'd shown up to our meetin' tonight at the train yard, you'd know. And I wouldn't know your...friend."

Wesley pressed his back farther against the bookshelf and blubbered. "P-please. Please d-don't kill me! He's the one you want!"

Marcel rolled his eyes. "You're useless. Did you know that?"

"Please don't. Please don't." The other man sank to the floor against the bookshelf and began to cry. "I don't want to die!"

"Wow. You have some friends." The dwarf turned toward Lisa and nodded. "Keep an eye on 'em, darlin'. I'll be right back."

She frowned at the sobbing Wesley but trained her laser gun on Marcel. "What was your plan after you made it up here?"

"I don't know. Wait for my men to kill you." He snarled his frustration.

A giant explosion wracked the building and made everyone stumble. The lights flickered.

She grimaced at him. "You seriously misjudged that."

"It would seem so." His nostrils flared as he glared at her.

Johnny ripped the heavy curtains down from the rod twelve feet above the top of the windows. Then he ripped off the heavy cords meant for nothing more than decoration and strode toward Lisa and their captives. "Tassels. Who the fuck likes tassels?"

"Those were very expensive," Marcel muttered.

"Great." He handed the cords to his partner and trained his weapon on the men again. "Then Wesley here can get tied up in expensive style. How about that, huh?"

The man cried out and broke into sobs again when she pulled him away from the bookshelf so she could wrap him in the curtain cords. He groaned and sniveled the whole time but didn't even try to struggle.

When she'd finished, she stood and aimed her laser gun at him. "This feels like a little too much, you know?"

"Naw. It's perfect. He can wait here while we go get what we came for."

Johnny grasped the back of Marcel's suit jacket and hauled him roughly across the giant room.

"W-wait! No!" Wesley screamed. "You can't l-leave me here. What am I supposed to do? Marcel. *Marcel!*"

"It might do y'all both some good to leave him here for a while," Johnny muttered as he jerked his captive through the hole in the wall.

"Please." The man scoffed. "You and I both know my chances of coming back are next to nothing. You'll kill me after you get what you want. And knowing Wesley, he'll probably cry himself to death."

The bounty hunter hauled the man down the stairs as the explosions and gunfire continued outside, albeit sporadically. "Well, you're right about one of those. You ain't comin' back for a long time. But I ain't gonna kill you—not as long as you do exactly what I say and don't pull any funny business. Understand?"

Marcel gritted his teeth and made no reply as he stumbled down the stairs, jerked forward every few steps by the dwarf's iron grip on the back of his collar.

When they reached the ground floor, the fighting had stopped. Bodies littered the drive in front of the warehouse. Both semis rocked on their frames as dozens of fists pounded on the inner walls of the trailers and even more voices shouted to be let out.

"Wow." Lisa lifted the laser gun and settled it on her shoulder. "I honestly didn't expect you guys to leave anyone…uh, alive."

Brandon wrinkled his nose. "Yeah, shooting them on the spot is fun and all, but we thought it would be better all round to keep some of them alive. You know, for whatever you guys have to do after this."

June pounded a metal fist against the side of one trailer and left it with a huge dent. The men inside shut up instantly. "This is fun too."

"And now we're gonna have a different kinda fun, ain't we?" Johnny shook Marcel by the collar. "I want those weapons. And don't even think about askin' me which ones. You know damn well."

"On the other side of the property," the man muttered. "About a mile."

"Then let's get walkin'."

The hounds raced around the side of the warehouse, licking their muzzles. "Johnny! Hey, you did it."

"Of course he did. Johnny's the dwarf."

"Hey, where we going now?"

Johnny nodded up ahead. "About a mile that way."

"Cool, cool. Hey, what about the other buyer?"

"Who's your other buyer?" Lisa asked.

"What?" Marcel lurched forward as Johnny yanked him again but frowned at the half-Light Elf.

"We know you were planning to sell to someone else tonight. Where is he?"

The man chuckled. "Still in my office tied in the curtains, I believe."

"Huh." Johnny shook his head. "Well, that was convenient."

CHAPTER TWENTY-SEVEN

Of course, the highly dangerous and sought-after weapons of mass destruction would be kept in something as unassuming as a barn at the back of Marcel Calloway's property. Granted, it was a huge barn and it wasn't housing livestock.

"Is this it?" Johnny asked as they approached the double-story building with two massive doors at the entrance.

"Oh. Whoops." Marcel rolled his eyes. "I must have forgotten where I put them."

"Get the damn thing open." The dwarf shoved his captive forward and he stumbled across the grass. He took a moment to compose himself and straighten his suit jacket before he approached the barn doors and flipped a little panel on the side open. The buttons beneath beeped when he punched a code in and the doors opened on their own.

"There. Happy now?" He spread his arms and backed away from the doors down the wall of the barn. "You won."

"Uh-huh." Johnny rubbed his mouth and stared at the massive crates inside the building. Some of them had been sealed with tempered glass to display the contents—giant mechanisms with obvious barrels, something that looked like a larger version of

Leroy's mechanical eye but the size of a car, heavy-hitting satellite missiles, and an entire stack of assault rifles and RPGs packed neatly in crates. "You have yourself a hell of a cache here."

"I know. And you've cost me a hell of a lot of money." Marcel whipped his hand away from the wall of the barn and yelped. The small pistol flew from his hand into the grass, and he grasped the wrist of his gun hand. His fingers gushed blood where they'd been sliced cleanly off after the second knuckles. Then, he screamed. "My hand!"

Clint still aimed his index finger at the arms dealer and shook his head slowly. "Bad idea."

The bounty hunter chuckled and approached the open barn to get a better look inside. "He only talks when it counts. I like it."

Brandon clapped his brother on the shoulder and gave him a little shake. Clint grinned at his twin and winked before he blew the nonexistent smoke away from the tip of his finger.

Marcel's shrieks cut off immediately and he toppled to his knees and finally sprawled in a heap.

"Oh, good. He fainted." Lisa whipped her light jacket off and approached the unconscious arms dealer to tie his wrist off as best she could.

Johnny stopped inside the barn and peered at the giant stash of weapons. "All right. Do y'all reckon you can get rid of these in the next, say...hour or so?"

Brandon chuckled. "You mean, like, get rid of them, get rid of them, or—"

"I ain't talkin' about takin' 'em to Florida, if that's what you're tryin' to get at." He turned and snorted. "And that ain't a subtle way to ask either."

"I'm only curious."

"I thought the major general wanted them," Leroy said.

"Uh-huh. And that's why we're getting' rid of 'em. So?"

"Hell yeah, we can," June said and stalked toward the barn. "It won't even take an hour."

"Great."

The Crystal borg wrapped both hands around one side of the doorway and pulled. The entire right-hand side of the barn ripped off with a crack of splitting wood and the shriek of metal beneath it. The wall hurtled across the field and she moved to the other side but paused when she realized everyone was staring at her. "What? It makes it easier to get them out all at once."

"It sounds good to me." Leroy shrugged and went to help her.

The twins nodded at Johnny before they did the same.

With Marcel's bleeding hand tied off to at least stop him from losing much more blood—and a low dose of healing magic to help it along—Lisa sat back on her heels and swiped her hair out of her face. "Okay. So now we call Bartlett and get this over with, right?"

"Not yet, darlin'."

The hounds sniffed around the unconscious weapon dealer's head, their tails wagging. "Johnny, he smells like oranges."

"What?"

Luther snorted. "Blood oranges."

"Bro, that was way too obvious to be funny."

"Aw, come on. Seriously, though, Johnny. There's something in his pocket. Not an orange."

Johnny nodded at Lisa and she reached into Marcel's front jacket pocket. The plastic case she pulled out of it looked like any other regular plastic case in which certain overly expensive pens were boxed. It did have a pen in it too—copper with a silver button at the tip. "Is this what you smelled?"

Rex bumped his nose against the box and sneezed. "Oh, yeah. Something orange in there, all right."

"I think we can explore that one later." Johnny crouched to take Marcel's arm and eventually draped him over his shoulders before he stood. "We're headin' to the front."

Lisa shrugged and slid the pen case into her back pocket.

"What about the borgs?"

A massive crate the size of a small sedan groaned as Leroy got his back under it and carried it across the field. "We got it. See ya by the trucks, boss."

"Oh, my God." She stared at the shifter borg who hauled the crate away like it was a backpack.

"Yeah, that's new too." With a snort, the bounty hunter turned back the way they'd come and whistled for the hounds. "Let's go, boys. The night ain't over yet."

They waited forty minutes at the front of Marcel's decimated warehouse before the borgs returned, looking incredibly pleased with themselves. "It's done already?"

"Oh, yeah." Brandon dusted his hands off. "You'll never guess—"

"Naw, don't tell me. I don't wanna know." Johnny pulled his phone out and dialed Bartlett's number.

"Johnny."

"You sound surprised to get my call, Colonel."

"Well, admittedly, none of us expected you to survive this. But at the very least we know where you are. And I'm assuming the job's done."

"Yep."

"I'll send a team out right now. Good wo—"

Johnny hung up and slipped the phone in his pocket with a dreamy smile. "It always feels good to hang up on a rankin' officer."

Lisa shook her head and hissed a laugh. "And he's still going to pay you."

"Hey, we finished the job, darlin'. That's all that matters."

When Bartlett's team arrived, Johnny hadn't expected the colonel to arrive with them. The man was the first to get out of the car, however, and he headed directly to the bounty hunter. "Where are they?"

"Well, we have a few dozen hired guns locked in those trucks. The arms dealer's been passed out on the ground since he got his fingers shot off." Johnny gestured toward Marcel with a sweep of his hand. "And the rest of us are here. Take your pick."

"The weapons, Johnny."

"Huh. I have no idea."

"Don't screw around with me, dwarf. This was your job."

"My job was to make sure those weapons don't get into the wrong hands. I did my job and I got you a boatload of prisoners —which are your responsibility now, seein' as you're the one who contracted the job. I merely find the guys. Feel free to tear the place apart, though. I don't mind."

Bartlett grimaced so hard his lips curled apart to reveal surprisingly white teeth. "You're this close to stepping over the line, Johnny Walker."

"Naw. I stepped over it decades ago, Colonel. You can ask Dorn about it later."

The man nodded at his team and they fanned out to go through the wreckage of the warehouse.

"Oh, yeah. And the other buyer's whimperin' upstairs on the third floor. I think you could point at him and he'd spill his guts about whatever you wanna know."

The colonel waved his hand in a dismissive gesture but didn't turn. "Get out of here before I change my mind."

"Yeah. Right." Johnny snorted and swung on his heel to march down the road. He stopped only to take the laser-gun cases from the cab of the first truck so he and Lisa could tuck the weapons snuggly inside. "Time to head out, y'all."

His partner studied Bartlett and his team with a frown before she jogged after the dwarf to catch up with him. The borgs trudged behind them down the road, and the hounds raced repeatedly from them to the field and back. "I don't get it."

"Get what, darlin'?"

"He didn't even try to keep you here until they found the weapons. I can't believe he let us walk out without asking more questions."

The bounty hunter raised his hand and wiggled his fingers. "They've been trackin' us the whole time."

"Yeah, I know. But what does that have to do with it?"

He took her hand and drew a deep breath of the cool night air that rapidly grew colder. "I think I have about a dozen new reasons why it pays to have cyborgs on the team, one of 'em bein' folks don't think to track someone they only see as a walkin' weapon."

Lisa looked over her shoulder at the borgs who marched in silence behind them like they hadn't put an end to an entire arms-dealing operation and saved any number of people considerable trouble and harm by destroying so many deadly weapons.

"That's why you had them get rid of the crates first. And with the tracker, Bartlett has proof that you and I never left Marcel's property."

"Uh-huh."

She laughed wryly and squeezed his hand. "You know, if it weren't for all the close calls we've had in the last week—and I mean extremely close calls—I'd think you'd planned every step of this from the beginning."

"Naw. You know that ain't my thing. I merely roll with the punches."

Lisa grimaced at his swollen lower lip. "Yeah. We'll have to take a look at those when we get back."

"I won't complain."

"Which makes me wonder… How, exactly, will we get back?"

The bounty hunter smirked and pulled his phone out. "Do you think a flat, empty road like this would work for a private landin' strip?"

CHAPTER TWENTY-EIGHT

One week later...

Johnny stepped out onto the back porch with a drink in his hand and took a deep breath of the pleasantly warm air. "Hell of a day, huh?"

Lisa followed him with their plated sandwiches. "It feels like every other day."

"That's the point." He descended the stairs and sat on a part of the obstacle course's underside he'd turned into a bench. She sat beside him and handed him his plate before she took a bite of her sandwich. "It looks like they're...adjusting well."

With a snort, the dwarf gestured with half a sandwich toward the four borgs sprawled on the lawn ten feet from Margo's hull. "Who knew TV would keep 'em from breakin' everythin' they can get their hands on?"

"At least it works."

"And it ain't inside the house so I'm good with it."

Johnny had almost refused to let the borgs tack an old bedsheet to Margo's roof—not because he cared about the bedsheet but because he thought it was a dumb idea in the first place. But then they'd had their first movie night out on the lawn. Leroy had projected the chosen movie through his eye after he'd hooked himself up to Margo for free cable and channel streaming.

This was now what the borgs did when Johnny didn't have a job for them around the property. Or a real job, which they hadn't had any more of. Then again, it had only been a week.

"Oh, go to that sci-fi channel," Brandon shouted and snapped his fingers to refresh his memory. "There's that show that's...it's about..."

"Screw that," June cut in. "We live the sci-fi channel. Go with Planet Earth."

"Yeah, we live in the middle of the nowhere in the swamp. How's that a better choice?"

Clint shook his head slowly. "History."

"Hey, you know what?" Leroy raised his hand for them to quiet. "How about whoever has the remote gets to pick the channel, huh? Oh, that's right. I am the remote."

His mechanical eye swiveled and widened, and the blue projection of the incoming shows burst from the lens to fill the entire bedsheet hanging from Margo's hull. The speaker Johnny had rigged up beside his giant metal intel server crackled to life and a woman anchor's businesslike voice came through loud and clear.

"Seventeen eyewitness reports of an unexplained phenomenon sighting over the Gulf of Mexico last week."

"Wait, wait. Shh." Brandon leaned forward over his crossed legs to get a better view. "This could be good."

"Some witnesses have already stepped forward to give their accounts of that night. Some think the bright lights in the sky were UFOs floating through our atmosphere. Others believe this was the work of magic, although its exact origins are still unknown."

Johnny swallowed his food and pointed at the borgs. "If this was y'all, it sure as hell better not come back around to point the finger at me."

Leroy tsked. "Trust us. No one will know."

"A large, unidentified explosion detonated in the waters of the Gulf of Mexico Tuesday night at approximately 11:00 pm. This was followed immediately by a burst of light in the night sky. Whether it was magic, other species beyond what we know from Oriceran, an unscheduled aircraft flight, or the work of networked drones, we still aren't sure. But there's one thing every witness statement around this phenomenon has in common.

"Each of them heard a crack immediately after the explosion off the coast. And shortly afterward, they each saw the same image in the sky. We at Channel Twelve News weren't quite sure what to make of these accounts until we received actual footage this morning of the similarly described light on Tuesday night. We're sharing that footage with you now."

The screen switched to a recording someone had taken with their phone. The guy's gasps of awe were barely audible but the explosion in the sky couldn't be mistaken. The light was blinding, there was the aforementioned loud crack, and when the explosion of light faded, something was left behind in the sky.

A smiley face of golden lights flared in a bright glow for no longer than five seconds before it disappeared.

The footage cut off and the news anchor returned.

"So there you have it, folks. Tuesday night was an inexplicable..."

Everyone seated in Johnny's back yard turned to stare at June, who stood with her arms folded as she looked directly ahead at the projector screen. Even Leroy turned, and the news station flickered out when his eye cut the connection off.

Lisa smothered a laugh.

Johnny cleared his throat. "June. Did you drop all Marcel's weapons of mass destruction in the Gulf of Mexico and then... uh, leave a callin' card?"

The Crystal borg broke into a wide grin none of the others had seen before. "Idiots."

Her boots flared with orange light and she launched out of the yard to land five seconds later on the deck of the boathouse with a metallic clang. Her laughter echoed across the swamp.

With a snort, Leroy returned his gaze to the sheet-turned-screen and activated the homemade TV.

THE STORY CONTINUES

Have the monsters and bad guys learned their lessons? Not yet. Continue Johnny, Lisa and the coonhounds adventures in _FOR DWARF'S SAKE, coming May 2, 2021._

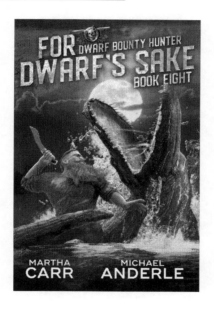

Get sneak peeks, exclusive giveaways, behind the scenes content, and more. PLUS you'll be notified of special **one day only fan pricing** on new releases.

Sign up today to get free stories.

AUTHOR NOTES - MARTHA CARR
MARCH 4, 2021

I first started writing with Michael Anderle in the beginning of 2017, which feels more like it was ten years ago. We were shooting from the hip and working as fast as we were able. I had a full-time corporate job back then and any writing had to happen very early in the morning, at night or on the weekends.

But I loved the creation of Oriceran and the stories of Leira and Correk and YTT and was thrilled to be writing something that might just get more readers.

And in an instant from the first book, The Leira Chronicles took off.

I did my best to write faster and in the first few months we had put out five books with more to come.

I remember coming up against a deadline, eating peanut butter on celery because it was high in protein and quick to make and eat. I took a break to walk the good dog, Lois Lane, and while we made our way down the street, I thought about the plot twist that needed a solution.

By November of that year, I was a little worn out. Maybe not burned out but crispy around the edges for sure.

Burnout is a real thing that happens to everyone. We push

ourselves to get something done at a breakneck speed but over time we use up our reserves till we hit a wall.

Sound familiar?

It should because we all do it at some point. Maybe it's parenting or it's a job thing or maybe an exercise routine. We get attached to a goal and it has a deadline, and we go for it. There's even a kind of thrill to actually making the goal.

As Anderle will be happy to tell you, I'm a little competitive and I'm fine competing with myself. But, at some point, I need a break. A breather to build the reserves back up and get back into life and gather new weird information about people, places and things that I can pour into books. Not a long breather because, come on, there's another book to put out. Life keeps on coming at you. But something deliberate to unwind.

Usually that means seeking out people to hang around and tell tall tales and have a few laughs. Or take a weekend and go somewhere. Of course, there was 2020, which needs no background for you to get that one. To decompress I played games with neighbors through Zoom or sat in another neighbor's front yard in her inflatable pools at a safe distance from each other. Or a few of us gathered around a fire pit in my backyard. And there were the few concerts from my garage and another garage up the street.

Hey, it was something and all those friendships have grown deeper this past year.

To fill in the cracks I even took up meditation, embroidery, yoga from YouTube, running, kayaking and recently, print making. It was a long year, and I made it through intact with a lot of new books.

The point is, if you're hitting a wall, it's okay. Take it in, feel it and then stand back up when you can and take a look around. No judging yourself or wondering if it's a sign of anything. It's not. There was just a lot to do and you did your best at getting it all done.

Instead, let's look at the whole thing like it was just happening, and not happening to you. You have choices and can use them to do something different. For me that starts with gathering information. What did I learn from it? I've learned over the past few years to delegate a lot more. At first that usually happened when I'd hear Michael laughing and he'd ask, "why are you still doing that?" Next I ask, what can I reasonably change and then take the plunge and do it.

I'm a big fan of quality of life and this past year has only made that stronger. Working a lot sometimes though is necessary, but I've also learned that if I made different decisions early in the planning, a lot of late night hours disappear, and things still get done.

Soon, the world will actually reopen – for real this time. (Remember when quarantine started, and it was supposed to be for two weeks and we all talked about how long that would be?)

When it does, I will still be here typing away, creating magic, but some of that time will also be spent doing other things whose only reward is fun. A surefire way to head off burnout. More adventures to follow.

AUTHOR NOTES - MICHAEL ANDERLE
MARCH 30, 2021

Thank you for reading through the story to these author notes at the end!

I've read Martha's author notes, and I remember talking to her about…well, her.

She has a gift when it comes to supporting others that was born of experience and effort on her part. She has been the receiver of support and the provider as well for more than a decade now, and I feel it comes out in her musings.

I'm not sure that is my gift whatsoever, but I appreciate (and occasionally envy) her way of providing support to those who might need it.

My version of burnout support is perhaps a bit more abrupt. It would go something like this:

"Burnout is real! I've experienced it, many of my collaborators experience it, and I now warn every collaborator to take a break between books 04 and 05 for sure, if not sooner. If you don't, your body WILL collapse at some point and make you pay and pay dearly the longer you push."

Now, that isn't to tell someone that they MUST stop or they MUST do anything, period. It is a suggestion that if you allow yourself a bit of downtime (in the beginning, it was a week minimum of goofing off after the last release), it helps increase the number of books you can complete.

My first burnout (sort of) was somewhere around books 07 to 09, I think. I know I've written author notes about this before, so I won't belabor my point.

For me, that episode was more that my mind went kinda blank. "What do I write? What do I talk about? This is boring!"

I would give Earlier Me different advice now in hindsight than I received at that moment. It would include advice I'm not sure Earlier Me would even listen to.

Does that make sense?

I know Earlier Me, and he was an obstinate guy. I'm not suggesting he was hard-headed, but you could shape diamonds using his skull. (Ba-doom *Ching!*)

Now I give advice three ways: short, fast, and to the point. Those who hear it are welcome to do whatever they wish with the advice, including ignoring it because I know what I was like back then.

Sometimes you are in a place to hear and use advice. Sometimes you hear advice, and you think it is baloney (and let's admit it, sometimes you are right to ignore the advice!)

What I don't ever want to become is the person who is upset when my advice is not acted upon because that means I've forgotten who "I" was when younger.

Sometimes, just sometimes, stubborn gets you places that advice will never allow you to achieve.

Like whether burnout is something you can deal with. It is. Through sheer force and determination, you can write books eight, nine, ten, eleven, and so on and so on until you finally break through to success.

Because you didn't listen to advice that said "Don't write more than four books a year."

But...please remember...the mind NEEDS rest. Know your

mind and when to give it rest, and burnout won't be something you need to fear.

If I told myself anything else, it would be, "Don't promise your fans twenty-one books in your first series minimum."

Ad Aeternitatem,

Michael Anderle

Solve a murder, save her mother, and stop the apocalypse?

What would you do when elves ask you to investigate a prince's murder and you didn't even know elves, or magic, was real?

Meet Leira Berens, Austin homicide detective who's good at what she does – track down the bad guys and lock them away.

Which is why the elves want her to solve this murder – fast. It's not just about tracking down the killer and bringing them to justice. It's about saving the world!

If you're looking for a heroine who prefers fighting to flirting, check out The Leira Chronicles today!

<u>AVAILABLE ON AMAZON AND IN KINDLE UNLIMITED!</u>

CONNECT WITH THE AUTHORS

Martha Carr Social
Website:
http://www.marthacarr.com
Facebook:
https://www.facebook.com/groups/MarthaCarrFans/

Michael Anderle

Website: http://lmbpn.com

Email List: http://lmbpn.com/email/

Social Media:

https://www.facebook.com/LMBPNPublishing

https://twitter.com/MichaelAnderle

https://www.instagram.com/lmbpn_publishing/

https://www.bookbub.com/authors/michael-anderle

ALSO BY MARTHA CARR

Other series in the Oriceran Universe:

THE LEIRA CHRONICLES

THE FAIRHAVEN CHRONICLES

MIDWEST MAGIC CHRONICLES

SOUL STONE MAGE

THE KACY CHRONICLES

THE DANIEL CODEX SERIES

I FEAR NO EVIL

SCHOOL OF NECESSARY MAGIC

THE UNBELIEVABLE MR. BROWNSTONE

SCHOOL OF NECESSARY MAGIC: RAINE CAMPBELL

ALISON BROWNSTONE

FEDERAL AGENTS OF MAGIC

SCIONS OF MAGIC

MAGIC CITY CHRONICLES

Series in The Terranavis Universe:

The Adventures of Maggie Parker Series

The Witches of Pressler Street

The Adventures of Finnegan Dragonbender

OTHER BOOKS BY JUDITH BERENS

OTHER BOOKS BY MARTHA CARR

OTHER LMBPN PUBLISHING BOOKS

To be notified of new releases and special promotions from LMBPN publishing, please join our email list:

http://lmbpn.com/email/

For a complete list of books published by LMBPN please visit the following pages:

https://lmbpn.com/books-by-lmbpn-publishing/